Making Sense of English

英文文法有道理！

入門版

A

Z

• Grammar

• English •

PREFACE

序

一直想寫這本書，是給國、高中生、給一般大眾看的！

因為，不希望再有人走冤枉路！不希望學英文變成只會背規則、考試，卻不知規則所表達的溝通目的，及規則和規則間可互通之處。

如果一開始學英文，就能建立正確的語法概念，把英文規則學通，通則靈，深則變，這就是「從理解到活用」的意義。

認識一個人必須先了解這個人的個性，學習語言亦同。

一開始就弄懂英文獨特的語性，了解中、英文基本差異，及英文形意搭配的原則，英文就能學得精準、全面，學習自然就有樂趣，學得有道理！

所以本書的野心很大：想讓每一個學英文的人都能「知其然，又知其所以然」。並達到事半功倍，舉一反三之效，避免死背，零散、不完整或不連貫的死規則。

筆者的目的很簡單：本書回答了我們在學習英語過程中可能遇到的問題。但當你鼓起勇氣問老師時，得到的回答總是千篇一律：「這是習慣用法，背起來。」我想告訴本書讀者：其實英語規則是可以理解的，規則是有道理的！

英文真的不難，好好花時間讀這本書吧。

想放棄前，先給自己一個機會讀這本書吧！

劉美君

CONTENTS 目錄

PREFACE 序 3

CHAPTER

0 中英文法大不同 7

英文的十大特點 9

（特性1） 英文句子，什麼都不能省略！ 9

（特性2） 動作不同，動詞有差！ 11

（特性3） 重點先講，主從有別 13

（特性4） 名詞出場，必有標記！ 17

（特性5） 動詞出場，時間清楚！ 19

（特性6） 事件有樣貌，做完了還是進行中？ 22

（特性7） 辨明真假，判斷可能 26

（特性8） 主動被動，句句講究 30

（特性9） 時空轉換，語意多變 33

（特性10） 規則為上，例外有深意！ 35

CHAPTER

1 文法是什麼？文法就是 形式和意義搭配的原則！ 37

1. 你想說什麼？ 38

2. 英文怎麼說？ 39

3. 還能怎麼說？ 41

4. 讀一段短文 46

5. 唱一首英文歌 47

6. 看一部影片 48

7. 做一點練習 49

CHAPTER

2 發生了什麼事？
動詞怎麼用？ 55

1. 你想說什麼？ 56

2. 英文怎麼說？ 57

3. 還能怎麼說？（進階篇） 62

4. 讀一段短文 69

5. 唱一首英文歌 72

6. 看一部影片 73

7. 做一點練習 75

CHAPTER

3 重點何在？ 79

1. 你想說什麼？ 80

2. 英文怎麼說？ 85

3. 還能怎麼說？（進階篇） 90

4. 讀一段短文 99

5. 唱一首英文歌 101

6. 看一部影片 102

7. 做一點練習 105

CHAPTER

4 究竟是指哪一個？ . 109

1. 你想說什麼？ 110

2. 英文怎麼說？ 111

3. 還能怎麼說？（進階篇） 120

4. 讀一段短文 126

5. 唱一首英文歌 127

6. 看一部影片 129

7. 做一點練習 131

CHAPTER

5 什麼時候的事？ 135

1. 你想說什麼？ 136

2. 英文怎麼說？ 137

3. 還能怎麼說？（進階篇） 146

4. 讀一段短文 150

5. 唱一首英文歌 151

6. 看一部影片 155

7. 做一點練習 156

CHAPTER

6 事件的進展如何？ . 159

1. 你想說什麼？ 160

2. 英文怎麼說？ 167

3. 還能怎麼說？ 176

4. 讀一段短文 188

5. 唱一首英文歌 189

6. 看一部影片 190

7. 做一點練習 190

CHAPTER

7 辨明真假
事實與假設 195

1. 你想說什麼？ 196
2. 英文怎麼說？ 199
3. 還能怎麼說？ 209
4. 讀一段短文 218
5. 唱一首英文歌 220
6. 看一部影片 221
7. 做一點練習 222

CHAPTER

8 誰該負責？
主動與被動 229

1. 你想說什麼？ 230
2. 英文怎麼說？ 230
3. 還能怎麼說？ 235
4. 讀一段短文 238
5. 唱一首英文歌 239
6. 看一部影片 240
7. 做一點練習 240

CHAPTER

9 在哪裡發生的？
介系詞該怎麼用？ . 245

1. 你想說什麼？ 246
2. 英文怎麼說？ 247
3. 還能怎麼說？ 260
4. 讀一段短文 266
5. 唱一首英文歌 267
6. 看一部影片 268
7. 做一點練習 269

CHAPTER

10 規則之外 273

1. 你想說什麼？ 274
2. 英文怎麼說？ 274
3. 還能怎麼說？ 281
4. 讀一段短文 283
5. 唱一首英文歌 284
6. 看一部影片 285
7. 做一點練習 285

CHAPTER

0

中英文法大不同

人有個性，語言有語性。「文法」或稱「語法」，就是語性的表現，代表語言能夠完成溝通的「標記原則」。代表的是語言能夠完成溝通的「標記原則」。那什麼又是標記？「標記」就是用固定的形式（form）來表達固定的語意（meaning）？有如交通號誌，紅燈這個形式表達了「停」的語意，綠燈這個形式則表達了「前進」的語意。固定的號誌（形式）搭配上固定的交通（語意），就成為大家都要遵守的交通規則。同樣的，學會一種語言，就是學會如何將固定的語言「形式」與固定的溝通「語意」做搭配。例如：中文說「貓追狗」，你一看就知道是誰追誰，因為中文用固定的SVO順序來表達誰對誰做了什麼。但是換成日文，順序就不一樣了，要說成「貓-狗-追」，動詞「追」要放在最後面。這是因為同樣的語意在日文裡的語序為SOV。由此可見，每種語言都有一套自己的「形式」和「語意」搭配原則，這就是文法規則：

形中文 ←———————— 意 ————————→ 形日文

中文形式 S-V-O	相同的語意	日文形式 S-O-V
貓 - 追 - 狗	← →	貓 - 狗 - 追

英文的十大特點

英文也有一套自己的搭配原則！這套原則和中文很不一樣，因此要學好英文，就要把這套原則搞清楚。到底英文和中文有何不同呢？本章要告訴你英文有十大要點，學會了就會讓你對英文瞭若指掌！

英文句子，什麼都不能省略！

中英文最大的不同就是：中文可以「省略」，但是英文「不能省」！什麼意思呢？請看看下面的對話：

┌─ **老師問學生** ──────────────────────┐

  師 吃飯沒？　　　　　（誰吃飯？）

  生 吃了！　　　　　　（誰吃了？）

  師 吃什麼？　　　　　（誰吃了什麼？）

  生 買的便當。　　　　（誰買的便當？）

  師 好吃嗎？　　　　　（什麼東西好吃？）

  生 還不錯！　　　　　（什麼東西還不錯？）

└──────────────────────────────┘

你發現了嗎？中文對話省略了好多東西：老師問「誰」？「誰」吃「什麼」？「什麼東西」好吃？都沒有說清楚，並將其省略！這是因為中文和英文有不同的「個性」，中文有點像「差不多先生」，只要對話者已經知道情境中的人事物，就可以省略不說；但是英文是個嚴謹的英國紳士，一絲不苟，條理分明，每樣東西都要說清楚：

A teacher asked a student

Teacher	Have YOU eaten LUNCH?
Student	Yes, I have eaten LUNCH.
Teacher	What have YOU eaten?
Student	I've eaten a boxed lunch I bought.
Teacher	Is IT good?
Student	It's not bad.

英文句子裡的主詞、動詞、受詞都不能省略，都得說清楚，都得「標記」出來！因此「誰」對「誰」做了什麼，兩個「誰」都不能省，即使前面已經提過了不想重複，英文也得用代名詞說清楚：

> 中文可以省　我買了本書，__很好看。我看了____，__很喜歡__。
> 英文不能省　I bought a book. It's good. I read the book and I like IT!

既然主詞、動詞、受詞都不能省，這樣的表達模式就構成英文的基本句式──SVO：

(**Subject**) + (**Verb**) + (**Object**)

問 Have you done the homework?

答 No, I haven't done it yet.

簡答 No, I haven't.

在 SVO 的基本句式下，英文嚴謹規定每個句子都要有主詞，即使沒有明確的主語，也要用虛主詞來表示：

> 中文可以無主詞　好美喔！ 有瀑布耶！
> 英文必須有主詞　It's beautiful! <u>There</u> is a waterfall!

究竟英文的句子形式還有哪些要注意的呢，請看第 1 章《文法是什麼》！

動作不同，動詞有差！

說英文時，「誰對誰」做什麼事不能省，當然「什麼事」也不能省，一定要說清楚「做」了什麼！「做什麼」就是動詞的選擇。動詞這麼多，到底要怎麼學呢？再來看看下面的對話：

老師問學生

師　你在做什麼？

生　我在打……，我打算……，我在想……，我想說……

師　你在打？打誰？

　　你打算？打算做什麼？

　　你在想？在想什麼事？

　　你想說？想說什麼話？

學生說了動詞，卻沒說完，老師只好一直問，希望補上沒說完的。可見動詞後面還有重要訊息，有了這些訊息，語意才完整！動詞後面要加上什麼東西和動詞的語意息息相關，因為動詞代表動作，不同的動作牽涉到不同的人事物，例如：

一個人的動作，與他人無關：

I jumped, I ran, I cried, I laughed, and I slept. ➡ 沒受詞，不及物！

牽涉兩個人，動作影響另一方：

I hit him, I kissed her, I broke the vase, and I ate the cake.

➡ 有受詞，及物！

這兩種動詞的區別在於是否有受詞，動詞後面要接受詞（受影響的人 or 物）的叫做「及物動詞」；動詞後面不需要加受詞的叫做「不及物動詞」（沒有受影響的人 or 物），這就是動詞最主要的兩種類別！

既然動詞大都是代表動作，那沒有動作的句子該怎麼辦？下面這些句子，都沒有「動作」，都是形容詞，中文句子不一定需要動詞，而英文句子中，主詞、動詞皆不可少，就只好以沒有動作性的 BE 動詞來連接形容詞：

中文用「很」：我很高，你很帥，他很聰明。

英文用 **BE** 動詞：I am tall. You are handsome. He is smart.

所以，當動作有對應的動詞可用時，不管是動態或靜態的，就用一般動詞；但當要表達身份、關係、形容特徵時，沒有動作時，就可用 BE 動詞：

有動作的動態動詞：

I visited my teacher.　　　　　　➡ 外在活動

I kicked the ball into the goal.　　➡ 肢體活動

I am thinking about the problem.　➡ 心智活動

沒有動作的靜態動詞：

I love English.　　　　➡ 心理狀態

I have a car.　　　　　➡ 擁有狀態

用於連接的 **BE** 動詞：

I am a student.　　　➡ 身份

He is my father.　　　➡ 關係

She is talented.　　　➡ 形容特徵

They are fond of music.　➡ 形容特徵

BE 動詞不能表達「做了什麼」，只是用來連接主詞和形容主詞的東西，所以稱為「連接動詞」。到底英文還有哪些不同類型的動詞，動詞後面所接的東西又有什麼差別，請看第 2 章《發生了什麼事：動詞怎麼用》。

3 特性 重點先講，主從有別

除了「不能省」以外，英文嚴謹的文法表現在溝通上還有一個特點，那就是無論講什麼，都要有「重點」，而且要「先講重點」！ 什麼是重點？請看以下的對話：

> **老師問學生**
>
> 師 昨天發生什麼事？
>
> 生 昨天下午三點 10 分上課鐘響的時候……
>
> 師 ？？？
>
> 生 劉小華突然肚子痛！

說了半天，最重要的是「發生什麼事」，在這裡要說的是「小華肚子痛！」這個重點放在最後。換成英文，就要先說重點：

> **Teacher** What happened yesterday?
>
> **Class Head** Mary was having a stomachache when the bell rang at 3:30 yesterday.

既然重點要先講，英文的說話順序常會和中文不一樣，因為中文的重點通常放在最後：

> 中文 請在八德路右轉！
>
> 英文 Turn right onto Bade Road!

開車找路的時候就要注意了！如果你是使用英文的GPS導航或是 Google Map，聽到 "turn right" 的時候，別急著轉彎，先聽完再說：

GPS：Turn right in 2 miles!　　　　　　　於兩英里後向右轉！
　　　Turn right at the next intersection.　下個路口向右轉。
　　　Exit the Highway in 10 miles.　　　　於十英里後離開高速公路。
　　　Turn to Highway 70 at the 2nd exit.　於第二個出口接到70高速公路。

　　所以，英文習慣重點先講：

　　這個「重點先講」的特性影響到英文文法的每一個層面，無論是詞組、簡單句、複雜句，英文都傾向把重點放在前面：

英文 — 重點在前	中文 — 重點在後
[A girl] who is beautiful	漂亮的[女生]
[A book] I bought yesterday	我昨天買的[書]
[One] of them likes dancing.	他們其中[一人]很喜歡跳舞。
[I went shopping] last night.	昨天晚上[我去逛街]。
[He is taller] than I am.	他比我[高]。
[I took the bus] to save money.	為了省錢，[我坐公車]。
[I am dancing] because I am happy.	我很開心，所以[我跳舞]。

　　既然要先講重點，英文在空間和時間的表達上，就要從最關鍵的「小處」著手！寫地址的時後要先寫與房子最直接相關的門牌號碼，然後才慢慢放大到路名、城市、國家。寫時間的時候也一樣，都是由小漸大、焦點在前。

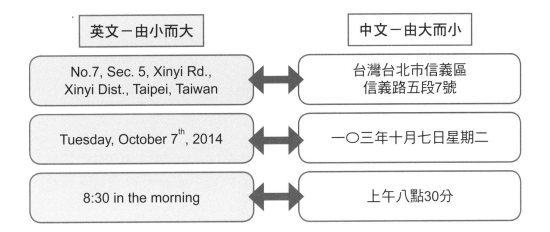

英文－由小而大		中文－由大而小
No.7, Sec. 5, Xinyi Rd., Xinyi Dist., Taipei, Taiwan	⟷	台灣台北市信義區 信義路五段7號
Tuesday, October 7th, 2014	⟷	一〇三年十月七日星期二
8:30 in the morning	⟷	上午八點30分

　　有一個前提就是必須分清楚什麼是重點，什麼不是，而且重點只能有一個。因此要是一個句子有兩個動詞，一定是一主一從；要是有兩個子句，也一定是一主一從，這是英文「重點為主，其餘為輔」的原則。每個句子都有一個重點，就是主要子句，主要子句最大，語意完整，可以單獨出現，但是附屬子句就必須加上額外的附屬標記，因為單獨出現時，語意就不完整，因此不能單獨使用：

獨立子句：I went to see a doctor. ➡ 語意完整，可以獨立出現
附屬子句：Although I went to see a doctor,...
　　　　➡ 語意不完整，不能獨立使用

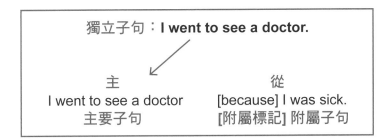

獨立子句：**I went to see a doctor.**

主　　　　　　　　　　　　從
I went to see a doctor　　[because] I was sick.
主要子句　　　　　　　　　[附屬標記] 附屬子句

　　所以英文有清楚的「主從之分」，主要子句就是語意的重點，完整獨立；附屬子句必須加上附屬標記，做為區別：

主要子句 ⬅ 附屬子句 帶附屬標記

15

★為什麼英文不能說 Because... so....?

中文可以說「因為……所以……」，英文卻不能說 "Because..., so...."，為什麼？

原因很簡單，因為中文沒有主從之分，英文卻是「主從有別」，兩個子句中必須一個為主，一個為從。由於 because 和 so 都是附屬連接詞，如果兩個子句都加上附屬連接詞，就都成了附屬子句，而沒有主要子句了！所以有了 because，就不能有 so；有了 although，就不能有 but，這樣才能保持一主一從的原則：

> 一主一從：
>
> **I went to Taipei** although it was raining.
>
> Although it was raining, **I still went to Taipei.**
>
> **It was raining,** but I still went to Taipei.

基於「主從有別」的特性，英文的動詞也一樣要分主從，句子裡只能有一個主要動詞，是唯一帶有時態標記的動詞，用來表達時間主軸，其他動詞在形式上都有別於主要動詞，可能是不定詞、動名詞或是子句補語，都是「主從有別」的表現：

主	從	
I planned	to see a doctor.	➡ 不定詞 to-V
I enjoyed	visiting friends.	➡ 動名詞 V-ing
I thought	that he was out of town.	➡ that-子句
I married her	because I love her.	➡ 附屬子句
I bought a book	which is interesting.	➡ 關係子句

到底英文還有哪些「主從分明」的講究，附屬子句又有哪幾種？請繼續看第 3 章《重點何在》。

名詞出場，必有標記！

特性 4

每種語言都有用來表達周遭的人、事、物、東西的名詞。在句子裡，每一次使用名詞時，如「貓」、「狗」、「書」、「桌子」、「椅子」，都要知道你說的「東西」所指為何？那麼要如何讓說話的另一方知道你指的是「哪一個」呢？請看以下對話：

小華在書店遇見小明

> **小華** 咦，你怎麼在這裡？
>
> **小明** 我來買書。

中文的一句買「書」，其實有四種可能：

可能一：一本你不知道的書　➡ a book　　單數，不定
可能二：那本你知道的書　　➡ the book　　單數，特定
可能三：一些你不知道的書　➡ some books　多數，不定
可能四：那些你知道的書　　➡ the books　多數，特定

中文可以「省」，所以在表達「某一本」的時候，也可以省略該名詞的細節。但是英文對於名詞有嚴謹的規定，名詞出現時，一定要有「數量」（不可數名詞除外）和「特定與否」的標記。名詞前面要加上冠詞，顯示

「單複數」和「對方是否知道指的是哪個東西」：

> **What did you buy?**
>
> I bought **a** book.　　　　　　　➡ 單數 不定（對方不知道的一本）
>
> I bought **the** book (you mentioned).　➡ 單數 特定（對方知道的那本）
>
> I bought **some** books.　　　　　➡ 複數 不定（對方不知道的一些）
>
> I bought **the books** (you mentioned).　➡ 複數 特定（對方知道的那些）

　　英文非常有原則，一旦名詞出現，就必須考慮名詞的單複數以及對「聽者」而言這樣東西是否「你知我知」。英文使用了固定明確的名詞標記：

> 不定冠詞 a / any / some　　　　　➡ 聽者不知道是哪一個
>
> 　　　　　　+ 名詞 +（複數標記s）
>
> 特定冠詞 the　　　　　　　　　➡ 聽者知道是哪一個

　　加定冠詞 the 表示聽者知道是哪一個；用不定冠詞 a、any、some，表示聽者不知道是哪一個。除了冠詞外，名詞本身也有標記，複數時要加上表示複數的 –s，例：book ➡ books。

● 何謂「特定」和「非特定」？冠詞 a 和 the 有何區別？

　　「特定」的意思其實就是「你知我知」。如果名詞所指的東西是聽者清楚已知的，就用 the 來標記（identifiable to the hearer）。「非特定」指的就是「我知而你不知」，如果認為聽者不知道並且無從辨認，就用 a 來標記（not identifiable to the hearer）。

　　使用冠詞 a / the 是很有效的方式，因為看到冠詞就知道所指的是否「你知我知」：

Who is he talking to?	他在跟誰說話？
He is talking to **a** girl.	（一位你不知道的女生）
He is talking to **the** girl.	（那位你知道的女生）
He is talking to **some / many** girls.	（一些／很多你不知道的女生）
He is talking to **the / these / those** girls.	（那些你知道的女生）
He is talking to **the** girl you mentioned.	（那位你才提過的女生）

英文名詞的標記還有什麼其他的功能和用法呢？請詳見第 4 章《究竟是哪一個？》。

動詞出場，時間清楚！

在表達一個事件時，除了要說清楚「誰對誰做了什麼」，事件發生的時間也很重要，一旦動作出現，必定牽涉到動作發生的時間，這就是時式的基本意義：

> 小明 我看到老師！
>
> 小華 什麼時候看到的？
>
> 小明 昨天晚上！

事件的發生一定有一個時間點，When？

只要有動作一定有時間，但是每種語言表達動作時間的方式不一樣，先來看看中文的表達方式：

> 小明 你這幾天做了什麼?
>
> 小華 我昨天讀書，今天讀書，明天讀書，天天都讀書。

中文利用不同的時間詞，如「昨天」、「今天」、「明天」、「天天」來幫助表達動作的時間，但是「讀書」這個動詞本身並沒有任何改變。然而在英文中，卻是直接利用「動詞」來表達發生的時間，發生時間不同，動詞形式就跟著變化：

英文 — 以動詞表達發生時間	中文 — 動詞與時間無關
I studied yesterday.	我昨天讀書。
I am studying.	我正在讀書。
I will study tomorrow.	我明天讀書。
I study every day.	我天天讀書。

英文以動詞來表達發生時間，動詞形式隨時間而改變，時間成為「動詞標記」的一部分，因此「看動詞」就知道事件是什麼時候發生的！但是動作發生的時間究竟有幾種區別呢？

時間的概念可分為四個區段，以說話當下的時間為基準，可分為「現在」（說話當下）、「過去」（說話之前）、「未來」（說話之後）以及「事實習慣」（過去/現在/未來都如此）。這四種時間概念的區別，可以放在時間座標中來理解：

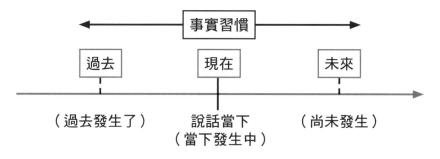

以上四種時間概念，搭配四種動詞的形式，準確表達事件發生的四種「時式」：

> 過去式：I cooked yesterday.　➡ 說話之前發生
> 現在式：I am cooking now.　➡ 說話當下發生
> 未來式：I will cook tomorrow.　➡ 說話之後才發生
> 習慣式：I cook every day.　➡ 無明確時間點，天天發生

這四種時式的區分，都要以「現在」為基準。什麼是現在呢？「現在」就是「說話當下」，我說話的當下就是我的「現在」，你說話的當下就是你的「現在」，所以「現在」這個時間是是會隨說話的人而變動的！為了表達不同的時間概念，英文的動詞有四種時式變化：

1）在說話之前發生的，就是「過去式」，通常在動詞後加 -ed：

　　V-ed：I cooked / talked / jumped.

2）在說話當下發生的，就是「現在式」，動詞保持常態：

　　V 原形：He is angry.

　　　　　　I feel happy.

但是要注意：動作類的動詞（cook, talk, jump...）如果發生在當下，一定是正在進行，就要用進行貌（V-ing）：

V-ing：He is cooking dinner now.

　　　　I am writing my homework.

3）在說話之後才發生的，則是「未來式」，在動詞前加上表未來的助動詞 will：

　　Will + V 原形：I will cook dinner for you.

　　　　　　　　　　I will visit you tomorrow.

4）若事件是一直重複發生，時間涵蓋過去、現在和未來，表達一種習慣或事實，則是「習慣式」，無論是不是動作，形式上都要用動詞常態：

　　The sun rises in the east.　➡ 每天都如此

　　I go to school by bus.　➡ 每天都如此

特別要說明的是：「現在式」和「習慣式」的時間概念不同，但是表達狀態時，動詞形式看起來會很像：

靜態動詞

現在式：I know the answer now.　　　　　➡ 現在知道

習慣式：I know the answer all the time.　　⇒ 一直都知道

在表達動作時，就可明顯看出「現在式」和「習慣式」的語意完全不同：

動作動詞

現在式：I am eating apples.　⇒ 現在正在吃蘋果

習慣式：I eat apples.　⇒ 事實如此：我平常是吃蘋果的

所以「太陽從東邊升起」這句話是表達一種事實，因為過去如此、現在如此、將來也如此；若是現在正在升起，就會用不同的形式：

現在式：The sun is rising in the east.　⇒ 太陽此刻正在升起

習慣式：The sun rises in the east.　⇒ 陳述事實

有了時間的基本概念後，就要進一步養成「用動詞標記時間」的習慣，每次使用動詞時，都要把時間納入考量，準確標記！動作的時間還有哪些其他的表達方式，動詞的過去式又有哪些變化呢？詳盡的內容請見第 5 章《什麼時候的事？》。

事件有樣貌，做完了還是進行中？

英文用動詞標記時間，時間的區別主要有「過去」、「現在」、「未來」和「習慣」這四種不同的時段，但是除了時間之外，描述事件時還可以選擇用不同的角度，來表達事件發生的「樣貌」。比如「昨天寫功課」這件事，可以用三種不同的觀點來描述，就會出現三種不同的表達方式：

三種觀點	中文	英文
➤簡單完整的描述	昨天我寫了功課。	I did my homework yesterday.
➤強調在持續進行中	昨天我在寫功課。	I was doing my homework yesterday.
➤強調說話前已完成	我寫完功課了。	I have done my homework (by now).

這三種方式以不同的角度來描述「寫功課」這件事，呈現三種事件的「樣貌」：簡單貌、進行貌、完成貌。這三種「時貌」（Aspect），搭配三種動詞的形式，表達了三種不同的語意：

時貌	語意	形式	例句
簡單貌	單純表達事件發生了	有時間標記的 V	I ate breakfast at 7 am.
進行貌	強調事件在持續進行中	BE + V-ing	I was eating breakfast at 7 am.
完成貌	強調事件在「參照點之前」已完成	Have/has + V-pp	I have eaten breakfast (by now).

➤什麼是「進行貌」？

　　「進行貌」強調動作的進行，通常有一個時間的「焦點」，強調在這個交會點上，事件正在進行（on-going）：

➤以說話當下為焦點，就是「現在進行式」：

 Q: What are you doing?   你現在在做什麼？
 A: I am reading.   我在看書。

➤以過去的時間為焦點，就是「過去進行式」：

 Q: What were you doing at 6 am? 你早上六點在做什麼？
 A: I was reading.   我在看書。

➤以未來的時間為焦點，就是「未來進行式」：

 Q: What will you be doing at 9 pm tonight? 你今晚九點會做什麼？
 A: I will be reading.   我會看書。

➤將焦點延伸至過去、現在、未來，就是「習慣性的進行式」：

 Q: What do you usually do?   你通常做什麼事？
 A: I am always reading.   我總是在看書。

　　因此，「進行貌」的表達，可依據事件發生的時段，分為「過去進

行」、「現在進行」、「未來進行」及「習慣進行」四種不同的可能：

習慣性的進行 I am always reading.

➢V-ing 進行貌與動名詞

進行貌和動名詞的形式相同，都是 V-ing，這是因為進行貌表示動作實際在持續進行中，如同存在於時間座標中，就像名詞一樣有時間的持久性，因此動詞可藉由改變為 V-ing 的形式變成名詞（即動名詞）：

Cooking is my hobby. 　　　烹飪是我的嗜好。

We both like *swimming*. 　　我們都喜歡游泳。

➢什麼是「完成貌」？

「完成貌」的描述觀點很特別，並不是要表達事件本身的時間，而是要強調事件在「另一時間之前」已經做完。「完成」的概念一定會牽涉到另一個時間點，判斷一件事是否完成，要看你從哪一個時間點來看！例如下午 2 點到 5 點是我上課的時間，如果從 3 點鐘這個時間點來看，課還沒上完，但是從 6 點鐘這個時間點看，課已上完了。因此「完成」與否取決於由哪一時間點切入，「完成」是相對於一個「參照時間」認定的（completed by a reference time）。

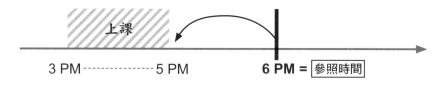

I have finished my class by 6 PM. 　我的課六點前就結束了。

「完成貌」表達的就是事件在「參照時間之前」完成的語意。所以「參照時間」才完成貌最重要的考量！依照「參照時間」是「現在」、「過去」或「未來」，就成為「現在完成」、「過去完成」及「未來完成」三種形

英文文法有道理！入門版

式，分別表達三種「之前完成」的語意：

➢ 現在完成式：現在「之前」已完成

　參照時間 = 說話當下

　I have done my homework (before now). ➡ 說話此刻之前完成了

➢ 過去完成式：過去「之前」已完成

　參照時間 = 過去某時間

　I had done my homework before I ate dinner. ➡ 吃晚飯之前就完成了

➢ 未來完成式：未來「之前」會完成

　參照時間 = 未來某時間

　I will have done my homework before I sleep. ➡ 睡覺之前應該會完成

➢ 由於習慣式並沒有一個明確的時間點，不能作為參照點，因此沒有習慣完成式。

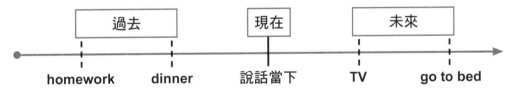

I had done the homework before dinner.　　I will have watched TV before bed.
I have done the homework and have had dinner.

　　所謂「時態」就是包含「時式」（Tense）與「時貌」（Aspect）兩種標記。如果將「進行」和「完成」兩種觀點與四個時段相結合，便會構成七種語意，搭配七種表達形式：

瞭解了進行貌和完成貌的不同，就要特別注意如何使用正確的時貌來表達不同的語意。有關時貌的其他組合及形意搭配的原則與用法，請詳見第 6 章《事件的進展如何》。

7 特性 辨明真假，判斷可能

英文的動詞可以標記時間和時貌之外，還可以加上表達對「真假可能」與「責任需要」的判斷，這樣的標記在中文裡也常見：。

真假可能的判斷
小明 你會去嗎？
小華 可能會去。
也許會去。
或許會去。

責任需要的判斷
小明 我不想去……
小華 你應該去。
你必須去。
你一定要去。

中文的「可能」、「也許」、「或許」、「應該」、「必須」、「一定要」表達的是說話者個人的主觀判斷，是一種對「可能性」或「責任義務」的判斷，通常放在動詞前面。在英文裡這些詞都被稱為「情態助動詞」，就是幫助表達主觀情態推斷。這些推斷情態的助動詞在語意上可分為三大類：

1）表達真假可能性的推斷： can、may、 might、will、would
2）表達義務需要的推斷：should、 must、ought to、has / have to
3）表達能力或許可的推斷：can、may

真假可能		
	現在或習慣	過去
可能	It can be hard.	It could be hard.
可能	It may be hard.	

一定是	It will be hard.	It would be hard.	
可能（較委婉）	He might do it.	He might have done it.	➡ 可能已經做了
可能會（較委婉）	He would do it.	He would have done it.	➡ 可能已經做了
一定要	He must do it.	He must have done it.	➡ 應該是已經做了

責任需要		
	現在或習慣	過去
應該要	He should do it.	He should have done it. ➡ 早就應該要做了
應該要	He ought to do it.	He ought to have done it. ➡ 早就應該要做了
必須要	He has to do it.	He had to do it. ➡ （過去）必須要做
一定要	He must do it.	無對應的過去式

能力／許可		
	現在或習慣	過去
能夠	He can do it.	He could do it. ➡ 當時有能力做
可以（有能力）	He may do it.	
可以（有許可）	You can leave now!	He could leave. ➡ 當時被允許
可以（有許可）	You may leave now!	

> 情態助動詞的特性：一詞多義

情態助動詞常有「一詞多義」的現象，例如 can 就有三種可能的語意：

1）有能力：I can speak English.

2）有可能：This can be a good choice.

3）有許可：You can use my car.

這三種語意其實是彼此有關聯的，如果你「有能力」做，就等於「有許可」去做，有能力或許可做，就很「有可能」去做：

有能力做	➡	有許可做	➡	有可能去做
I can do it.		You can do it now.		It can be done.

may 則通常表達兩種語意：

有能力做	➡	有許可做	➡	有可能做
She may do it.		You may go now.		I may see you tomorrow.

➢事實與推測

情態助動詞都是表示說話者的推斷，加了這些助動詞的句子就變成了「推測」，而非確實發生的事。請看以下例句：

> 事實： I visited Mary today. ➡ 確實去拜訪了
> 非事實：I should / must / can / may / might / will / would visit Mary today.
> ➡ 應該去，但是並未確實發生

事件是否確實發生了是溝通上很重要的訊息，因此在語法上也有明確的標記方式。其中，動詞時態就是透過時間上的認定來表達「確實與否」：

若是事件發生在過去、或正在進行、或已經完成，那動詞本身的時間就證明「確實發生」了：

事實	現在進行：I am writing a letter. 過去式： I wrote a letter. 完成式： I have/ had written a letter.	➡ **事件確實發生**

非實	未來式：I will write the letter. I will have written the letter. I would write the letter	➡ **事件尚未發生**

➢條件與假設

最常見的「非事實」不外乎「條件」與「假設」。這兩種情況都「不是

事實」，都可用附屬連接詞 if（如果），但語意上還是有區別的：「條件句」通常是指未來有可能出現的情況，表達一種「萬一成真」的前提；而「假設」通常是指「與事實不符」的情況，是表達一種遺憾或追悔。請看以下對話：

> 條件句：如果明天下雨，我就在家吃飯。　　➡ 可能發生
> If it rains tomorrow, I will eat at home.
> If it will make you happy, I will do it!
> 假設句：如果我是他，我會跟她去看電影。　　➡ 不可能發生
> If I were him, I would go to the movie with her.
> 如果我昨天去賣場，我就會遇見她了。
> If I had been to the supermarket, I would have met her.

由於「條件」及「假設」都是非事實，因此在時間標記上必須要與確實發生的事件有所區別。有可能出現的「條件句」並沒有明確的時間點，所以通常用沒有既定時間的「習慣式」來表示「可能情況」：

> 條件式：未來有可能發生，但時間未知
> 習慣式：If it **rains** tomorrow, I will not go out for dinner.
> 　　➡ 習慣式表可能
> 未來式：If you will go, I will go.　➡ 強調未來將發生

換成「違反事實」的假設句，則會有兩種情況：與「現在」的事實不符還是與「過去」的事實不符，兩種情況都要在時態的標記上與「現在」有所區別：

➤若是違反「現在」的事實，就在時間上往前推移，以「過去式」來表達但願如此的「非現在事實」：

> 與現在事實相反的假設：
> 現在事實：I **am** not rich.　　　　　　　　　　➡ 用現在式
> 非現在事實：If I **was** rich, I **would** buy the house.　➡ 用過去式

➤若是與過去事實相反的假設，就不能用過去式，而是要再往前推移，用「過去完成式」來表達但願當時如此的「非過去事實」：

> 與過去事實相反的假設
> 過去事實：I **didn't** see her. ➡ 用過去式
> 非過去事實：If I **had seen her**, I **would have** told her the news.
> ➡ 用過去完成式搭配非事實的助動詞

情態助動詞幫助說話者表達各種主觀的推斷，在語意上自然造成「純屬推測，並未成真」的認定，至於情態助動詞更詳細的用法和語意區別，請詳見第 7 章《辨明真假：事實與假設》。

8 特性 主動被動，句句講究

一個動作的發生，一定有做動作的人，有時也會有一個受動作影響的人，例如打人的事件，一定有「打人的」，也有「被打的」，一方是事件的「主導者」，一方是「受害者」。打人這事件可以從「主導者」的角度來描述，也可以從「受害者」的角度來描述：

> 師 發生甚麼事？
> 生 女生罵男生！ ➡ 以「主導者」為主詞
> 男生被罵了！ ➡ 以「受害者」為主詞

這兩種不同的描述角度就是「主動」和「被動」最大的區別。在英文裡「主動句」和「被動句」在動詞形式上有明顯的差異：

> 主動句：The dog <u>chased</u> the boy. ➡ V_{tense}
> 被動句：The boy <u>was chased</u> (by the dog). ➡ BE + V_{pp}（過去分詞）

「狗追男孩」還是「男孩被狗追」在英文的動詞上要有清楚的標記。

「主動句」用一般動詞，「被動句」要用 BE 動詞加過去分詞（BE + V$_{pp}$），所以請注意：被動句的主要動詞變成 BE，而不是一般動詞。這其實是有原因的，因為打人的動作出現後才會有被打的結果，所以「被動句」其實是表達動作的「結果狀態」，不是在描述「打」這個動作，為了描述打了之後的「狀態」，所以要用表示狀態的 BE 動詞。

英文的每一個句子都有主、被動之分，每句話都要考慮主詞和動詞的關係，若是被動的關係，一定要有被動的標記。但是中文的「被動句」卻不一定有「被」：

> 中文的被動句不一定有「被」：
> 報紙送來了。➡ 報紙是「被」送來的
> 功課寫完了。➡ 功課是「被」寫完的

英文的被動句一定要有被動標記：

主動句 S$_{主導者}$ + V + O	被動句 S$_{受控者}$ + BE + Vpp
I bought a pen. （我買了一枝筆。）	**The pen** was bought. （筆買了。）
Mom prepared dinner for me. （媽媽為我做晚餐。）	**Dinner** was prepared for me. （晚餐準備好了。）
She sent a book to him. （她送了一本書給他。）	**The book** was sent to him. （書送到他那了。）

筆不會自己買、晚餐不會自己準備、書也不會自己送，因此當這些角色出現在主詞位置時，英文都必須用被動式來表達，英文嚴謹的要求主詞和動詞的關係必須要釐清！這種「責任清楚」的標記原則可以從中英文的對照看出，所以千萬不要因為中文沒有「被」，就忘了要釐清主詞和動詞的關係喔！

● 分詞也有主、被動之分

「分詞」是動詞的一種形式，基本上分為「現在分詞」和「過去分詞」，通常和 BE 動詞合用，作為修飾語：

現在分詞 V-ing：The book is <u>interesting</u>. ➡ 主動的語意
過去分詞 V-en：The book is <u>torn</u>. ➡ 被動的語意

「現在分詞」和「過去分詞」這樣的名稱，有時會造成誤解，以為和時間有關，其實這兩者的區別並不是在於發生在「現在」還是「過去」，而是在表達「主動」和「被動」的區別。現在分詞就是「主動分詞」，表達主動的語意；過去分詞就是「被動分詞」，表達被動的語意，請比較以下的分詞構句：

主動句： I helped my mom and I washed the dishes.
⬇
主動分詞：<u>Helping</u> my mom, I washed the dishes.
為了幫媽媽的忙，我洗了碗。

被動句： I was helped by my mom and I washed the dishes.
⬇
被動分詞：<u>Helped</u> by my mom, I washed the dishes.
在媽媽的幫忙下，我洗了碗。

完整的句子可以被簡化為分詞，有一個很重要的條件，那就是要有相同的主詞，分詞的主詞要和主要子句的主詞一致：

主動分詞 Teaching at a high school, <u>she</u> became more outgoing.
V-ing （她）在高中教書後，<u>她</u>變得比較活潑。
（X）Teaching at a high school, <u>her job</u> is secure.

被動分詞 Taught by a good teacher, <u>she</u> made progress in English.
V-en （她）被一位老師教導後，<u>她</u>的英文進步了。
（X）Taught by a good teacher, <u>her English</u> improved.

以上的分詞又稱為「簡單分詞」，單純表達主語相同的關聯。然而，分詞構句也可將時間的先後帶入，用完成貌來強調「之前」已經發生，稱為「完成分詞」，形式上用 Having + V-en：

完成分詞　　主動：Having worked for 20 years, he retired this year.
Having V-en　　（他）在工作了20年後，他退休了
　　　　　　被動：Having been fired by his company, the man
　　　　　　　　　　disappeared.
　　　　　　（他）在被公司解雇後，他就失蹤了

「主動」和「被動」是英文最基本、最重要的語意區別，無論說什麼，每一句話都要釐清主詞和動詞間是什麼樣的關係，每一個被動關係都要有明確的被動標記。這是最需要注意的！其他有關主、被動的形意搭配原則，請看第 8 章《該誰負責：主動與被動》。

時空轉換，語意多變

介系詞是語言中很特別的一類詞，介系詞都來自空間方位，上、下、前、後、裡、外等，但這些詞也可以用在時間的描述上，例如我們可以說：

他的位子在我的「之前」，也可以說聖誕節在新年「之前」。位子是空間的概念，聖誕節卻是時間的概念，這種「空間」和「時間」相互連結的例子，生活中無處不有。請再看以下對話：

小明　期末考快要**到**了。
小華　時間**過**的真快，希望暑假快點**來**！
小美　時間不停的**走**，想**追**也**追**不上！

對話中的動詞「到、過、來、走、追」原本都是表達空間移動，時間不會真的「來到」你家，但是這些空間動詞都被用來描述「時間」。這是因為「時間」是抽象的，很難理解，除非借用具體的「空間」詞彙來描述，才比

較容易理解。這種「時空轉換」的特性，在英文的介系詞用法上相似。以英文最常見的三個介系詞 in、at、on 為例，每個介系詞各有其獨特的「空間概念」及「原型圖像」：

介系詞	空間原型	概念圖像	例子
in	在空間範圍內	空間容器（container）	in a city in a box in a room
at	在空間定點	空間實點（point）	at the bus stop at the entrance at the shop
on	在空間接觸面上	空間平面（surface）	on the floor on the table on the road

簡單的說，這三個介系詞各自有其專屬的空間概念：

in：在範圍內（in a boundary）

at：在定點 （at a spot）

on：在接觸面上（on a surface）

這些基本的空間概念，可以延伸到其他的生活範疇，而產生看起來不一樣的語意，這就是為什麼介系詞似乎牽涉到多變的語意。但是其實介系詞的核心概念並沒有變，變的是從空間轉換到時間或其他的範疇：

英文文法有道理！入門版

透過認知轉換，介系詞的原型空間概念，可以延展至其他範疇，以表達看起來不一樣的語意：

- in 可由「在空間範圍之內」延展至「在時間範圍之內」，如：“Finish your homework in a minute.”（在一分鐘內完成作業。）接著可再進一步延伸至抽象範圍，表達出「涵蓋於內」的語意，如：“She is in love.”（她戀愛了。）或是顏色的範疇：“She is in red.”（她穿全身紅的。）。

- at 可由「立於空間定點」延展至「時間的定點」，因此可說 “Let's meet at 8 o'clock.”（我們八點碰面。）而定點的概念可以再延伸至能力的「定點」或情緒的「定位」，如：“She is good at math.”（她數學很好。）“I am surprised at her English.”（我對她的英語能力很驚豔。）

- on 可由「在空間接觸面上」的概念延展至「時間的接觸面上」，因此可說 “She is always on time.”（她總是準時。）“We will have a meeting on Monday.”（我們周一會開會。）而接觸面的概念亦可再延伸至某一主題或焦點的「面向」，如：“She is working on the project/ report / topic.”（她正在做那個計劃／報告／專題。）

以上只列舉了英文三種最常見的介系詞，至於其他更多介系詞的空間原意及延伸用法，請參照第 9 章《在哪裡發生的：介系詞該怎麼用》。

10 特性 規則為上，例外有深意！

語法是一套為了溝通而產生的「形意搭配」的法則，這套法則必定存在著一定的共通性，以便能夠讓說話者清楚了解彼此傳達的訊息。「形意搭配」的法則是固定的，然而人是活的，可能會為特殊的需要而巧妙的運用語言的規則來達成特殊的溝通需求，這就是為什麼語法規則總有例外！

規則的形成，是大多數情況下所使用的原則，例如 love 和其他的情感動詞一樣，都是表達一種心理狀態，是心動，不是行動，所以通常不會用於進行貌：

> I love her.　　　➡ 不會說：*I'm loving her.
> I like McDonald.　➡ 不會說：*I'm liking McDonald.

I'm loving it!

　　這是一個通則，在大多數情況下大多數人為了大多數的目的所使用的原則。但是當麥當勞想要創造一個新的廣告亮點，好讓「心動」變成「行動」時，他就故意說：I'm loving it!

　　這個所謂的例外，並不是破壞規則，而是規則的特殊運用。為了一個特殊的目的，採取了特殊的搭配方式，故意將 love 加上「-ing」，把心動變成了行動。

　　這個效果能夠達成正是因為「-ing」這個形式固定搭配了進行貌的動態語意（on-going）。所以語法要學通就是要了解什麼樣的形式搭配什麼樣的語意，規則是常態，而例外卻是有特殊涵意！

　　再舉一例：food 這個詞的常態用法是集合性的概念，是「食物」的總稱，為不可數名詞，但是若要特別強調多種、個別、不同的食物，就有可能加上 -s：

> Many plants are eaten as <u>food</u>.　➡ 食物的總稱
> Some <u>foods</u> are not from animal or plant sources.　➡ 多種類的食物

　　所以，可數不可數的區別是以認知和使用的常態來區分，但有時為了表達特別的語意，就可能打破常規。台灣許多外文系的名稱是 "Department of Foreign Languag<u>es</u> and Literatur<u>es</u>"。有沒有注意到 literature 加了「-s」？文學一詞 literature 是指文學這個文體，通常是用來表達不可數的概念，但為什麼外文系卻用 Literatur<u>es</u>，難道連自己系所的名稱都搞錯了嗎？道理其實是一樣的，外文系為了表達少數特殊的語意，強調要教的是多種多樣的文學，就故意加上「-s」。藉由複數的標記表達多元化的文學研究，表示文學還可再細分為不同的文學類型。

　　所以，「規則」是溝通的常態，是大多數情境中，為大多數目的所使用的表達方式，也就是所謂的「majority rule」；「例外」就是少數特殊情境下，為了少數目的，所使用的特殊搭配方式。其他有關規則與例外的說明請看第 10 章《規則之外》。

文法是什麼？

文法就是
形式和意義搭配的原則！

♀))) 1. 你想說什麼？

單元1 主詞／動詞／受詞

當你看見一個奇景，一隻胖貓在追一隻瘦狗，你會說什麼？

> 哇，貓追狗耶！
>
> 哇，胖貓追瘦狗！
>
> 哇，一隻貓在追一隻狗！

不管你怎麼說，都不會說成顛倒的：「狗」追貓！為什麼？

因為語言的「先後順序」代表不同的角色，能清楚表達誰追誰，誰打誰，誰愛誰……

主詞	動詞	受詞
↓	↓	↓
貓	追	狗。
她	打	他。
我	愛	你。

英文呢？也一樣！

主詞	動詞	受詞
↓	↓	↓
I	love	you.
Mary	hit	Tom.
A cat	chases	a dog.

「主詞」（**S**ubject）就是最主要的角色，通常是主動做事的，放在動詞前面。

「動詞」（**V**erb）就是表達動作，交代做了什麼事。

「受詞」（**O**bject）就是接受動作的人物，放在動詞後面。

有了完整的主詞、動詞、受詞（S-V-O），就表達一個完整的事件，就是一個完整的英文句子。電影「阿凡達」最後一句話，就是最好的例子：

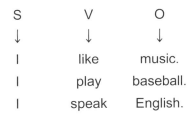

S-主詞	V-動詞	O-受詞
↓	↓	↓
I	see	you.

同理：

S	V	O
↓	↓	↓
I	like	music.
I	play	baseball.
I	speak	English.

2. 英文怎麼説？

➤**超簡原則1：主、動、賓不可少，也不可多！**

英文和中文的「先後順序」一樣，都是 S-V-O（主詞-動詞-受詞），但是有一點很不一樣：中文可以省，英文不能省！請看看以下的對話：

> **老師拿著一本很受歡迎的書問學生**
>
> **師** 喜歡嗎？
>
> **生** 喜歡！

請注意，師生對話中，「誰」喜歡「什麼」（你喜歡這本書嗎？）其實都沒說出來，但學生都明白！這是因為中文對話情境中已知的成分可以省略不說，所以老師的問句中省略了主詞（你）和受詞（這本書）。

但是英文不行！老師的問題換成英文，就不能省，必要的語意成分（主詞、動詞、受詞）都要表達清楚：

Teacher Do you like the book?

Student Yes, I like it.

No, I don't like it.

所以，英文的表達方式是很嚴謹明白的，像一個嚴謹的英國紳士，該說的都得清楚說出來，這就是「主、動、賓（受詞）不可少，也不可多」的原則！

小結（中英比一比）：中文可以省，英文不能省！

> **超簡原則2：代名詞作主詞、受詞形式不同**

「先後順序」有助於表達主詞和受詞的不同，但英文在使用「代名詞」時（如：我喜歡他。），為了方便區別，主詞和受詞的「形式」必須不一樣，作主詞的代名詞以「主格」形式出現，作受詞的以「受格」形式出現：

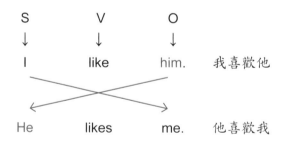

```
  S        V        O
  ↓        ↓        ↓
  I       like     him.    我喜歡他

 He      likes     me.     他喜歡我
```

英文代名詞有主格、受格形式之分：

主格代名詞：單數 I、 you、he、 she、it
　　　　　　複數 we、you (you all)、they
受格代名詞：單數 me、you、him、her、it
　　　　　　複數 us、you (you all)、them

I see you.	我看見你（妳）。
You see her.	你看見她。
She sees him.	她看見他。
He sees them.	他看見他們（她們）。
They see us.	他們看見我們。
We see it.	我們看見它。
It looks good.	它看起來很好看。

有沒有注意到只有兩個代名詞的形式保持不變：第二人稱 YOU 和代表東西的第三人稱 IT，主格受格同形！

小結（中英比一比）：中文代名詞形式不變，但英文代名詞的角色不同，形式就不同，有主格、受格之分。

 ## 3. 還能怎麼說？

> **英文句子一定有主詞，到底主詞有何講究？樣貌為何？**

簡單來說，主詞就是事件的「主角」，其呈現內容有數種型態，人、事、時、地、物均可當主詞，但其概念為【名詞性】的：名詞（N）、動名詞（V-ing 將動作轉變成名詞）、不定詞（to-V 表示「要做的事」）或名詞子句（Noun clause 名詞性的事件）等皆可做為主詞。

> **英文句子裡的受詞也不能省，到底受詞有何講究？樣貌為何？**

至於受詞呢？就是「接受動作」的第二主角。能夠「接受動作」的當然也是名詞，受詞除了常見的名詞（N），也可為動名詞（V-ing）、不定詞（to-V）或名詞子句（Noun clause）。

(1) 例句解說：主詞

一句話的主詞，可以有下列不同形式：

[The police officer] 主詞 chased the bad man.

➡ 主詞為一般名詞 [The police officer]。

[Seeing Lady Gaga] 主詞 drives me crazy.

➡ 主詞為動名詞 [Seeing Lady Gaga]

[To play basketball with my classmates] 主詞 **is exciting**.

➡ 主詞為不定詞 [To play basketball with my classmates]。

[It] 主詞 **is exciting to play basketball with my classmates.**

➡ 前一句主詞太長了，為避免頭重腳輕，用代名詞 [It] 做主詞，代替 [To play basketball with my classmates]。

[It] 主詞 **is convenient [to shop online]** 主詞.

➡ It做為虛主詞，代替後面訊息較複雜的不定詞。

[Whether it will rain tomorrow] 主詞 **is really important.**

➡ 主詞為名詞子句

[There] are five people in the room.

➡ 主詞為處所詞 [There]，加上 BE 動詞，引介時空中存在的事物。存在的人物才是語意重點，所以動詞單複數要配合後面的名詞。

[There] is a game in the afternoon.

➡ 下午有一場比賽，明確的空間處所詞+BE（There is / are...）表明時間中存在的事物，這是時空轉換的結果。

(2) 例句解說：受詞

受詞和主詞一樣，也可以有不同的形式：

I painted **[my room]** 受詞. ➡ *受詞為一般名詞*

Jessica enjoys **[swimming]** 受詞. ➡ *受詞為動名詞*

To exercise every day means **[to keep healthy]** 受詞. ➡ *受詞為不定詞*

I just want to know **[what they talked about]** 受詞. ➡ *受詞為名詞子句*

　　主詞、受詞都是名詞，要向「名詞」對齊，因為主詞與受詞都是參與事件的「主角」，其本質等於「名詞」性的人事物，都得標記為「名詞」。

　　一句話的是否有受詞，跟動詞語意息息相關，因為動作分為兩種類型：及物（＝及於另一物）與不及物（＝不涉及另一物）。「及物」就是有觸及或牽涉另一物的動作，當然要加受詞語意才完整：

I met a young woman.

I like English.

如果只說 "I like..."，別人一定要問 "You like WHAT?"

別忘了英文的主詞、受詞都不能省，一定要說清楚講明白！

有些動詞本身語意就帶有受詞，跟動作的產出是同形同意，因此 I sang a song. 也可說 I sang. 就足以表達其意了，所以此類動詞可以是及物，也可以是不及物動詞。

(3) 例句解說：含有受詞意味的動詞

I danced. ➡ I did **a dance**.

I sang. ➡ I sang **a song**.

I turned. ➡ I made **a turn**.

➢英文的基本句式

英文有幾種句式？

基於主動賓不可少也不可多的原則，英文嚴格說來只有一種基本句式，那就是：

主詞 + 動詞 + 補語 （補充語意的必要元素），簡稱為 S-V-C：

(**Subject**) + (**Verb**) + (**Complement**) ➡ (**S-V-C**)

補語（complement）是補充語意的必要元素，可能是受詞（＝賓語 object），或是其他形式的補語（Ｘ），例如：

I like math. ➡ S-V-O （Ｏ：名詞）

I like hiking. ➡ S-V-O （Ｏ：動名詞）

I like to hike. ➡ S-V-X （Ｘ：不定詞 to-V）

進一步說，基於動詞有及物和不及物的區別，英文基本句式（SVC）有四種可能形式：

S-V: I *exercised.* ➡ 不及物動詞不加受詞

S-V-O: I *read* a book. ➡ 及物動詞加受詞

S-V-X: I *read* to learn. ➡ 動詞後加不定詞補語

S-V-O-X: I *want* them big and strong. ➡ 受詞後再加受詞補語

除了搭配動詞語意的補語（complement）之外，句子裡還可加上其他額外的附加訊息（adjunct），如：時間、目的、方式、地點等：

I *exercised* for three hours.	➡ 時間（duration）
I *exercised* for my health.	➡ 目的（purpose）
I exercised with caution.	➡ 方式（manner）
I *exercised* at the gym for three hours.	➡ 地點+時間（place + duration）
I *ran* from my house to the market.	➡ 起點+終點（source + endpoint）

　　英文的每一個句子都是在描述一個事件，事件有**動作**與**狀態**之分，也有**及物**與**不及物**之分（詳見第 2 章），因此句子的形式會依**動詞語意類型**的不同，加上需要搭配的補語（S-V-C）：

➢一般動作動詞：

1）不及物：He sang. ➡ S-V

2）及物＋受詞： He sang a love song. ➡ S-V-O

➢**BE 動詞**：

3）BE+名詞補語： It is a love song.

　　➡ S-V-C（It = the song, S + BE + NP）

4）BE+形容詞補語： It is melodic.

　　➡ S-V-C（It = the song, S + BE + AdjP）

5）BE+連動補語： It is beautiful to hear.

　　➡ S-V-C（The song is beautiful to hear. S + BE + Adj + to-V）

註：C=補語, NP=Noun Phrase（名詞片語）, AdjP=Adjective Phrase（形容詞片語）

➢感知判斷動詞

6）It sounds beautiful. ➡ S-V-C（感知判斷 V + AdjP 形容詞補語）

7）It sounds like heaven. ➡ S-V-C（感知判斷 V + like 介系詞+名詞補語）

➢**虛主詞+BE**

8）It is beautiful to hear the song. ➡ S-V-C（It 虛主詞 = to hear the song）

　　= To hear the song is beautiful. ➡ S-V-C（主詞為不定詞 to-V）

　　= Hearing the song is beautiful. ➡ S-V-C（主詞為動名詞 V-ing）

　　➡ 事件性主語（即主詞），可用不定詞或動名詞

➢分詞作形容詞補語：

9）主動分詞：The song is inspiring.

　　➡ S-V-C（S + BE + 主動分詞）

10）被動分詞：He was inspired by the song.

　　➡ S-V-C（S + BE + 被動分詞 + by 主動者）

　　➡ 所謂的被動句（BE 動詞為主要動詞）

➢處所倒裝句（先強調空間地點）：**X-S-V**

11）Here you are. ➡ X-S-V（倒裝：You are here.）

12）In the room are five students. ➡

　　X-S-V（倒裝：Five people are in the room.）

13）There are five students in the room. ➡

　　X-S-V（倒裝：Five students are there in the room.）

➢從「處所倒裝」到「存在句」There is / are：

　　There is / are原為空間倒裝句，透過 時空轉換 的認知機制，空間存在可延伸為時間上的存在或廣意的存在：

14）There are five games tomorrow . ➡ X-V-S 時間存在

15）There are five members in the team . ➡ X-V-S 廣意存在

　　➡具體的空間詞 there is / are 經由語意轉換，成為表達「**時空存在**」的固定用法：

16）There is a movie I want to see tonight. ➡ X-V-S 存在一部電影

17）There are rumors about his promotion. ➡ X-V-S 存在一些謠言

　　基本上, 英文以句子為本，每一個句子都表達一個事件，說明誰對誰做了什麼（Who does what to whom?）。英文要求參與事件的每一個角色都要說清楚，所以「主動賓不可少」，要清楚標記事件的主詞+動詞+補語（S-V, S-V-O, S-V-C）。正因為主詞不能省，英文常出現帶虛主詞的句式。以下再用兩例進一步分析為什麼常見「虛主詞」句子。

？為什麼要用虛主詞 It is.... ？

通常使用虛主詞 "It is..." 大多因為主詞本身就是一個事件，語意較複雜，如果放在句首，可能影響溝通：

It is impossible [to do all the work in one day].

➡ 虛主詞 It 代表後面的不定詞子句

= [To do all the work in one day]主詞 is impossible.

➡ 不定詞子句作主詞

It is impossible [for me to do all the work in one day].

➡ 虛主詞 It 代表後面的不定詞

= [For me to do all the work in one day]主詞 is impossible.

➡ 不定詞子句作主詞

　　因為主詞不可少，而這兩句話的主詞又是較長的事件性主語，為了避免頭重腳輕，所以選擇用「虛位」的主詞 It（虛主詞）放在句首，來代替後面提到的真正主詞 [to do the work in one day]。

　　總結，英文和中文很不同。**中文是「情境導向、能省則省」**，只要有明確的情境，已知的主詞或受詞便可省略。但**英文屬於「語句為本、嚴謹標記」**，什麼都不能省，到底「誰」對「誰」做了什麼事都必須交代清楚，句子內每一個參與角色都需要一一標記。因此，請記住中文重情境，英文嚴句子！

 4. 讀一段短文

As I was going to St. Ives,	當我正要去聖艾夫斯市時
I met a man with seven wives.	我遇見了一個有七位太太的男士。
Each wife had seven sacks.	每個太太都有七個麻布袋。
Each sack had seven cats.	每個麻布袋裡都有七隻貓。
Each cat had seven kits.	每隻貓都有七套工具。
Kits, cats, sacks and wives:	工具、貓、麻布袋和太太們：
How many were there going to St. Ives?	到底有多少東西正要去聖艾夫斯市呢？

說明：

說英文的原則是主詞、動詞、受詞不可少，也不可多！所以從上面這首經典英文童謠短文的前四句可以清楚找到英文表達的原則：SVO。

I *met* [a man with seven wives].
S V   [O]

Each wife *had* [seven sacks].
　　S　　V　　　[O]

Each sack *had* [seven cats].
　　S　　V　　　[O]

Each cat *had* [seven kits].
　　S　　V　　　[O]

5. 唱一首英文歌

Desperado　　　　　（by Eagles）	亡命之徒　　　　（老鷹合唱團）
Desperado	亡命之徒
Why don't you come to your senses	你為什麼不能用理性來思考呢？
You've been out riding fences for so long now	你現在已經把自己用圍籬隔絕自己很久了
Oh, you're a hard one	喔！你是個固執的人
But I know that you've got your reasons	但我知道你有你自己的理由
These things that are pleasing you	那些可以令你開心的事
Can hurt you somehow	可能會不知怎麼地也會傷了你
Don't you draw the Queen of diamonds boy	難道你不抽走那張方塊皇后的牌嗎？
She'll beat you if she's able	她如果有機會就會把你打敗擊垮
The Queen of hearts is always your best bet	一直以來紅心皇后都是你手中王牌
Now it seems to me some fine things have been laid upon your table	現在對我來說似乎那些美好事物都在你眼前
But you only want the ones you can't get	但是你卻只想要那些你無法得到的

從以上的歌詞中，也能發現在「主動賓」不可少的原則下，英文的主詞

和受詞以多種不同形式出現：

1. You*'ve been out riding* [fences] for so long now
   S   V   [O]

2. But I *know* [that you've got your reasons]
     S V   [O] 名詞子句為受詞

3. These things [that are pleasing you] *can hurt* [you] somehow
             S 主詞含有形容詞子句   V   [O]

4. Don't you *draw* [the Queen of diamonds boy]
         S   V   [O]

5. She*'ll beat* [you] if she's able
   S   V   [O]

6. But you only *want* [the ones you can't get]
       S   V   [O] 含有形容詞子句的受詞

 # 6. 看一部影片

電影名稱：《舞力全開 3 "最後決賽"》（Step up 3 Finale Dance）

Part 1：主動賓不可少，也不可多！

> 精選對白：
>
> 1. And I *wouldn't have* [the courage to do that] without you.
>   S   V   [O]
>
> 2. Samurai*'s wiping up* [the floor] with these guys.
>   S   V   [O]
>
> 3. You *can trust* [me].
>   S   V   [O]
>
> 4. Oh! Oh, *are* you *kidding* [me]?
>   S   V   [O]
>
> 5. I *will take care of* [everything] until you get back.
> S   V   [O]
>
> 6. I *know* [you have dreams, too]. ➡ 我*知道*[你也有夢想]。
> S V   [O] ➡ 名詞子句為受詞 O

Part 2：什麼時候用「虛主詞」？

這句對白的中文翻譯是：「但現在該是我們這些評審來決定誰將把這 10 萬元帶回家的時候了。」從此句中可看出 it 代表後面整句「to V」的不定詞片語 "to decide who's going home with this $100,000."。

當主詞造成「頭重腳輕」或是搞不清楚誰當作主詞時（如描述天氣狀況等），英文就以代名詞 it 作為主詞。把 it 放在主詞位置上，滿足了語法標記之需求，但地位不同於典型主詞，而是代替另一個語意較為明確的名詞，就是所謂的「虛位主詞」。

Part 3：

除了 it 之外，語意較為特殊的主詞還有表示空間存在的 There 和 Here。如果不僅要表達「存在」，還要強調人物的「出現」，英文會用空間倒裝句搭配較動感的來去動詞來引介此號人物。如影片中的對白：

 7. 做一點練習

Part 1：請將下列句子圈出主要主詞（主要動詞已加底線）並註明主詞類型：名詞、代名詞、動名詞、不定詞、虛主詞、名詞子句、處所詞。

(1) I *ate* the apple yesterday.

(2) The little girl *sang* a song.

(3) The boy *waved at* us.

(4) Jessie *put* a sausage in the oven.

(5) Surfing the net *is* fun.

(6) It *is* interesting to play basketball with you.

(7) The movie *amazed* me.

(8) There *are* two movies I want to see.

(9) To keep the body in good health *is* a duty... otherwise we shall not be able to keep our mind strong and clear. *Quote from Buddha*

(10) Saying nothing sometimes *says* the most. *Quote from Emily Dickinson*

(11) That I am not a member of any Christian church *is* true; but I *have never denied* the truth of the Scriptures, and I *have never spoken* with intentional disrespect of religion in general, or of any denomination of Christians in particular.

Quote from Abraham Lincoln

答案：(1) I, 代名詞 (2) The little girl, 名詞 (3) The boy, 名詞 (4) Jessie, 名詞 (5) Surfing the net, 動名詞 (6) It, 虛主詞 (7) The movie, 名詞 (8) There, 處所詞 (9) To keep the body in good health, 不定詞 (10) Saying nothing, 動名詞 (11) That I am not a member of any Christian church, 名詞子句

Part 2：請圈出主要子句中的受詞

1. I am a crocodile. I can wiggle my hips. Can you do it?

   ~From Head To Toe by Eric Carle

2. Old McDonald had a farm, Eieeioh. And on his farm he had a cow, Eieeioh.

   ~ Old MacDonald Had A Farm

3. You shall have an apple,

   You shall have a plum,

   You shall have a rattle,

   When papa comes home.

   ~Nursery RhymeYou Shall Have an Apple

4. Look into my eyes

   You will see what you mean to me

   Search your heart, search your soul

   And when you find me there

   You'll search no more

Don't tell me it's not worth trying for

You can't tell me it's not worth dying for

You know it's true

Everything I do, I do it for you

~(Everything I do) I do it for you - Bryan Adams

答案：1. hips, it 2. farm, cow 3. an apple, a plum, a rattle 4. my eyes, me,

your heart, your soul, me, me, trying, dying, Everying, it, you

Part 3：克漏字

> ### The Garden Party 花園派對
>
> ---
>
> **a. There　　b. her mother　　c. was trimming　　d. hired**
>
> ---
>
> Mrs. Trotter (1) _____ a wonderful hat to wear to the garden party. The hat was covered with leaves and ferns. Mrs. Trotter had (2) _____ a parrot to sit on the top.
>
> Little Rosalind Trotter was sitting by the window with her friend the breeze. "What's a garden party?" Rosalind asked (3) _____.
>
> Her friend the breeze became still to listen.
>
> "A party in a lovely garden," said Mrs. Trotter. "(4) _____ will be roses, lilies and peacocks strutting around a fountain."
>
> （聯經出版）

答案：(1) c (2) d (3) b (4) a

Part 4：中英大不同

A. 請將下列英文句子翻成中文，並將主詞、動詞與受詞標示出來

1. People have no sympathy for Villains. They prefer them small and weak. They don't realize how a bit of danger brightens things up.

~The New House Villain 新家樹上的大壞蛋（聯經出版）

中文翻譯：

答案：大家一般對大壞蛋沒有什麼同情心，他們寧願大壞蛋又小又弱。
大家不瞭解，有些危險性才可以炒熱氣氛。

[People] have [no sympathy for Villains].
　S　　V　　　　　O

[They] prefer [them] small and weak.
　S　　V　　O

[They] don't realize [how a bit of danger brightens things up].
　S　　　V　　　　　　　O受詞為名詞子句

註解："They don't realize how a bit of danger brightens things up." ➡ 動詞
　　　realize 後的受詞通常為名詞子句。"They prefer them small and weak" 句
　　　中的主詞 they 指的是一般人，受詞 them 指的是 Villains。

2. The narrow track to the old swing bridge didn't always follow the river.
Sometimes it looped into the forest and we would be walking over
giant tree roots or through patches of mud and ferns.

~Stories of the Wild West Gang

當我們瘋在一起：無可救藥的偉斯特家族1（聯經出版）

中文翻譯：

答案：往舊吊橋的狹窄小路，不總是沿著河流走，有時[它]會繞進森林
　　　裡，所以我們得走在巨大的樹根上，或是通過有泥巴跟蕨類植物
　　　的地方。

[The narrow track to the old swing bridge] didn't always follow the river.
　　　　　　　　　　　S　　　　　　　　　　　　V　　　　　　　O

Sometimes [it] looped into the forest and [we] would be walking
　　　　　　S　　V　　　　　　　　　　　　S　　　V

over giant tree roots or through patches of mud and ferns.

註解：中文是主題為大、主題為先的語言。因此，此題中[往舊吊橋的狹窄小
　　　路]是整段主題，後面句子圍繞主題而鋪陳，所以主題非常明確而可以
　　　省略。但英文是主詞為大，主動賓不可少，每個句子都有清楚明確的主
　　　詞、動詞、受詞。

B. 請將下列句子中翻英。

1. 每天彈鋼琴是很好玩的。

答案：1. Playing the piano every day is fun.

2. It is fun to play the piano every day.

3. To play the piano every day is fun.

註解：英文句子中主詞若有頭重腳輕的現象可以用虛主詞 It 代替，成為形式上的主詞，實質語意內涵則在後面子句中。

2. 的確，他持有（possess）這戒指很多年，也曾經使用過。

答案：Of course, he possessed the ring for many years, and used it.

~魔戒首部曲：魔戒現身（聯經出版）

註解：中文可以省，「這戒指」已清楚明確的提到過，後面即可省略不提（也曾經使用過）；但英文句子中主動賓不可省，所以再次提到戒指時，還是要用代名詞 it 來清楚標記受詞（and used it），it 一定要翻譯出來。

CHAPTER

2

發生了什麼事？
動詞怎麼用？

⏣))) 1. 你想説什麼？

單元1 主詞／動詞／受詞

　　如第一章所言，英文一個句子表達一個事件，而事件的核心就是「動詞」!

　　「動詞」用於表達人所從事的各種「活動」，或周圍發生的各種「變化」。比如說，貓和狗都在跑，這到底是什麼動作？是「跑」、「跳」、「追」還是「趕」？動詞就是用來描述所認定的動作，句子中的其他成分則是在幫助完整表達發生了什麼事。

　　動詞的功能既是用來表達「所認定的動作或是狀態」，選擇動詞的同時也要確定動作或狀態所牽涉的參與者，是貓追狗還是狗追貓？是人遛狗還是狗遛人？這就影響主詞／受詞的選擇。

　　「動詞」標記不同的動作，不同的動作會有不同的語意要求，牽涉不同的參與角色。例如，「追／趕」和「跑／跳」就是兩種不同的動作：追、趕一定會「及於另一物」，一定有個追趕的對象（受詞），屬於及物動詞；但是跑、跳只牽涉動作者自身，不會及於另一物，不涉及其他人或物（沒有受詞），所以是不及物動詞。

　　及物與不及物動詞代表兩種不同事件類型。不及物的事件「不及於另一物」，例如："The dog jumped." 「跳」jump 這個動作，不會牽涉其他人物，不須搭配受詞。而及物的事件必然「及於另一物」，一定要有受詞，例如："The dog bit the cat." 「咬」bite（過去式 bit）這個動作一定有對象，就需要交待承受動作的人物，如此語意才完全。所以及物動詞後面須接「受詞」來表達動作的「承受者」。

　　及物動詞和不及物動詞為兩種不同的事件類型，整理如下：

| 只涉及自身 | I ran / slept / dance / wander. |
| 涉及他人 | I hit / kick / miss / admire **him**. |

不及物：動作不及物另一物 ➡ V 不帶受詞

及物：動作及於另一物 ➡ V + O 帶受詞

 ## 2. 英文怎麼說？

▶**超簡原則 1：動詞語意決定用法**

動詞的用法是由語意決定，最基本的語意區別就是及物與不及物之分，代表兩種「事件類型」。要學會動詞的用法就必須了解動詞要表達的語意，所代表的「事件類型」。以 want 為例，want 可表達三種語意：想要什麼東西（+ 名詞），想要做什麼（+ 動詞不定式），想要某人（+ 名詞）做某事（+ 動詞不定式）。既然有三種語意，動詞後就有三種用法，表示三種不同的事件結構，要求三種不同的參與角色。

1.「及物類事件」：動作及於另一物，語意成分為：主動者 + 所及之物。

➡ I	want / like / take / have	the car.
主詞 +	動詞 +	名詞性受詞
(主動者)		(所及之物)

2.「想望類事件」：投射於未來想做的計畫／希望／目標，語意成分為：想望者 + 想做之事（to-V）

➡ I	want / plan / intend / hope	to quit.
主詞 +	動詞 +	不定動詞
(想望者)		(想望之事)

3.「支配類事件」：意圖操控他人去做某事，語意成分為：支配者 + 受支配的人 + 要做的事（to-V）

➡ I	want / ordered / asked / forced	him	to quit.
主詞 +	動詞 +	受詞+	不定動詞
(支配者)		(受支配的人)	(去做的事)

57

學動詞不需要死記用法，而是要理解語意，因為用法是為了表達完整的語意。為了表達「想做」的語意，就要交代想做「什麼」，動詞後就要加上不定詞 to-V，說明下一步的「目標」；而為了完整表達「支配」的語意，則需說清楚是要支配「誰」去「做」什麼事，用法上就必須加上受詞及不定詞 to-V。

有此可知，動詞有不同的用法形式是為了表達不同的語意類型。

> **超簡原則 2：動詞後加原形 Base-V、不定詞 to-V、動名詞 V-ing、或是名詞子句 that-CL（clause），各有不同含意。**

1. 原形動詞

「原形」就是指不帶任何時態標記的「裸」形式。就像一個人沒穿衣服，失去穿著的自主性，所以原形動詞也沒有自主性，失去「單獨陳述事件」的功能，只能依附於帶有時態標記的主要動詞之後。英文的「使役動詞」後要加原形動詞，就是表示「完全操控」的意思。

I made him clean his room. ➡ 我叫他打掃房間（我一要求他就去打掃）。
I had him water the flowers. ➡ 我叫他去澆花（我一要求他就去澆花）。

這裡的主要動詞 made 和 had 為「使役動詞」，後帶「原形動詞」，表示有「立即有效的操控」：只要 made 成立，clean 就成立；兩者「同時同地」發生，有直接緊密的關係，表達「完全且立即」的操控。

2. 不定詞 to-V

To 的基本語意表示空間上的「位移目標」，go to/ move to 後面接地點方位，表示移動的目標。從空間目標轉換至時間目標，移動方向就成為「未來要做的事」，投射在未來的時間點上。想望動詞後要接不定詞 to-V，表達下一時間點想做的事，也就是「時間上的目標」：

I went to the market. ➡ 空間目標（要去的地方）
I went to buy a sandwich. ➡ 時間目標（要去做的事）

例如：

Julie plans **to study** abroad. ➡ 計畫要去國外念書。
Vicky decided **to go** to Taipei by train. ➡ 決定要搭火車去台北。
Henry would like **to play** basketball with his classmates.
➡ 想要跟他的同學去打籃球。
My parents urged me **to hurry up**. ➡ 我爸媽催促我要快一點。

以上例子中都用不定詞補語（to-V）表達想要做的事，表示下一個時間點的心願，都屬於未來目標。

3. 動名詞 V-ing

動詞倏乎即變，詞尾加上「-ing」表示在時態上的進行事件。進行中的事件確實發生，在時間上必然「存在」；就如同名詞一般，保有時間上的延續性。因此動詞加上「-ing」就變成了名詞，成了「動名詞」，表達動作性的實體。動詞後如果接動名詞作補語，表示該事件已然進行，必然存在。以下例句的動詞補語形式上都是 V-ing，表示具有時空存在的實體性。

Enjoy + N → Enjoy + V-ing
I enjoy the novel.　➡　I enjoy reading the novel.
I enjoy hot spring bath.　➡　I enjoy taking hot spring baths.

能夠 enjoy 的東西，必然是已存在的實體，因此 enjoy 後可直接加名詞（the novel）。但如果要用動作性補語，就要以 V-ing 形式表達如名詞般存在的「動作實體」（reading the novel），才能符合 enjoy 的語意。

同樣地，在表達動作的開始、結束或完成時，必然牽涉到動作本身的進行，就必須用「動名詞 V-ing」，因為開始做的事就開始進行，結束的動作必然已存在，完成的工作也是已進行的，形式上都需要 V-ing：

Jessica started the song. ➡ Jessica started **singing the song**.
　　　　　　　　　start + V-ing是指「開始進行」
Ms. Lu stopped the class. ➡ Ms. Lu stopped **teaching the class**.
　　　　　　　　　stop + V-ing是指「結束進行中的事件」

Mary finished her homework. ➡ Mary finished **doing her homework**.

finish + V-ing是指「做完」了，完成
進行中的工作（completed the job）

　　同樣的，spend、practice、mind、avoid、keep 後面都需要接 V-ing，就是所謂的「動名詞」！因為這些動詞語意都牽涉動作的進行，動名詞就是指動作如同名詞般在時間中存在，例如 spend 指的是花時間「做」某件事，花時間的同時就是動作在進行中：

Mike spent one hour swimming. ➡ 花一小時進行游泳這件事
Mike practiced swimming for one hour. ➡ 練習游泳進行了一小時
Mike kept swimming for one hour. ➡ 持續游泳游了一小時

　　所以，動詞加上 -ing 變成動名詞，讓它具備名詞功能，也標記了動作的進行與存在。但如果是要表達開始或結束以後的「目的」，那就不一樣了。下一刻要做的是「未來目標」，就要搭配不定詞 to-V：

Jessica started to sing the song. ➡ 開始唱歌（開始的目的是要唱歌）
Ms. Lu stopped to teach the class.
➡ 停下來去教課（停了先前的動作是為了要教課）

4. 名詞子句 that-CL

　　有些動詞需要另一個事件做補語，例如想「什麼」或說「什麼」。這個事件就要用 that 所接的子句來標記，表達一個時空明確及語意完整的獨立事件：

I think [that William must practice playing the guitar for hours every day].
He said that [he would not go to the party tomorrow].
The good news is [that my classmate, Jacky, won the Best Project Award].

➤**超簡原則 3：「動態動詞」表活動 vs. 「靜態動詞」表狀態**

　　動詞語意範圍包含隨時間而變化的「活動」或是相對穩定的「狀態」兩類。

動詞	特性	舉例
動態動詞：表達活動	1. 隨時間改變 2. 可搭配 ongoing 的進行式	外在體力活動：chase、catch、run、jump 內在心力活動：miss、consider、worry、think
靜態動詞：表達狀態	1. 無明顯進程 2. 較持久不變 3. 較抽象的心理或認知狀態 4. 不涉及動作 5. 不用在進行式	感知動詞：know、have、understand、forget 情緒狀態：like、envy、care、love、prefer、mind

請看例句：

1. 動態可進行：

　　Jay Chou is singing at the concert right now.

　　Ruby was eating and watching TV in the living room.

2. 靜態無進行

　　Those fans love Jay.

　　We care and respect our parents.

3. 動態 vs. 靜態

　　The children were shouting "Mr. Smith, we love you! Happy Teacher's Day!".

➤**超簡原則 4：動詞後補語的形式不同，語意就不同。有些動詞後面可以接 to-V，也可以接 V-ing，到底為什麼呢？**

(1) continue 繼續……有兩種用法：

　a. They continued **to play** badminton after lunch.

　　➡ 中間可能中斷了一段時間沒有打羽球，然後午餐後再繼續打羽球。

61

b. They continued playing badminton for the whole afternoon.

➡ 整個下午都在打球沒有中斷。

(2) start 到底開始了沒？

　　a. Fortuna started to walk her dog.

　　➡ Fortuna 開始要去溜小狗。（強調目的）

　　b. Fortuna started walking her dog.

　　➡ Fortuna 開始遛狗了。（強調動作已進行）

(3) stop 停下來做什麼？

　　a. Tina stopped to clean her room. ➡ 停下先前的工作去打掃房間。

　　b. Tina stopped cleaning her room. ➡ 停止正在打掃的動作。

(4) persuade / urge：此類為「勸說動詞」，要勸說某人「去做」某事，是勸說的目的，需用 **to-V** 表達「期望達成」的目標。

　　My father persuaded / urged me to apply for the new university.

(5) dissuade / prevent / stop sb from V-ing：此類為「勸阻動詞」，要讓人停止正在進行的動作，所以後面要接 **V-ing**，表達所要阻止已在進行的動作。

　　My parents dissuaded / prevented me from smoking. ➡ 阻止我抽菸

 # 3. 還能怎麼說？

動詞根據語意可分為十大類，分別表達十種不同的事件類型。

英文動詞的十大語意類型：

(1) 狀態連接動詞（be Verb）：表達狀態、關係、屬性、身份

　　這類動詞也稱作連綴動詞（Linking verb），用於靜態連結，連接主詞（Subject）和後續成分（形容詞或名詞），因為沒有動作所以沒有動詞可用，只能用連接動詞來描述狀態或狀態變化，例如：

> 狀態：be、seem、appear
> 狀態改變：become、get、turn into

後面可接描述特徵屬性的形容詞：

Jerry is / seems / appears tall. （外在）
Jerry is / seems / appears happy.（內在）
My dad's face turned green. （外觀變化）
He got/ become angry. （內在變化）

還可以用名詞表示身分、屬性或關係，例如：

My mother is a vegetarian. （狀態屬性）
She became / turned into a vegetarian. （狀態改變）

(2) 及物與不及物動詞

此類動詞區別在於「事件是否及於另一物」，如果動作有及於他物，則須於後面加上動作的接受者，也就是受詞；若無受詞，不及物動詞只要有主詞即可。而外在動作與內在心智活動都有及物與不及物的區別：

動態動詞（內外活動）
不及物：I swam / danced / cried.
及物：I saw / invited / visited John.

靜態動詞（無動感、無進行）
不及物：I agree / know / regret.
及物：I envy / love / respect him.

(3) 使役動詞：表完全操控

使役動詞指後面結果完全被操控而產生的，無自主性，故要接原形動詞，表示被操控後要「立即行動」；或接形容詞補語，表示「立即變化」。

make	+受詞	+動詞原形 （立即動作）
I made	him	**cry**.
I made	him	**leave**.

make	+受詞	+形容詞 （立即變化）
I made	Mary	**happy**.
I made	his day	**miserable**.

(4) 想望喜好動詞：表達個人意願、喜好、傾向、決定等。

> 想望動詞+ to-V
>
> I want / plan / desire / prefer to **take a week off**.
>
> I decided / made up my mind **to travel around the world**.

　　個人想望喜好表示「嚮往的事」，但尚未發生，故用不定詞 to + V 表達「下一個時間」目標，強調時間上有先後之分。

(5) 支配請求動詞：表達「意圖操控」。

　　此類動詞帶有支配他人，要求他人採取行動；但不保證一定能成功操控，僅能以 to-V 表達期望達成之目標。

> 支配動詞 + 受詞 + to-V
>
> Frank ordered / forced / persuaded me **to take a rest**.
>
> ➡ 我不一定 take a rest
>
> Linda asked / told / required me **to take a break**.
>
> ➡ 我不一定 take a break
>
> I ordered him to leave, but **he didn't**.
>
> ➡ to-V 表期望目標，但不保證一定發生

(6) 感官知覺動詞：表達感知活動與經驗

　　a. 此類動詞為透過五官所感受的知覺經驗，分為「可自控」與「非自控」：

可自控

Please **look at** the beautiful flowers.

Please **listen to** what he is going to say.

➡ 可刻意去聽或看，可自主決定

非自控

I **see** some beautiful flowers there.

I **hear** what he says.

➡ 眼睛/耳朵自動接收到影像或聽到聲音，非自主決定

因此，可自主的動作才可命令他人去做，才可用於祈使句。例：

A: **Look**! There is a ladybug over there! Can you see it?

B: No, I don't **see** it!

以上例子說明我們可以要他人用眼睛「去看」一隻瓢蟲（Look at the ladybug!），但對方不一定「看得到」（may not see it!）

此種自主與非自主差別適用最重要的兩種感官：「聽」與「看」。

b. 其他次要的感官，如聞 smell、嚐 taste、摸 feel 等就可用同一個詞
表示：

可自控

Smell it!（祈使句）

Taste it!

非自控

It **smells** so good! Do you **smell** the scent?

It tastes yummy. Can you taste the sweetness?

c. 感官經驗的對象可為名詞、動詞或子句

1. 名詞：

例：I heard **the good news** yesterday.

The boy looked at **the dog**.

2. 動詞：

(1) 原形動詞：I heard them sing.

➡ 時空相依（感官動詞本身有主導性，以原形動詞來標記感知）

(2) 進行式： I heard them singing.

➡ 共時進行（表示在聽覺範圍之內，所察覺的現象正同時同地進行，有現場直擊感受）

3. 子句：I heard that they were singing.

➡ 完整事件（用以強調感知活動和感知現象間可為各自獨立的事件）

I heard that they have left. 從聽見到「聽說」（強調訊息, 而非感官）

I heard that they will arrive tomorrow.

➡ 從聽見到「聽說」(兩個事件在時空與人物上不必相連)

d. 語意轉換：從視力到腦力、感官到認知，**see** 也可以表達「理解明白」的意思。

例：I see.

I saw [that you had a good point in your argument].

➡ 表示理解認知、非真正看到

(7) 樣貌呈現動詞（look-like verbs）：連綴動詞（表達外物樣貌）

此類動詞有 look like、sound like、smell like、feel like⋯⋯等，傳達「外在物體」的樣貌，描述外物所引發的五官感受（It looks...、It sounds...）。因此主詞為「外物」，動詞形容所感受到的樣貌特徵，所謂「連綴」，就是連結客觀的「外物」和主觀的「樣貌感受」。

連綴 V + 形容詞
It looks pretty.
It sounds funny.

連綴動詞 + 介系詞 like + 名詞
It looks like a bat.
It tastes like coffee.

(8) 思考溝通動詞：你「想說」什麼？

「思考溝通」為人最基本活動，「說的話」通常和「想的事」相通，因此「我想說……」、「我認為……」，後面要加一個補充說明的子句，用來引述說明思考的內容。子句以 that 為前導，區隔主要動詞和補語，並提示後續將有完整事件，又分為「直接引述」與「間接引述」兩種。

> 「直接引述」
>
> "I didn't know how to get to the MRT station," Henry said.
>
> The author wrote: "There is no happiness without pain."
>
> ----
>
> 「間接引述」
>
> Copernicus（哥白尼）said / claimed / explained that [the Earth is round].
>
> He thought / guessed / remembered that [his boss had promised to promote him].

(9) 給予授受動詞：表達物件的傳遞與接收

此類動詞描述兩方間「給予/接受」互動關係，含有「物件傳遞」的動作。

> a. 給予者 + V + NP給予物 + to NP接收者
>
> My mom gave / sent / mailed a letter to me.
>
> b. 給予者 + V + NP接收者 + NP給予物
>
> My mom gave / sent / mailed me a letter.

例句 a，給予物為「直接」受控物品，接收者「間接」收到信件，故用 to 來標記 receiver（接收者）角色。

例句 b，接收者放於動詞後，強調接收者之「直接受益」角色。

說話時究竟該選 a 或 b 之句型，需判斷「接收者」和「接收物」孰重孰輕？在訊息傳遞過程中，最自然傾向「已知」先於「未知」，由熟知訊息帶出「新訊息」：

在已知接收物前提下

A: Who will you give **the book** to? （接收物 the book 已知）

B: I will give **it** to John .

在已知接收者前提下

A: What will you give to **John**? （接收者 John 已知）

B: I will give **him** a book .

(10) 享受感謝動詞：享受行動的樂趣

英文有兩個動詞很特別，在中文裡沒有直接的對應詞，那就是 enjoy 和 appreciate。這兩個動詞是表達對「行動」的感受，後面要用 V-ing，表達享受或感謝的對象為真實存在或已發生的事件：

I enjoyed **talking** to you. ➡ 享受和你的談話

I appreciate your **spending** time with me. ➡ 感謝你花時間陪我

I'd like to thank you for **recommending** the book. ➡ 謝謝你的推薦

在英文中，要感謝或享受的是行動本身或他人所做的事，故 enjoy/appreciate 的對象為「事」而非「人」。但 thank 可以用於感謝「人」。

例：

1. I appreciate **it (事)**. ➡ It will be appreciated if you come.

2. I enjoyed **your company (事)**. ➡ Your company is enjoyable.

3. I thank **you (人)** for coming here. ➡ thank 人 for 事

4. I appreciate **your coming** here **(事)**. ➡ appreciate 事

5. **Your coming** here **(事)** is appreciated. ➡ It is appreciated that you came here.

其實 thank you 本身為一種「行動」（speech act），與 apologize 一樣，說出來就等於做出來了：

I apologize to you for my negligence.

➡ apologize to 人 for 事（為了某事向某人道歉）

I apologize for not being able to help you.

➡ 為某事道歉

多樣用法，多樣語意

　　有些動詞可表達多樣語意，不同用法可表達不同的類型語意，如 remember 為「多義」詞：

I remember his name. ➡ 記得什麼？ ➡ 及物語意＋名詞

I remember his coming to visit us.

➡ 記得什麼？ ➡ 及物語意＋動名詞

I always remember to turn off the light.

➡ 記得要做什麼？ ➡ 如同想望類動詞＋不定詞

I remember that he moved to Hsinchu in year 2000.

➡ 記得什麼事？ ➡ 如思考溝通動詞＋that子句

 4. 讀一段短文

(1) Polar Bear

Polar bear, Polar bear, what do you hear?

I *hear* a lion **roaring** in my ear.

Lion, Lion, what do you hear?

I *hear* a hippopotamus **snorting** in my ear.

~*Polar Bear, Polar Bear What do you Hear, Bill Martin; Eric Carle*

　　說明：

　　感官知覺動詞後面可接動詞進行式，如 hear +受詞+ V-ing 表在聽覺範圍之內，所察覺到同時同地，正在進行的現象，有現場直擊感受。"I hear a lion roaring in my ear." 表示我聽到一頭獅子正在我耳邊怒吼。"I hear a hippopotamus snorting in my hear." 則是表示：我聽到一頭河馬在我耳邊嘶氣打呼。

(2) My Magical Maui

MY MAGICAL MAUI
(by Laura Thomas)
(Kelowna, B.C.)

What I am about to tell you happened many years ago. I was just a young girl, and the Hawaiian Islands were my vacation playground every summer.

I loved the island of Maui, and the ocean was home to me. When I snorkeled, I pretended I was entering a secret world, filled with mysterious creatures.

"A tiny turtle!" I shrieked through my bulky mask. I followed him through shoals of yellow tangs, and hundreds of other glorious, rainbow-colored fish. As I allowed myself to glide gracefully next to the tiny turtle, I felt his flipper touch my hand. I stayed close, and the two of us swam and swam in a watery waltz.

Eventually, I **decided** to pop my head above the water to clear my mask while Tiny munched on some green stuff. I looked back at the beach.

> 註解："decide to do something" 決定要做什麼（動詞 decide 後面接不定詞 to V，表示決定要做的事）

"My mom will be in a panic, Tiny. I have to go. But I'll be back tomorrow, okay?"

It's hard to explain, but I believe Tiny smiled at me!

I didn't tell anyone about my turtle, and that night, I dreamed a wonderful dream about Tiny showing me the whole ocean. When I woke up, I almost dragged my parents to the beach, and then flip-flopped into the clear blue water.

"Be careful, Lucy!" called my mother.

"Sure, Mom!" I replied.

I swam out to a safe depth, and then waved to my parents. When I reached my usual area at the big, black rocks, Tiny was waiting. My heart flipped as he smiled at me again, and then **asked me to follow him**. Not with words, of course, but I just knew.

> 註解：asked 為支配請求動詞，ask sb to V，意圖操控後面對象去做某事。

Tiny took me on a magical journey; we swam through giant coral reefs, slithered alongside slimy eels, and **saw a thousand starfish resting on a rock**. But Tiny saved the best until last. Basking in the reflection of the summer sun above us, I discovered a whole family of turtles!

> 註解：saw [a thousand starfish]resting on a rock
>   O   V-ing
>
> saw 非自控感官知覺動詞，"a thousand starfish" 為受詞，"resting on a rock" 的 resting 為與 saw 共時進行的動作。

I balled the net up in my fist, as I didn't want any other turtle getting caught. Tiny was safe, and I **realized** I **had been gone for quite some time**, so I waved to the turtle family and rose to the surface.

> 註解："I realized [I had been gone for quite some time]" 中 realize 為靜態活動動詞，為抽象的心理或認知狀態，不會用於進行式。realized 後接名詞子句 "[I had been gone for quite some time]"，表達時空明確且語意完整的一個獨立事件。子句補語前可用 that 為標記,或省略 that，語氣更直接。

………

But as my heart started pounding, I sensed the biggest turtle beneath me. I gently reached down to hold the edge of her shell, and she **started to move**, slowly at first. Tiny followed as I held my breath and we propelled through the water with ease. This was a ride I would never forget.

> 註解："started to move" 表示開始要移動（強調目的）

I spotted my parents pacing the shore by the time I got close. As soon as it was shallow enough for me to stand, Tiny and the big turtle swerved away. I stood on wobbly legs, and as I looked up, Tiny poked his head out of the water and **gave me one final smile**.

That was the last time I ever saw Tiny, but it was the best day of my life. I **told my parents what had happened**, and even **showed them the net**, but they just **thought** I'd been playing imaginary games. ……

> 註解：
> 給予者+給予收授動詞+接收者+給予物
> (1) gave [me] one final smile 的 gave 為授與動詞，授與的物品為 one final smile，接收者為 me，是動作傳遞的收受者。
> (2) told [my parents] what had happened 的 told 為授與動詞，授與的物品為 what had happened，接收者為 my parents，是動作傳遞的收受者。
> (3) showed [them] the net 的 showed 為授與動詞，授與的東西為 the net，接收者為 them。

From:http://www.short-story-time.com/my-magical-maui.html

（*https://goo.gl/LjbEHm*）

71

5. 唱一首英文歌

Last Christmas

Last Christmas I gave you my heart
But the very next day you gave it away
This year to save me from tears
I'll give it to someone special

Once bitten and twice shy
I keep my distance
But you still catch my eye
Tell me baby, do you recognize me
Well it's been a year
It doesn't surprise me
Merry Christmas
I wrapped it up and sent it
With a note saying I love you I meant it
Now I know what a fool I've been
But if you kiss me now
I know you'll fool me again

Last Christmas I gave you my heart
But the very next day you gave it away
This year to save me from tears
I'll give it to someone special

A crowded room and friends with tired eyes
I'm hiding from you and your soul of ice
My god I thought you were Someone to rely on
Me, I guess I was a shoulder to cry on
A face on a lover with a fire in his heart
A girl on a cover but you tore her apart
Maybe this year, Maybe this year,
I'll give it to someone special

Cause Last Christmas I gave you my heart
But the very next day you gave it away
This year to save me from tears
I'll give it to someone special

Last Christmas I gave you my heart
But the very next day you gave it away
This year to save me from tears
I'll give it to someone special
And last Christmas...

And this year...
It won't be anything like, anything like
Last Christmas I gave you my heart
But the very next day you gave it away
This year to save me from tears
I'll give it to someone special

從這首歌歌詞中發現授予動詞 give 及思考溝通動詞 think / guess 的用法：

1. 授予動詞

    (1) Last Christmas I gave you my heart.

    (2) I'll give it to someone special.

英文文法有道理！入門版

說明：

"Last Christmas I gave you my heart" ➡ 我（給予者 I）給你（接收者 you）我的心（給予物 my heart），這句話的直接受詞是接收者（you）。但下一句 "But the very next day you gave it away"，但隔天你就把它（my heart）送走了…… ➡ 給予物 it 成了直接受詞。

在給予的事件中，最「直接」受控的是物品，接收者是「間接」收到物品（to you），但也可以調過來。究竟誰做直接受詞要看誰是已知的訊息（在前），誰是新的訊息（在後）。"This year to save me from tears" 所以今年為了不再哭泣，"I'll give it to someone special" 我決定要把我的心（it）給另一個特別的人（to someone special）。

2.思考溝通動詞

(1) My god I **thought** you were Someone to rely on
(2) Me, I **guess** I was a shoulder to cry on

說明：

「我想說……」、「我認為說……」，為表達思考溝通的補語，後面接子句，通常以 that 為前導，區隔主要動詞並提示後續將有完整事件。但在歌詞或口語中，that 常常被省略。"I thought (that) you were Someone to rely on"，表示「我曾認為我是那個你可以依賴的人」，"I guess (that) I was a shoulder to cry on"「我猜想我是你可以靠著哭泣的肩膀」。

 # 6. 看一部影片

Ted 泰迪熊

Part 1：思考溝通動詞

精選台詞：
I guess Santa paid attention to how good you were this year, huh?

中文翻譯：我猜想聖誕老公公有注意到你今年表現有多好，是吧！

說明：為表達思考溝通內容，於 I guess 後面直接加子句，是另一個獨立而完整的事件，就是 "Santa paid attention to how good you were this year."。

請注意 paid attention to 後面直接用名詞子句 how good you were this year，表示注意到的現象，這個倒裝子句本質上是名詞性的補語（pay attention to something）。

Part 2：使役動詞

精選對白：

There was something about that bear [that made him feel as if he finally had a friend] with whom he could share his deepest secrets.

中文翻譯：有件關於那隻熊的事，就是那隻熊讓他覺得終於有個可以跟他一起分享內心深處祕密的朋友了。

說明：此句中使役動詞 made 後面要接完全被操控而產生的結果，因為是這隻熊讓他覺得他有朋友可以分享內心祕密了，是熊造成此結果，所以 "the bear made him feel..."。受詞 him 無自主性，故後面要接的是原形動詞，表示完全受控「必然」產生此種感覺。

Part 3：想望喜好動詞

精選對白：

I just wanted John and I to be friends.

中文翻譯：我只是想要約翰和我成為朋友。

說明：want 表示個人想望喜好「嚮往的事」，但尚未發生，此句中 I 只想要 John 和 I 可以做到「下一個時間」的目標 "be friends"，故用「to + V」，強調時間上有先後之分。

 **7. 做一點練習**

....

Part 1：請將下列句子加底線的主要動詞下方註明動詞類型：使役動詞、想望喜好動詞、及物語意、不及物語意、連綴動詞

(1)So many dreams are swinging out of the blue

We'll <u>let</u> them come true.

Forever young, I <u>want</u> to be forever young.

＜Forever Young，德國爾發村合唱團＞

答案：let 使役動詞；want 想望喜好動詞

(2)Hey Jude, don't <u>make</u> it bad

<u>Take</u> a sad song and make it better

<u>Remember</u> to let her into your heart

Then you can <u>start</u>

To make it better

＜Hey Jude，英國披頭四樂團＞

答案：make 使役動詞（+形容詞），表立即變化的結果補語，make it bad 讓它變糟

take後面接名詞，為及物動詞，take a sad song表選首悲傷的歌

remember/ start：想望喜好類語意動詞+不定詞（表下一個目標動作）

(3)I'm <u>driving</u> around in my car

I'm <u>driving</u> too fast

I'm <u>driving</u> too far

<u>I'd like to change</u> my point of view

I <u>feel</u> so lonely

I'm <u>waiting</u> for you

But nothing ever <u>happens</u> and I wonder

＜Lemon Tree，德國傻瓜花園樂團＞

答案：driving（drive）：不及物；I'd like to 想望喜好動詞；change：及物；feel：連綴動詞；wait：不及物；happen ：不及物。

Greedy Cat and the Sneeze 貪心貓打了個大噴嚏

be, is, clean, give, is, strong

"The real problem, I have to say, ___ too many dinners every day. This cat ____ like a pudding with feet. Katie, don't _____ him so much to eat."

"Sorry," said Katie. "That was wrong. I was only trying to make him _____."

"He'll ____ strong," said Dad, "if he eats less. Now, Katie dear, let's _____ up this mess."

（聯經出版）

答案：is, is, give, strong, be, clean

Part 3：中英大不同

A. 請就下列中英文對譯，觀察中英文動詞使用上不同

We Are The World	四海一家
（by USA for Africa）	（原唱：美國援非大合唱）
We **are**[1] the world	四海一家
We **are**[1] the children	神的子民
We **are**[1] the ones	我們就是
Who **makes**[2] a brighter day	創造更光明未來的人們
So **let**[3]'s **start**[4] giving.	所以我們要開始奉獻

B. 請將上面句子的劃線動詞寫出其語意類型及搭配用法。

答案：

1. are：為 linking verb，就是狀態連接動詞（BE 動詞），表達身分關係或屬性，連接後面的名詞或形容詞，屬於「靜態」連結，不牽涉到動作。

2. makes：此處為「製造」的意思，並非使役動詞，為及物動詞，後面接名詞（製造出什麼東西）。

3. let：為使役動詞，後面用原形動詞，「讓誰」做什麼事。Let's 為 let us 的縮寫，後接原形動詞。

4. start：此處為及物語意，後接動名詞，表示「開始進行」的事（giving= 給予）。

CHAPTER

3

重點何在？

🗣️))) 1. 你想說什麼？

單元1 簡單句 vs. 複雜句

前一章提到：一個動詞表達一個動作，一個事件。如果你看到下面這個場景，你會說什麼？

"Nobita and Doraemon are flying!"（大雄和哆啦A夢在飛！）這就是一個簡單獨立的句子，描述一個單一獨立的事件！

你可能覺得這件事太奇妙了，不禁又加了一句："It is amazing! Nobita and Doraemon are flying."（太神奇了！大雄和哆啦A夢在飛！）說話就是這樣，用一個一個句子，來表達想說的話。有時兩個句子也可以合併在一起，變成一個較長的句子："It is amazing that Nobita and Doraemon are flying!" 這是一個形式意義都較複雜的句子，包含兩個小句（＝子句）。由此可知，英文句子的種類有兩種：簡單 vs. 複雜句。

> 簡單句：有些句子比較簡單，表達單一的事件 who does what to whom 只牽涉一個動詞，就形成語意完整的表達：
> Nobita is flying.
> Nobita plays baseball.
> Doraemon comes from another planet.

複雜句：有些句子比較複雜，牽涉兩個以上的動詞，表達兩個以上的動作或事件：

Nobita likes to fly.（喜歡＋飛）

Doraemon plays a trick to fool Nobita.（耍個小把戲＋愚弄大雄）

They told me that Nobita and Doraemon flew to school.（告訴＋飛行）

複雜句就是把兩個動詞放在一起，或是把兩句話加在一起，變成一句話。前面說的例子就是把兩句獨立的話合併在一起，變成一句話：

It is amazing that Nobita and Doraemon are flying!

（注意：合併時一定有額外的標記）

有件事很神奇，那就是大雄和哆啦A夢在飛行！

由此可知，英文句子可根據動詞的多寡，分為簡單句及複雜句。

簡單句是最基本的組合，依【主、動、賓不可少】的原則，由一個主詞，一個動詞、或加一個受詞組成，表達單一事件。簡單句可以「簡單」到只有動詞的祈使句，如 Look!

複雜句就是較複雜的組，把兩個以上的簡單句合併在一起，成為一句話，所以一定有兩個以上的動詞，或是兩個以上的子句。看看下面這些句子，哪些是簡單句？哪些是複雜句？

Tina is a singer.	簡單句（只有一個動詞）
Tina sings well.	簡單句（只有一個動詞）
Tina sings English songs.	簡單句（只有一個動詞）
Tina sings a song to cheer herself up.	複雜句 （牽涉兩個動詞，兩個事件）
Tina sings a song when she feels sad.	複雜句 （牽涉兩個動詞，兩個事件）
Tina sings a song while doing her homework.	複雜句 （牽涉兩個動詞，兩個事件）

當我們把兩個動詞或兩句話加在一起時，自然出現一個問題，到底哪一個比較重要？哪一句是重點？英文嚴格講究誰為「主要」，誰為「次要」！一句話裡只能有一個重點，只能有一個「主」（main clause），其餘皆為「從」（subordinate clause）。請看看下面的例句，哪一部份在語意上是「主要重點」呢？

Tina sings a song to cheer herself up.	Tina唱一首歌（為了讓自己開心）
Tina sings a song when she feels sad.	Tina唱一首歌（當她覺得不開心時）
Tina sings a song while doing her homework.	Tina唱一首歌（一邊做功課時）

「主要重點」是全句語意上的核心，形式上也完整獨立。Tina 唱歌是重點，其餘部分是從屬訊息，都是在補充說明唱歌的目的、時間、情境。又如：

I heard Tina singing English songs.	我聽見[Tina唱英文歌]。
I know that Tina can sing English songs.	我知道[Tina會唱英文歌]。

我「聽見」、我「知道」是重點，其餘部分則補充說明聽見什麼、知道什麼。「主從有別」就成為英文語法的重要特點。

主從有別：
英語講究「主、從」在標記形式上有區別。語意上的「主要重點」在形式上就是「主要子句」，帶有正常的時態標記，單獨出現時形式語意都是獨立而完整的，不需額外的標記。但是次要訊息則一定要有明確的「次要標記」，形式上可能帶有明顯的附屬連接詞（if、although、when、because……），子句補語標記（that）或是無定標記（不定詞、分詞）成

為「從屬子句」。

附屬連接標記：Vicky bought a lot of new books_主要子句 [because_從屬連接詞 she enjoyed reading]_從屬子句.

子句補語標記：Vicky thinks [that_補語標記 books are the most enjoyable companions]_從屬子句.

不定詞標記：Vicky bought a lot of new books [to read_不定詞 in the summer break].

分詞標記：Vicky bought a lot of new books, [using_分詞 her pocket money].

　　上例中主要重點是 Vicky bought a lot of new books，這句話可單獨存在，語意完整；但是從屬子句 because she enjoys reading 僅表達原因，帶有額外的從屬標記 because，無法單獨出現，如果只說 *Because she enjoys reading 根本沒說完，語意也不完整。由此可知，「主、從」在形式上大有區別！

單元3 什麼是重點？重點放哪？

　　既然每句話都要有「重點」，說英語時就必須決定什麼是重點，而且重點要先說：“I saw a cat chasing a dog when I went to 7-Eleven after school this afternoon." 這和中文的溝通習慣很不一樣！中文說：小花今天下午放學後，在 7-Eleven 等公車時，看見一隻貓追一隻狗，這句話的重點是「看見貓追狗」，但是中文放到最後才說！中文通常先交代事件的背景細節，再進入主題。英文則剛好相反，先把重點講清楚，再將時地因果等其他細節逐一增添上去，先主後從，由小漸大，由重點到細節，層層展開，這就是英文的常態！

英文：<u>I saw a cat chasing a dog</u> in front of 7-Eleven while I was waiting for my bus this afternoon.

中文：今天下午放學後，我在 7-Eleven 前等公車時，<u>看見一隻貓追一隻狗</u>。

由此可看出英語的溝通特點是「重點在前」，再加上「主從分明」的要求，形式上就出現「主從有別」的標記特色。如果有兩個動詞，一定是「一主一從」，只有一個主要動詞；如果有兩個子句，也一定是「一主一從」，只有一個主要子句。而且順序上通常是「先主後從」：

兩個動詞：Nobita　**likes**　to fly.

| 主要動詞 帶有時態 | 不定詞補語 無時態 |

兩個子句：**Nobita likes to fly**　when he feels down.

| 主要子句 無額外標記 | 從屬子句 帶附屬連接詞 |

綜合上述，英文講究「主從分明」、「重點先講」，一個事件中不論出現多少動詞，只能有一個主要動詞（帶有時態標記）；一句話中不論出現多少要交代的事件，也只能有一個焦點事件做為主要子句。在形式標記上，主要子句（即焦點事件）也只能有一個主要主詞與主要動詞：

必要重點　＋　次要背景

| 主要子句 | 附屬子句 |

↓

主要主詞＋主要動詞

說英文時，要養成英文說話的習慣：重點先說，細節隨後，主從有別，標記不同！除了用對等連接詞 and / or 來連結地位平等的子句以外，其餘附屬子句都要有附屬標記。

2. 英文怎麼說？

單元1 什麼是主要子句？如何標記？

　　一個句號代表一個句子。英文句子中只能有一個「焦點事件」，就是主要子句。那麼究竟怎麼表達主要子句呢？所謂主要就是焦點、重點；主要子句就是一個句子中可以單獨存在的「獨立子句」，語意完整，形式獨立，不須額外標記。

1. I bought a new cell phone.	語意完整，形式獨立，為獨立子句	
2. I bought a new cell phone	which is expensive.	關係(附屬)子句
	because I lost my old one.	因果(附屬)子句
	when I went shopping yesterday.	時間(附屬)子句
	to replace the old one.	不定詞(附屬)補語
	spending a lot of money.	分詞(附屬)補語
主要子句 （無特別標記）	**附屬子句** （帶附屬標記）	

單元2 什麼是主要動詞（main verb）？如何標記？

　　無論是主要或附屬，一個子句只能有一個主要動詞，表達主要動作及發生的時間；形式上只有這個主要動詞可以帶時態，所以主要動詞就是帶有時帶態標記的動詞：

I went to the theater　　to watch the movie "Dangal".

主要動詞 (帶有時態)	其它動詞 (無時態標記)

　　在了解英語「主從分明」、「重點先講」特點後，以下就四個原則進一步說明如何寫出語法正確句子。

➤ 超簡原則 1：「主要子句」為報導重點

主要子句為全句的『報導重點』，負責報導溝通事件之重點，傳達主要事件、發生時間、主要參與人物及主題訊息，可獨立出現，無須附屬子句標記，為『獨立子句』；至於『附屬子句』在語意上用來介紹背景，傳達時間、原因、條件、前提等訊息，故形式上需有附屬標記。

"Jeremy played basketball with the kids <u>when</u> he came back to Taiwan."

一個句子『主、動、賓』不可少，因此主要子句中必有一個『主要主詞』和一個搭配的『主要動詞』，在主從分明的原則下，主要子句是無須特別標記的重點子句。上述例句："Jeremy played basketball with the kids"為主要子句，"when he came back to Taiwan" 則是帶有 when 標記的附屬子句，僅介紹事件發生的背景時間，語意上不完整，無法單獨存在。

➤ 超簡原則 2：「主要主詞」為全句核心人物

主要子句的主詞為全句『核心人物』，搭配『主要動詞』。在分詞構句中，『主要主詞』亦為分詞主詞。

例1. <u>Deciding</u> to keep a puppy, **Vicky** wanted to make a doghouse by herself.

➡ Deciding 為分詞，該分詞的主詞為全句的主角Vicky。

例2. <u>Being encouraged</u> to learn dancing, **Jessica** decided to take dancing lessons.

➡ Being encouraged… 為分詞，該分詞的主詞為全句主角Jessica。
Jessica被鼓勵去學跳舞，之後她決定去上舞蹈課。

例3. <u>Compared to human rights</u>, **animal rights** have been largely neglected.

➡ Compared to human rights 的主詞為 animal rights，兩個在比較的東西是 animal rights 及 human rights。

➤ 超簡原則3：「主要動詞」表達主要動作及標記主要時間

「主要動詞」（main V）表達主要動作，而且是句中唯一帶有『時態標記』的動詞。以下例句中的 heard 為「主要動詞」，且帶著『過去式

（past）』時間標記的完全動詞（finite V），後面接的原形動詞 sing 或進行樣貌 singing 都無時間標記，則為不完全動詞（non-finite V）。

例：I **heard**past a bird sing beautifully.

➡ 聽見鳥兒唱歌 (V-base原形：同時發生)

I **heard**past a bird singing beautifully.

➡ 聽見鳥兒正在唱歌 (V-ing：共時進行on-going)

主要動詞的時間功能

主要動詞負責描述全句的主要動作並且設定『時間主軸』，成為其他動詞對齊的參考時間。

問題一：如果在過去說了一件未來想要做的事，要用什麼時態呢？

回答：取決於『主要動詞』時間是否為貫穿全句的『主軸時間』。說話的內容有可能以說話當下的時間為基準。

例1. Mandy **told** me that she **would** go on a trip to Japan next week.

➡ 向『主軸時間』對齊

例2. Mandy **told** me that she **will** go on a trip to Japan next week.

➡ 以『當下時間』為參考

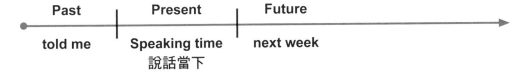

問題二：直接引述或間接轉述會影響次要動詞的參考時間嗎？

回答：

直接引述

He **said**, "I **will** go with you if I don't have to pick up my daughter."

➡ 兩句時間各自獨立，用引號隔開兩句，將當時說話的『原音重現』即可。

間接轉述

He **said** that he **would** go with me if he **had** time.

➡ 向『過去時間』對齊。

He **said** that he will go with me if he doesn't have to take dancing lessons.

➡ 向『現在說話時間』對齊。

因此主要動詞須與全句『主角』搭配，主要負責下列三項任務：

(1) 描述主角的動作或狀態

(2) 配合主角的人稱、單複數須一致

(3) 標記全句時間主軸，以此時段為基準，次要動詞須向其對齊

➤ 超簡原則 4：「主從有別」，要標記次要子句

主從的順序和標記：主從 vs. 從主

主要子句語意完整，可單獨存在，但次要的附屬子句須有「附屬標記」，標記方式如下：

(1) 附屬連接詞（subordinator）為最常見方式：

If		
When		
While	**+** 附屬子句,	主要子句（main clause）.
Because	（subordinate clause）	
As soon as		
In case that		

a. 功能

√ 表『因果』 because, since, for the reason that, so...

√ 表『條件』 if, only if, in case that, provided that, as long as...

√ 表『時間』 when, while, as soon as, at the time that...

b. 順序

主從的順序和標記： 主從 vs. 從主

√ 重點在前：【主要子句】+ 附屬子句

例：[We won't go mountain climbing next Saturday] **if** it rains heavily.

重點在前

√ 重點在後：附屬子句（+逗點）+ 【主要子句】

例：**If** it rains heavily next Saturday, [we won't go mountain climbing].

重點在後

說明：英文習慣重點先講，順序為「先主後從」，若順序為「先從後主」，則需要使用逗點加以標記說明。

(2) 無時間標記的分詞或不定詞（non-finite V）

分詞或不定詞句無法單獨報導事件重點或時間，屬於附屬形式，**無時間標記**功能，分詞表達『同時進行』，而不定詞表達『目的』，與主要子句共用同一主詞。

例1. We went mountain climbing last Sunday, spending some time with nature. ➡ 表『同時進行』

例2. We went mountain climbing last Sunday, to spend some time with nature. ➡ 表『目的』

(3) 帶有名詞子句或關係子句的標記（complementizer）

Part A. 名詞子句

當動詞後接子句當補語時，通常中間會以指示代名詞 that 做為補語標記，標示其為附屬，而 that 後接的名詞子句為另一事件，可做為『思想溝通』類事件之內容補語。

Kevin thinks **that** going skiing is easy. ➡ thinks 表達『現在認定的事實』

Kevin thought **that** going skiing is easy. ➡ thought 表示『過去認定的事實』

Kevin thought **that** going skiing **was** easy. ➡ "thought...was" 表示『過去如此認定，但現在可能改變想法了。』

Part B. 關係子句

關係子句（relative clause）也是附屬子句，用關係代名詞（who/which）來標記，以修飾要形容之名詞。包括：where、in which、whichever、wherever、whatever 等等……。

(4) 關係子句

✓ 定義與用法：關係子句是以關係代名詞 who、which、that 開頭的的形容詞子句，用來修飾、限定、解釋或說明相關名詞（即先行詞）。

✓ 修飾主詞：

英文：**The girl** [who was elected the class leader] took dancing lessons.

中文：【那位被選為班長的】女孩上舞蹈課。

√ 修飾受詞：

英文： Jeremy saw **a dog** [which was running after a cat.]

中文： Jeremy 看見一隻【正在追貓的】狗。

 ## 3. 還能怎麼說？

關係子句的形意搭配原則有幾種類型呢？要搭配何種語意呢？

➤關係子句（Relative Clause）是如何形成的？

　　基礎篇裡已提到關係子句是一種附屬子句，是由關係代名詞 who、which、that 所起始的形容詞子句，在句子裡扮演修飾名詞的角色。由於是用來修飾、限定、解釋或說明相關名詞，因此關係子句在句子裡的作用相當於形容詞，故又稱為「形容詞子句」。為了方便理解英文關係子句的形成，我們用中文句子來解釋概念：

　　例：那個女孩是我表妹。

　　　　那個女孩在講電話。

　　　➡ 那個【在講電話的】女孩是我表妹。

　　從中文的例子來看，【在講電話的】就是一個關係子句，對女孩做限定修飾。既然兩個句子同時都提到了「那個女孩」，將其中一句結合關係代名詞（who / which）變成形容詞子句，用來形容另一句話中的名詞，對該名詞加以限定、形容、解釋、說明，以補充該名詞的訊息，即為關係子句。接下來讓我們看看英文的例子：

The man is my teacher. He is talking to my father.

　　上述的句子中，兩個主詞都指向同一個主角，也就是 "the man"。既然主詞都為同一主角，那麼兩句話可合為一句來說明同一主角所做的事。因此英文就想到了一個方法，也就是用關係子句來合併這兩個句子：

The man [who is talking to my father] is my teacher.

　　這樣的關係子句有一個特色，就是子句中少了一個名詞，這個「失蹤」的名詞由關係代名詞 who 來「代替」，指向前面的名詞 "the man"，也就關係子句的先行詞。

➤關係子句的「標記」

前面提到關係代名詞是用來代替「前面的」名詞,那麼依照名詞在關係子句中的位置及語意分類的不同,關係代名詞就有不同的「標記」,就好比人在不同場合就有不同穿著:

名詞	主格	所有格	受格
人	who	whose	whom/ who
物	which	whose	which
人或物／人+物	that	X	that

在關係子句中,最關鍵的標記就是「關係代名詞」(relative pronoun)。關係代名詞主要有以下三個功能:

1. **代替名詞**,標記前面名詞所屬的種類:即人、物或「人＋物」。
2. 在關係子句中作為**組成成分**。
3. **連接**名詞與關係子句。

關係代名詞代替子句內失蹤的名詞,作為人或物的「替身」,因此也有「格」(case) 的分別。所謂的格是名詞或代名詞因語義角色不同而產生構詞上的變化。主格標記的就是擔任「主導者」的主詞,受格標記的就是擔任「受影響者」的受詞,所有格則是標記領屬的關係。除了格位上的不同,英文更貼心的標記失蹤的名詞是人、物或「人＋物」的區別:

名詞為人	
主格	I bumped into <u>an old friend</u> [**who** was shopping at SOGO Department Store].
受格	I bumped into <u>an old friend</u> [**whom** I often went to a movie with before].
所有格	I bumped into <u>an old friend</u> [**whose** wife used to live next door to me].

名詞為物	
主格	I have <u>a cute dog</u> [**which** was born in summer].
受格	I have <u>a cute dog</u> [**which** I often go to the park with].

所有格	I have met a cute dog [**whose** owner is a college student].

名詞為人+物	
主格	I unintentionally hurt the man and the dog [**that** were crossing the street].
受格	I have already found the man and the dog [**that** I am currently looking for].

溝通就是透過一連串的標記來表達意義的過程。同時表示人和物的關係代名詞 that，用來標記名詞子句的功能，和表示人的 who 和表物的關係代名詞 which 有所區隔。從關係詞的標記中，我們可以看見英文標記系統的原則：形式搭配語意，想要把話說清楚，就要用適當的標記形式來表達；

1. 關係代名詞為關係子句中的主詞：

I bumped into an old friend [**who** was shopping at SOGO Department Store].

I bought an interesting book [**which** was published recently].

➡ 關係子句中少了一個名詞，此『失蹤』的名詞則由關係代名詞來代替，則為【替身】，做為關係子句中的主詞之用，限定前面的 "an old friend"，屬於主格，不能省略以免造成理解困難。

2. 關係代名詞為關係子句中的受詞：

I bumped into an old friend [~~whom~~ I often went to a movie with before].
可省略

I bought an interesting book [~~which~~ my teacher recommended].
可省略

➡ 關係代名詞代替關係子句中失蹤的名詞做為【替身】，在關係子句中 whom 為受詞替身，故為受格，可以省略，不會造成理解困難。

3. 關係代名詞為關係子句中所有格形容詞：

I bumped into an old friend [**whose** wife used to live next door to me].

以上用法，做主詞的 who 可以代替 whom，that 可以代替 who、whom 或 which 之主、受格，而 who/ which 當主詞時，不能像受詞一樣省略，以免造成誤解。

4. **關係代名詞可搭配適當介系詞，此時關係代名詞為受詞，因前有介系詞不能省略，以免造成理解困難。**

John is the person [with **whom** I went hiking last weekend].

I went to a convenience store [in **which** I ran into one of my classmates].

若關係代名詞前面搭配介系詞，可等同於【疑問副詞】，又稱【關係副詞】。

・in which = where

➡ I went to a convenience store **where** I ran into one of my classmates.

・by which = how

➡ This is the formula **how** the problem can be solved.

➤關係代名詞的可省略與不可省略

在這一節，我們從溝通的角度出發，來探討關係代名詞的可省略與不可省略。

■關係代名詞什麼時候可以省略？為什麼？

首先，讓我們先來看看下面的例子：

I bumped into an old friend [**whom** I often went to a movie with before].

＝I bumped into an old friend [⊠ I often went to a movie with before].

I forgot to bring the book [**which** you are interested in].

＝I forgot to bring the book [⊠ you are interested in].

關係代名詞代替受詞時，可以省略。而關係代名詞當主詞時，不能像受詞一樣省略：

I bumped into an old friend [**who** was shopping at SOGO Department Store].

（✗）I bumped into an old friend [was shopping at SOGO Department Store].

為什麼會有這樣的區別呢？從溝通的角度來看，who 代替主詞時標記關係子句中的主角，因此主角不能缺席。

➤關係代名詞什麼時候不可以省略？為什麼？

關係子句中如遇到子句中的片語，可將片語中的介系詞拉到關係代名詞前，如下例所示：

例：I forgot to bring the book [**which** you are interested **in**].

＝I forgot to bring the book [you are interested **in**].

＝I forgot to bring the book [**in which** you are interested].

雖然關係代名詞在這裡是受詞，但因為介系詞在關係代名詞前，關係代名詞便不可省略，否則語句會不合語法：

例：（✗）I forgot to bring the book [in ⊠ you are interested].

為什麼當介系詞出現在關係代名詞前面時，關係代名詞就不能省略呢？這是與介系詞的標記功能有關。簡單來說，就好比及物動詞後一定要接受詞，表示動作及於另一物的概念；介系詞也一樣，後面一定要接名詞。介系詞和名詞之間的關係，就好比及物動詞和受詞間的關係，兩者密不可分，因此當介系詞移到關係代名詞前面時，關係代名詞也就不能被省略了。

另一個關代不可省略的關鍵在於區分限定子句與非限定子句的區別，關於限定子句與非限定子句的不同，請參考下節。以下的非限定要不要改成「補述」。

➤限定與非限定關係子句的不同功能與使用時機

在關係子句中有分【限定】及【非限定】用法，以下說明兩者使用功能與時機。

【限定】就是『眾中選一』，從一個較大的集合中，利用關係子句來『限定』、標示出所指的子集合：

The girl [who we met at the park yesterday] is my classmate.

➡ 昨天遇見好幾個女孩，在公園遇見的那個是我同學，[who we met at the park yesterday]用來限定標示指定的那一個女孩。

許多人在理解限定和非限定的關係子句時，很容易死記。其實，限定和非限定的關係子句最主要在標記上的區別只是在於關係子句前有逗點和沒逗點而已。要了解限定和非限定子句的不同，首先就要了解，逗點到底在關係子句中扮演著什麼樣的角色？請參考以下例子：

例：I have three brothers who live in Taipei.

　　我有【三個住在台北的】兄弟。➡ 還有其他兄弟！

　　➡ 說話者可能有不只有三個兄弟，但其中三個住在台北。

限定關係子句，顧名思義，指的是限定範圍意思。當名詞的範圍太廣時，我們用限定子句來縮小名詞的範圍，也就是前面提到的『眾中選一』的意思。

第二個例子恰好是屬於非限定的用法，表示『不須限定』或『非用於限定』的意思。通常用於沒有其他可能人選的情況下，做『後位補充』：

例：I have three brothers, who all live in Taipei.

　　我有三個兄弟，【他們都住在台北】➡

　　只有三個兄弟。

　　➡ 說話者總共只有三個兄弟，由逗號引導

　　　的關係子句扮演著補充說明的角色。

95

簡單的歸納,限定與非限定關係子句的區別如下:

	限定關係子句	非限定關係子句
先行詞	範圍廣	範圍明確
功能	縮小範圍	補充說明

逗號加關係代名詞,扮演著補充說明的標記,因此在溝通上也就不能省略。這就是為什麼,我們會說在「非限定性關係子句」中,關代不可以省略的原因了。

「非限定」用法剛好相反,表示『不須限定』通常是要描述指稱的人選沒有其他,而且已經很明確,無其他可能,故無須「限定」,其關係子句只是做『後位補充』,前後均會加上逗點「,」。

Princess Diana, who was Prince William's mother, will be always remembered.

➡ 黛安娜王妃是威廉王子的母親,將永遠會被世人記得。她只有一位 only one,所以關係子句用補充說明用法,前後用逗點格開,"who was Prince William's mother"屬非限定關係子句。

➤非限定性用法的使用時機

1. 當關係代名詞代表整個主句內容時:

I missed the train, which upset me a lot.

我錯過了火車,(這件事)令我感到很煩悶。

2. 當先行詞指的是世界上獨一無二的事物或專有名詞時：

Princess Diana, who was Prince William's mother, will be always remembered.

黛安娜王妃，威廉王子的母親，將會永遠被世人記得。

3. 當先行詞指的是唯一的某個親屬時：

I miss my father, who will be always remembered.

我想我爸爸，我永遠都會記住他。

➤That 標記幾種子句？何時可省略？為什麼？

A. that 的三種溝通功能

a. 做為動詞後的補語標記

Judy told me [**that** she doesn't like math].

（茱蒂告訴我她不喜歡數學。）

b. 做為關係子句的關係代名詞

Cathy had dinner with the girl [**that** looked like a police officer].

（凱西跟一位很像警員的女生一起吃晚餐。）

➡ that 代替關係子句主詞

Louis visited the man [**that** I saw in front of the post office yesterday].

（路易斯去拜訪那個昨天我在郵局前看到的男生。）

➡ that 代替關係子句受詞

c. 做為名詞後同位補語標記

My parents discovered **the fact** [**that** my brother failed math last semester].

（我的父母發現了我弟弟上學期數學當掉這件事。）

B. that 省略與否

只要不妨礙溝通或影響理解，that 通常可以省略。唯獨下列兩種情況，that 不能省略。

◆ 關係主詞不可省:

➡ 因為代替主詞時，that 標記關係子句中主詞，主角不能缺席。

I read the novel **that** is very interesting.

（我讀了那本很有趣的小說。）

◆ 同位修飾不可省，省略 **that** 會誤以為是兩個分開的句子造成理解困難：

➡ 若為出現在名詞後做補充說明時，不可省。

I learned the fact [**that** he told a lie]. 　（我發現他說了謊這件事。）

C. 做為關係代名詞 that 和 which 用法有何不同？

That 和 which 兩者皆可以在限定用法的關係子句中當關係代名詞─主格或受格用法，that 可代替人或物，但 which 的先行詞多為物：

There was an old lady **who/ that** swallowed a fly.

有一個老太太吞了一隻蒼蠅。

There was an old dog **which/ that** swallowed a bug.

有一個老狗吞了一隻蟲。

但是，在非限定用法的關係子句中，關代就不會用 that，只會用 who(m) 或是 which。

Jacky has a blue car, which was bought in America.

➡ Jacky 只有這部車，無需限定，為非限定關代子句，不能用 that，只能用 which。

Jacky has a blue car which/ that was bought in America.

➡ Jacky 還有其他車子。限定關係子句的關代可用 which 或 that。

That 還可以用來連接名詞子句，當附屬連接詞 （complementizer）使用，但 which 無法連接名詞子句：

He realized **that** he has grown into a man.

他發現他已經長成一個大人了。

➤ 關係子句的句法位置

關係子句跟一般形容詞在句法位置上有何不同？讓我們來一起看看下列的例子：

I saw a 【beautiful】 girl.

I saw a girl 【who is standing around the corner】.

在第一句話中，形容詞 beautiful 描述的女孩的特質，擺在名詞的前

端。在第二句話，關係子句擺在名詞的後端，後位修飾前端的名詞。講到這裡，不曉得各位讀者有沒有一個疑惑，那就是為什麼在英文中，關係子句會擺在名詞的後方呢？那是因為英文在表達的過程中，重點要先說，細節隨後。所以 "I saw a girl" 這個重點要先說，然後才用關係子句來修飾名詞 "a girl"。

另一個相關的現象是：語言使用要避免「頭重腳輕」的情況

例1：Please turn **it** off.

（╳）Please turn off **it**.

例2：It is important **to study hard and study smart**.

To study hard and study smart is important.

什麼是頭重腳輕呢？即英文習慣把較長的文字向後移動，前面先點出重點，後面在詳述細節讀起來比較自然。所以在第一個例句中，英文的使用者不允許代名詞置於片語動詞後。第二個例句，英文則用虛主詞來代替原來主詞表達的不定詞片語，讓它成為延遲的主詞（delayed subject）。關係子句的形成也是為了避免「頭重腳輕」這個現象，同時也充分體現了英文「主從分明，重點在前」的原則！

 ## 4. 讀一段短文

The Boy Who Cried Wolf
an Aesop Fable

[1]There once was a boy who kept sheep not far from the village. [2]He would often become bored and to amuse himself he would call out, "Wolf! Wolf," although there was no wolf about.

> 註解[1]： There once was a boy [who kept sheep not far from the village].
> 英文特點為『主從有別、次要句子要標記』。"There once was a boy" 為主要子句，"who kept sheep not far from the village" 為次要子句（關係子句）；who 為關係代名詞，為 "kept sheep not far from the village" 關係子句的主詞，用來修飾前面的名詞 "a boy"，不能省略。
>
> 註解[2]： He would often become bored and to amuse himself he would call out,
> 第二句中 "to amuse himself he would call out..."
> "to amuse himself"表示他大喊 "Wolf! Wolf" 的目的是為了娛樂自己，此時的 "to amuse himself" 為 non-finite V 不定詞構句，沒有時間標記，無法單獨報導事件重點或時間，亦為一種附屬形式。

The villagers would stop what they were doing and run to save the sheep from the wolf's jaw. [3]Once they arrived at the pasture, the boy just laughed. [4]The naughty boy played this joke over and over until the villagers tired of him.

> 註解[3]: Once they arrived at the pasture, [the boy just laughed].
>
> 『主要子句』是報導的重點，可獨立出現，主要溝通報導重點事件、參與人物或主題訊息，第3句中 "the boy just laughed"的 "the boy" 是主要主詞，laughed 是主要動詞，"Once they arrived at the pasture"介紹發生的時間背景。而英文標點符號是配合『主從分明』、『重點在前』來標記，把主要子句放在後面為『反常順序』，因此要加上逗號。
>
> 註解[4]： [The naughty boy played this joke over and over] until the villagers tired of him.
>
> 第4句中 "The naughty boy played this joke over and over" 為主要子句，"The naughty boy"是主要主詞，"played this joke"是主要動詞，"until the villagers tired of him" 介紹發生的時間背景。而在此句中，主要子句放在前面為『正常順序』，符合英文『主從分明』、『重點在前』原則，故無須加上逗號。

[5]One day while the boy was watching the sheep, a wolf did come into the fold. The boy cried and cried, "Wolf! Wolf!"

No one came. The wolf had a feast of sheep that day. [6]No one will believe a habitual liar even when he is telling the truth.

> 註解[5]：One day while the boy was watching the sheep, a wolf did come into the fold.
>
> 第5句中 "a wolf did come into the fold"為主要子句，"a wolf" 是主要主詞，"did come into the fold"是主要動詞，"One day while the boy was watching the sheep" 負責發生時間的背景介紹。而英文標點符號是配合『主從分明』、『重點在前』來標記，把主要子句放在後面為『反常順序』，因此要加上逗號。
>
> 註解[6]：No one will believe a habitual liar even when he is telling the truth.
>
> 第6句中 "No one will believe a habitual liar" 為主要子句，"No one" 是主要主詞，"will believe" 是主要動詞，"even when he is telling the truth"負責發生時間的背景介紹。主要子句放在前面為『正常順序』，符合英文『主從分明』、『重點在前』原則，故無須加上逗號。

From: http://www.storyit.com/Classics/Stories/boycriedwolf.htm
(https://bit.ly/2PRTxdR)

5. 唱一首英文歌

https://goo.gl/98rm3D

As Long As You Love Me (Backstreet Boys)

Although loneliness has always been a friend of mine

I'm leaving my life in your hands

People say I'm crazy and that I am blind

Risking it all in a glance

And how you got me blind is still a mystery

I can't get you out of my head

Don't care what is written in your history

As long as you're here with me

*I don't care who you are

Where you're from, what you did

As long as you love me

Who you are

Where you're from

Don't care what you did

As long as you love me

Every little thing that you've said and done

Feels like it's deep within me

Doesn't really matter if you're on the run

It seems like we're meant to be (*)

I've tried to hide it so that no one knows

But I guess it shows

When you look into my eyes

What you did and where you're coming from

I don't care

As long as you love me baby (*)

說明：

1. Although loneliness has always been a friend of mine, I'm leaving my life in your hands.

   主要子句為 "I'm leaving my life in your hands"，"Although loneliness has always been a friend of mine"為附屬子句（次要子句），Although 為附屬連接詞，用來標記次要子句。

2. People say I'm crazy and that I am blind risking it all in a glance

   "People say" 動詞 say 為補語，後面省略了 that 這個補語標記。帶了另一事件，為表達『思想溝通』類事件所要求之內容補語，"I'm crazy and that I am blind risking it all in a glance" 為帶有名詞子句的標記。而觀察此處的動詞時態 "people say" 表示人們現在說的事實且認定 "I am crazy and blind" 的現在事實。

3. Don't care what is written in your history As long as you're here with me

"Don't care what is written in your history" 為主要子句，"As long as you're here with me" 為附屬子句（次要子句），"As long as" 為附屬連接詞，用來標記次要子句，符合英文「主從有別、次要子句要標記」的特點。

4. I don't care who you are, where you're from, what you did.

"I don't care" 為主要子句，"who you are, where you're from, what you did" 為間接問句的名詞子句。"I don't cate" 為主要事件，以說話當下為基準，但在間接引述的間接問句中 "who you are, where you're from" 時間點向【主要事件】-- "I don't care" 對齊，指的是【現在的事實】。"what you did" 時間點向【主要事件】對齊，指的是【你過去做的事】。

5. Every little thing that you've said and done. Feels like it's deep within me.

"Every little thing" 為 "that you've said and done" 關係子句形容的名詞，that為關係子句 "that you've said and done" 中的受詞，可以省略，不造成理解困難，主要子句為 "Every little thing feels like it's deep within me."。

 # 6. 看一部影片

派特的幸福劇本（預告片）
SILVER LININGS PLAYBOOK (Trailer) Festival 2012
https://goo.gl/THWWYT

1. What? What's this?

2. Did you tell me you took him out? -The court said yes.

   註解：Did you tell me you took him out?

   "Did you tell me you took him out?"句子中包含「that+名詞子句」" Did you tell me【that you took him out】?"，that 為動詞後的補語標記，that 省略不至於造成理解困擾。

3. Yeah but what did the doctor say?

4. Can I do an interview for a school project about mental illness?

5. No.

6. I'm ready.

7. I feel motivated. I don't feel so angry all the time.

8. The whole time you're rooting for this Hemingway guy to survive the war

9. and to be with the woman that he loves.

10. It's 4 o'clock in the morning, Pat. I can't apologize.

11. I will apologize on behalf Earnest Hemingway.

12. because that's who's to blame here.

> 註解：I will apologize on behalf Earnest Hemingway because that's who's to blame here.
> 此句符合英文特點【主從有別，次要子句要標記】，主要子句為 "I will apologize on behalf Earnest Hemingway"，次要附屬子句身分特殊，必須加上特殊標記 because 說明傳達造成主要子句的原因，符合英語【重點先講】、【先主後從】的大原則，所以不需要在從屬子句前加上逗點。
> 另外，若 because 和 so 同時出現，會使得這句話沒有主要子句，主人從缺且語意和結構都不完整，因此須遵從【主從分明】的標記原則，because 和 so 只能擇一使用。

13. Yeah. Have Earnest Hemingway call us and apologize to us, too.

14. Pat, you have to have a strategy. I hate my illness, I want to control it.

15. I hope you're ok with Veronica's sister coming over.

> 註解： I hope you're ok with Veronica's sister coming over.
> 句子中包含「that+名詞子句」，"I hope【that you're ok with Veronica's sister coming over】"，that 為動詞後的補語標記，that 省略不至於造成理解困擾。

16. Tiffany and Tommy? -Just Tiffany.

17. What happened to Tommy? -He died.

18. How'd he die? -Please don't bring it up.

19. Hey Tiffany! -This is Pat.

20. You look nice. -Thank you.

21. How'd Tommy die?

22. What meds are you on? -I use to be on Lithium and Seroquel.

23. I was on Xanax.

24. You ever take Klonopin? Klonopin, yes.

25. I'm tired I want to go. Are you gonna walk me home or what?

26. You have poor social skills.

27. You have a problem. -I have a problem?

28. You say more inappropriate things, than appropriate things.

29. Doc, she's crazy.

30. Whoa! What the hell!

31. She knew where I was. She followed me.

32. What don't you run somewhere else? -Calm down crazy!

33. Maybe she just needs a friend.

34. You want to have dinner at this diner?

35. Pick me up at 7:30.

36. So, how's your job? -I just got fired actually.

37. Oh, really how?

38. By having sex with everybody in the office.

39. Everybody?

40. I was very depressed after tommy died. -We don't have to talk about it.

41. Thanks. -How many were there?

42. She's a mess. You got to be careful. She does a lot of therapy.

43. I go to a lot of therapy. Am I messed up?

44. I just got to get a strategy you know?

45. Me too.

46. So there's this dance thing. I can only do it if I have a partner.

註解：I can only do it if I have a partner.
"I can only do it" 為主要子句，"if I have a partner"為附屬子句，此句符合英文特點【主從有別，次要子句要標記】，次要附屬子句 "if I have a partner"身分特殊，必須加上特殊標記 if 說明傳達造成主要子句的原因，符合英語【重點先講】、【先主後從】的大原則，所以不需要在從屬子句前加上逗點。

47. Wait. I'm not going to dance with you.

48. So, is this the girl you wrote about?

註解： "is this the girl"為主要子句，"the girl"為 "you wrote about"關係子句形容的名詞，whom 為受格關係代名詞，為關係子句 "you wrote about" 中的受詞替身，可以省略，亦不造成理解困難。

49. You wrote about me? -She's fine.

50. She is my friend with an "F."

51. Captial "F"... ...for friend.

52. What are you so up about? I'm happy.

53. Look I'm my best self today,

54. and I think she's her best self, and that's a good thing.

> 註解：I think she's her best self
> 句子中包含「that+名詞子句」，I think【that she's her best self】，that 為動詞後的補語標記，that 省略不至於造成理解困擾。

55. I know don't want to listen to your father. I didn't listen to mine

56. but life reaches out with a moment like this,

57. it's a sin if you don't reach back.

> 註解：it's a sin if you don't reach back.
> "it's a sin"為主要子句，"if you don't reach back" 為附屬子句，此句符合英文特點【主從有別，次要子句要標記】，次要的附屬子句 "if you don't reach back" 身分特殊，必須加上特殊標記 if 說明傳達造成主要子句的原因，符合英語【重點先講】、【先主後從】的大原則，所以不需要在從屬子句前加上逗點。

58. This is what I believe to be true.

59. you have to do everything you can

60. and if you stay positive, you have a shot at a silver lining.

> 註解： if you stay positive, you have a shot at a silver lining.
> " you have a shot at a silver lining" 為主要子句，"if you stay positive" 為附屬子句，此句符合英文特點【主從有別，次要子句要標記】，次要附屬子句 "if you stay positive" 身分特殊，必須加上特殊標記 if 說明傳達造成主要子句的原因。因為英語【重點先講】、【先主後從】的大原則，此句則為反常順序，所以需要在從屬子句後面加上逗點。

 ## 7. 做一點練習

Part 1：選擇題

( ) 1. The engineer _____ is reading a novel on the sofa is Fortuna's brother.
   (A) when   (B) which   (C) who   (D) what

( ) 2. It is reported, bananas, _____ are very common in Taiwan, are expensive in Japan.

(A) who   (B) what (C) that   (D) which

(　　) 3.　Did you see the blind woman and her guide dog _____ are sitting on the bench over there? They are both my neighbors.

(A) which   (B) who   (C) what   (D) that

(　　) 4.　Students must listen to their teacher _____ he or she teaches in class.

(A) before   (B) because   (C) when   (D) though

(　　) 5.　The doctor tells the sick lady her body will get worse and worse _____ she keeps smoking.

(A) if   (B) when   (C) though   (D) because

答案：(1) C (2) D (3) D (4) C (5) A

Part 2：合併句子

6.　Tina brushed her teeth at 6:30 am. Tina went to school at 7:00 am.（請用 after 合併）

_____

7.　She likes to help others. Many classmates like her.（請用 because 合併）

(1) Because _____.

(2) Many _____.

8.　She told me the fact. My favorite singer got married.（用 that 合併）

_____

9.　I decided to buy that bicycle. The bicycle has pink tires.（用關係代名詞合併）

_____

10.　The dress looks so good. Judy wore the dress at the party.（用關係代名詞合併）

_____

答案：

6.　After Tina brushed her teeth, she went to school.

　　= Tina went to school after she brushed her teeth.

7.　She likes to help others. Many classmates like her. (請用because合併)

(1) Because <u>she likes to help others, many classmates like her</u>.

(2) Many <u>classmates like her because she likes to help others</u>.

8. She told me that my favorite singer got married.

9. I decided to buy that bicycle which/ that has pink tires.

10. The dress which/that Judy wore at the party looks so good.

Part 3：克漏字

關係代名詞可重複

who	when	who	in which

Once (1)_____ a Lion was asleep, a little Mouse began running up and down upon him; this soon wakened the Lion, (2)_____ placed his huge paw upon him, and opened his big jaws to swallow him.

"Pardon, O King," cried the little Mouse: *"forgive me this time, I shall never forget it: who knows but what I may be able to do you a turn some of these days?"*

The Lion was so tickled at the idea of the Mouse being able to help him, that he lifted up his paw and let him go.

One day, the Lion was caught in a trap, and then the hunters (3)_____ desired to carry him alive to the King tied him to a tree while they went in search of a wagon to carry him on.

Just then the little Mouse happened to pass by, and seeing the sad plight (4)_____ the Lion was, went up to him and soon gnawed away the ropes that bound the King of the Beasts.

"Was I not right?" said the little Mouse.

改編文章來源：

http://www.taleswithmorals.com/aesop-fable-the-lion-and-the-mouse.htm

(https://bit.ly/2PZOJTs)

答案：(1) when　(2) who　(3) who　(4) in which

註解：

(1) when是附屬標記指的是時間【當⋯⋯時候】，介紹事件的時間背景，

"Once <u>when</u> a Lion was asleep" 為附屬子句，無法單獨存在。"a little

Mouse began running up and down upon him" 為主要子句，負責報導重點

事件，符合英語【主從分明】原則。

(2) "this soon wakened the Lion, who placed his huge paw upon him" 句子中 the Lion是關係子句形容的名詞，此處關係代名詞 who 為關係子句中主詞，前面加上逗點，為非限定用法，做補充說明之用，而此處的 who 為關係子句主詞之替身，不可以省略。

(3) "the hunters [who desired to carry him alive to the King] tied him to a tree" 句中 "who desired to carry him alive to the King" 為關係子句，關係代名詞 who 為關係子句中主詞，而此處的 who 為關係子句主詞之替，不可省略。

(4) "seeing the sad plight [in which the Lion was]" 句中獅子陷入 plight（困境），介系詞 in 放至關係代名詞 which 前，因此此處 which 不能省略。

CHAPTER

4

究竟是指哪一個？

𝄞)) 1. 你想説什麼？

英文裡的 a / an 和 the 有何不同？英語如何決定名詞是單數還是複數？
可數名詞與不可數名詞如何區辨呢？

去哪裡?

去圖書館

問 你剛才去哪？

答 我去圖書館！

請問你知道是哪一個圖書館嗎？如果在學校，應該就是學校的圖書館。
如果在其它地方呢？會是哪一個圖書館呢？ 中文似乎沒有說清楚！

英文不一樣, 每一個名詞所指的是哪一個人或物，對方知道與否，一定
得說清楚。

Q: Where did you go?
A: I went to the library.　➡ 你知道的那個（也許是學校的或市立的圖書
　　　　　　　　　　　　　　　 館，反正是你知道的）

　I went to a library.　➡ 某一個圖書館（可能是你不知道的）

在『貓追狗』事件中，世界上貓和狗那麼多，到底是哪隻貓或哪隻狗？
英文在溝通時，必須要講清楚兩件事：
  1）是一隻（a cat）還是多隻（two cats）？這就是單數和複數的區別。
    （注意：母音開頭的單數名詞要用 an，例：an elephant，這是為了
    發音方便！）

2）是對方認得的（**The** cat is chasing the dog.），還是不認得的（**A** cat is chasing a dog.）？這就是 a/ an 和 the 的區別。

如果有人說 ："I saw **a cat**." 那就只是告訴你他有看到一隻貓，究竟是哪一隻，無需讓你知道，也無須說明；如果對方說："I saw **the cat**." 就是清楚地告訴你，是你知道的那隻 （也許之前提過／看過／養過），也就是「我知你知」的那隻。如果看到的不只一隻呢？ 那就是多數，要用複數名詞（名詞後加複數標記「-s」）：

I saw **some cats**. ➡ 你不認得的一些貓
I saw **the cats**. ➡ 你認得的那些貓

英文的名詞出場，一定要有明確的標記！ 標記什麼呢？標記「單複數」和「認得與否」。

 ## 2. 英文怎麼說？

英文標記「單複數」和「認得與否」就是在名詞前須加上『冠詞』（「冠在」名詞前的標誌）：分為限定冠詞（the）及不定冠詞（a/an 或 some），藉由清楚的形式的來表達名詞的指涉意義：

單數：

I saw a cat. ➡ 不定冠詞 a 表示單數且「你不認得」
➡ ➡ 就是貓的其中一隻，我知但你不知
I saw the cat. ➡ 特定冠詞 the 表示「我知你知」的那一隻

複數：

I saw some cats. ➡ 不定冠詞 some 表示複數（+s）且「你不認得」
➡ ➡ 一些貓，你不認得的
I saw the cats. ➡ 特定冠詞 the 表示「我知你知」的那些貓

英文名詞有了明確的冠詞標記，就可以清楚表明所指的人事物。以下就三個超簡原則做進一步說明：

➢ 超簡原則 1：冠詞如號誌！『你知我知』決定 a/ an 或 the 的使用

　　語言中名詞是用來指涉周遭的人事物，在名詞前加上不定冠詞 a / an 或定冠詞 the，在溝通上可以幫助提示對方是否知道所指的人事物（Identifiable to the hearer or not？）。所以英文名詞前的冠詞標記，是很方便簡潔的「號誌」，直接提示指涉對象。到底指涉對象有幾種？一般溝通可能有下列四種的指涉類型：

1. 某類東西，你我都不確知是哪一個

   I want to buy **a** computer.

   ➡ 我想買一台電腦，但你和我都還不知道是哪一台

2. 某個東西，我知道但你不知道哪一個

   I bought **a** computer.

   ➡ 我買了一台電腦，但你還（你沒看過／聽過／說過）

3. 確知的東西，你我都知道哪一個

   I bought **the** computer.

   ➡ 我買了那台你知道的電腦（你看過／聽過／說過）

4. 確知的東西，藉由限定說明後，你也有充分訊息知道是哪一個

   I want to buy **the** computer [I saw at the computer store yesterday]關係子句.

   ➡ 我想要買的電腦是我昨天在店裡看到的那台

　　因此，冠詞如號誌，在名詞前提供簡潔明確的提示。而決定用什麼冠詞標誌，主要關鍵就在於判斷對方是否「確知所指」（Identifiable to the hearer or not？）。如果認定聽者確知所指的是哪個，也就是「我知你知」的狀況下（= identifiable to the hearer），就用定冠詞 the；如果認為聽者不知道指哪個，也就是自己或對方「不確知」的狀況下（= unidentifiable to the hearer），名詞前就用不定冠詞 a/ an 來標記。請看以下對話：

A: What did you do last night?

B: I watched **the** animal show on TV.

　　➡ 認定聽者知道是哪個節目（我知你知）

B: I watched **an** animal show on TV.

　➡ 認定聽者不知道是哪個節目（你不知）

> **超簡原則 2：如何認定聽者「確知與否」？第一次提到的就必須用 a/ an 嗎？**

　一般說故事開頭都是：Once upon a time in a far-away country, there lived a handsome prince. One day, the prince met a beautiful princess and....

　在第一次介紹新的人物時，因為之前沒聽過，所以通常使用不定冠詞 a / an，之後再提到時，就會用 the，因為聽者已可「確知所指」。然而，不是所有第一次提到的都得用 a / an，只要有足夠理由相信對方可以辨識指認，就可以用定冠詞標誌 the。以下用兩個例子作說明。

　例一：兩個人不久前一起去逛街，一天早上碰面的第一段對話：

A: I bought **the dress**!
B: Really? You did buy it! I like the dress, too.

　對話中 A 是第一次提到 dress，就用定冠詞標誌 "the dress"，表示兩人都確知所指，因為曾一起逛街，彼此都知道是哪件洋裝。這是基於共同的經歷或背景知識，說話者有足夠理由認定所指的對聽者來說，是已知的（known）、可辨識指認的（identifiable），即可用 the 來標記。

　例二：若兩人沒什麼交集，A 不確定 B 知道是哪件洋裝，就會用不定標誌 "**a** dress" 來表達意思：

A: I bought a new dress yesterday.
B: You did! I'd like to see it.

　A 知道這件洋裝對 B 來說是不明確且未知的（unknown）、無法辨識的（unidentifiable），故用 a 來標記「不確知」的名詞。

❓ 我根據什麼可以判斷對方是否「確知所指」？

綜合而言，語言學者 Givón (1993) 認為根據下列三種情況，說話者可以認定聽者知道所談論的對象：

➤ 情況一：同處一個時空環境下的人、事、地、時、物（Shared situation）：

- The speaker & hearer: *I, you, we*
- Demonstrative: *this whiteboard, that desk*
- Adverbs of time: *now, later, tomorrow*
- Adverbs of place: *here, there*

在同一個環境或溝通情境中的人，因為有共同的時空訊息及具體參照，很容易明白當下指稱的人、事、地、時、物。

例證：你和朋友都在同一間畫廊，你跟他說 "Look at the painting."，對方就能夠明白是指哪幅畫。

➤ 情況二：共享的言談對話（Shared discourse）

溝通時，我們所說的內容及前後文，就是共同參照的訊息。初次談及某事的時候，聽者對所指一無所知，所以第一次介紹到的人、事、物大都用 a/an，之後再提到時，才用 the 或是人稱代名詞（he/ she/ it）來指稱。

例證：I met **an old friend** yesterday afternoon in front of **Taipei 101**. **She** enjoys shopping and drinking coffee a lot. So, **the friend** and I went to have afternoon tea in **a** beautiful café near **the** area.

➤ 情況三：共同的背景知識（Shared background knowledge）

處於相同社會或文化中的人，擁有共同的背景知識。日常生活中，會形成一套共有的**知識框架與認知基礎（schema）**。

- Shared universe: *the Sun, the Earth, the Mars*
- Shared experience: *the President, the Mayor, the boss*
- Shared knowledge frame:

*He bought **a** house, but **<u>the</u> living room** was too small.*

*He was sick and sent to **<u>the</u> emergency room**, and **<u>the</u> doctor** ....*

日常的認知框架會涉及相關訊息的傳遞與理解，已提到的某個概念會激活相關的其他概念，即使沒明確提過，也可視為已知訊息：

例證：提到 "a house" 就會想到 "the living room" 或 kitchen；提到生病就可連想到 "the hospital"、"the emergency room"、"the doctor" 或 "the nurse"。這些場景知識會把相關的概念激活，成為「已知」的訊息，而可直接用 the 標誌。

➤ **超簡原則 3： 名詞出場，必有標記！**

英語的名詞出現，用於具體指涉時，一定要有兩種標記：1. 標示單複數；2. 標示確知與否。對於確知名詞 the 的用法，無需死背規則，只要理解the是一種必要標誌，凡是「你知我知」、有確定指涉對象的，都要加上the：

(1) 用在確指的專有名詞（proper nouns）：the Capital of France、the United States，原本的普通名詞變成大寫，做為專有名詞，表示只此一家，你知我知的那家。

   （注意： united states 小寫時是普通名詞，泛指任何聯合州府，只有大寫時才指美國！）

(2) 地球上獨一無二的、你我確知的那一個（the unique one）：the Sun、the Moon、the Earth、the Great Wall（這些都是你知我知、全世界人類共享的那一個）

   （注意：sun / moon / earth / wall小寫時都是普通名詞，泛指任何恆星／衛星／地球／牆垣，只有大寫時才指獨一的那個太陽、月亮、地球、長城。）

(3) 獨一無二的江河、海洋、海峽、海灣、群島、山脈、沙漠等專有名詞： the Taiwan Strait、The Pacific Ocean。

(4) 用在絕無僅有的序數詞，最高級形容詞和方位名詞之前：
   Jessica won **the** first prize. ➡ 第一名只有一位

Daniel is **the** best actor in **Taiwan**.

➡ 最……的只有一位；方位也是固定明確的，都是你知我知的確指。

(5) 用在單數名詞前，加以限定確指，代表你知我知的那一類：

The computer is a very important invention.

➡ 確指一種東西，你知我知的類型

(6) 用在形容詞前，加以限定確指，代表你知我知的那一類，等於複數名詞：the old、the young、the rich、the dead。

The poor need more help from the government.

➡ 窮人需要政府更多協助。

(7) 用在姓氏前，加以限定確指，表示確知的一家人：

The Browns often go on a picnic. 　布朗一家常去野餐。

The Lees are all intelligent scholars. 　李家一家都是聰明的學者。

(8) 用在計時、計量的名詞前，加以限定確指，表示確知的單位：

He is paid by **the** month. ➡ 以月算薪水，你知我知的度量

(9) 用在常識經驗範圍內已知的事物：

the government、the school、the congress、the train station、the neighborhood、the church、the community center

➡ 生活範圍內共同確知的事物

We went to an Italian restaurant. **The** waiter was friendly!

➡ 經驗範疇內明確相關的事物

(10) 用在上文或之前已提過的人事物：所指的對象已介紹過，因此明確可辨。

In this cold and darkness there went along the street <u>a poor little girl</u>, bareheaded, and with naked feet. When she left home she had slippers on, ...but **the** <u>poor little thing</u> lost them as she scuffled away across the street. （節錄自《賣火柴的女孩》The Little Match Girl）。對讀者來說，女孩這個人物第一次出場時是 "**a** poor little girl"，接下來就是明確可辨的人物，是你知我知已提過的那一位，所以用 "the poor little thing"。

➤ **超簡原則 4：可數與不可數差別在於是否可以「個體化」。**

名詞出場的標記中，最重要的就是要標示單數或複數。單數即「單一個

體」、複數則為「多個群體」。然而單複數的概念只適用於「可數」名詞，也就是可以「個體化」的事物。若名詞本身是不可數的（不能個體化），就沒有單複數的區分了：

可數名詞：單一的個體

- 具體的人事物：a man/ two men; a table/ two tables; an apple/ two apples; a video/ two videos
- 計量的單位及度量詞：a meter/ two meters; an inch/ two inches; a foot/ two feet; a day/ two days
- 可切分的事件名詞：a phone call/ two phone calls; a class/ two classes; a game/ two games

不可數名詞：不可分的整體

- 個體細微，很難細分的物體：sand、rice、flour、powder
  （注意：這類名詞的計量，通常會用度量詞，例："four tablespoons of cocoa powder"）
- 液體或氣體：water、oil、air、gas
  （注意：這類名詞的計量會用容器或度量詞："four cups of water"、"ten gallons of oil"）
- 抽象概念：patience、love、courage
  （注意：這類名詞的計量可用中性的數量詞："a lot of patience"、"abundant love"）

　　嚴格來說，可數不可數的分別並不是物理上「可不可數」，而是在於使用上是否傾向「個體指涉」。比方說，rice 和 sand 都是不可數名詞，但硬要數也可以數得出來有幾顆，只是大多人在使用 rice 一詞時，通常不是指單一的個體，而是把一堆米當成整體來看，不會細分。另外，氣體或液體也都無法再細分或個體化，因此 water 和 rain 都是不可數名詞，這是同時考量物理性質和使用原則的結果。

❓ 有首老歌名叫 "Rain and Tears" （雨水和眼淚）：同樣是液體，water 和 rain 是不可數, 但是眼淚 tears 卻是可數，這是怎麼回事？

"Rain and tears" 本質上都是液體，但在使用上，根據認知觀察到的現象而有所不同：眼淚可以是一滴一滴個別掉落下，就像珠子一顆一顆地落下，實際經驗中也的確可看到一滴眼淚掛在臉上，但雨水通常量大而連續，很難單獨切分。所以認知上 tears 較可細分，就當可數名詞；water 和 rain 較難細分，即為不可數。

這首老歌《Rain and Tears》描寫失戀的悲傷，雨水和淚水假裝不了，歌詞很有意思：

Rain and **tears** are the same,	雨水和淚水雖都是水
But in the sun you've got to play the game.	在太陽底下卻得玩花樣
When you cry in winter time,	在冬季掉淚
You can't pretend. It's nothing but the rain.	不能假裝沒事說是雨水

另外，"rice and noodles" 米飯和麵條，為何一個不可數一個可數？原因很簡單：米飯很難細分，吃的時候也無須細分；但麵條個體性比較明顯，可以一條條的享用，因此說 "rice and noodles"。

總結一下可數與不可數名詞的差別：

名詞	可數	不可數
具體還是抽象？	概念具體	概念抽象
個體性顯著？	個體性顯著（可細分）	個體性不明顯（不加細分）
用於指涉個體？	通常指涉個體	通常指涉整體
例子	tears / noodles / drops	rice / flour / sand; water / rain

❓ 複數名詞如何標記？ 字尾都是加 -s 嗎？ 有哪些不規則形式？

複數名詞的標記：複數名詞一定要搭配複數形式

・規則搭配：一般要加 -s 或 -es

（1）字尾發音和 /s/ 不同的：就只加「–s」，字尾 s 的發音可能是無
　　　聲 /s/ 或有聲 /z/，因為發音跟著字尾走：

　hats 發音 /s/

　blogs 發音 /z/

　ways 發音 /z/

　computers 發音 /z/

　TVs 發音 /z/

　oaths 發音 /s/

（2）字尾發音和 /s/ 相近的，如字尾為 -s /s/、-z /z/、-sh /ʃ/、-th /-tʃ/、
　　　-ge/ -dge /dʒ/ /dɪ/ 等之後，要加「-es」，發音為 /ɪz/，以便發音：

　buses 發音 /z/

　axes 發音 /ɪz/

　buzzes 發音 /ɪz/

　houses 發音 /ɪz/

　lashes 發音 /ɪz/

　churches 發音 /ɪz/

　pages 發音 /ɪz/

　judges 發音 /ɪz/

> **不規則搭配：有幾種類型**

母音 + y 結尾 ➡ -<u>ies</u> 　如：babies

-fe/ -f 結尾 ➡ -<u>ives</u> 　如：knives

其它

mouse ➡ mice

foot ➡ feet

alumnus ➡ alumni

bacterium ➡ bacteria

woman ➡ women

child ➡ children

 3. 還能怎麼説？

(1) 名詞前一定要加上冠詞嗎？

　　記得前面說「名詞出場，必有標記」？ 這是說當名詞用來指「出場」的個體，前面一定要加上 a 或 the，用來提示「聽者」所指的是哪個個體。但如果名詞<u>不是</u>用來指涉「出場」的人事物，而是描述詞彙本身的「概念類型」或一個「不知名的群體」，其實並沒有「出場」的問題，聽者根本無須辨明指涉對象，名詞前也就不需要加標示了。下列兩種情形不牽涉「個體指涉」，沒有名詞「出場」，當然就不用在名詞前加上冠詞。

> 複數名詞表示「不知名」的群體，無須辨明個體：

例：I see cats in the park.

➡ 不須細究是哪些貓，只是告訴聽者看到一群「不知名」的貓。

I see the cats in the park.

➡ 指涉「出場」的群體，告訴聽者是他知道的那一群貓。

> 單數名詞表概念類型，沒有「出場」的個體：

例₁：I like summer more than winter.

➡ 這句話的夏天、冬天只是概念類型，不是指某年的夏天或冬天。

I like the summer we spent in France.

➡ 我喜歡我們在法國渡過的那個夏天。

例₂：Jerry likes to eat purple rice. 　➡ Jerry喜歡吃紫米這種東西。

Jerry likes to eat the purple rice his sister bought for him.

➡ Jerry 喜歡吃姐姐替他買的那種紫米。

(2) 單數或複數名詞在冠詞使用上有差別嗎？

在不同的使用情境下，單複數的不同會有不同的語意解讀，請看下列例子：

> 情境 1：使用單數名詞

A: What did you do lately? 你最近在做什麼？

B: I sold **a designer bag** on the internet. 我在網路上賣了一個名牌包。

➡ 單數名詞表一次性的事件，業餘好玩而已

> 情境 2：使用無冠詞的複數名詞

A: What did you do lately? 你最近在做什麼？

B: I sold **designer bags** on the internet. 我賣名牌包。

➡ 說話者最近的工作可能就是賣名牌包

💡說明：

在以上情境中，使用「複數」名詞時，必然牽涉「複數」事件，因此解讀為工作。這是多數名詞與多數事件的關連，傳達出「重複從事」的額外訊息，推論說話者可能以此為工作。

> 情境 3：單數名詞前加上 the

A: What did you do lately? 你最近在做什麼？

B: I sold **the designer bag**. 我賣了那個名牌包。

➡ 認為聽者知道是賣哪一個包包

> 情境 4：複數名詞前加上 the

A: What did you do lately? 你最近在做什麼？

B: I sold **the designer bags**. 我賣了那些名牌包。

➡ 賣了聽者知道的那些包包

❓ (3) 專有名詞前要不要加限定冠詞 the 呢？

定冠詞 the 用於指涉「你知我知」的特定對象，而專有名詞也有「專屬的」特定對象，兩者間有何關連呢？

專有名詞和「the+N」有異曲同工之妙，都指向確知的人事物，所以若在專有名詞前再加冠詞 the 是多此一舉，沒有必要；但是在少數特殊情況下，可能有另外的考量。以下分三類來介紹專有名詞的使用：

a) 第一類：大寫且獨一的人名、地名、機構名稱，因為「只此一家，別無分店」，聽、說者都知道所指的單一對象，名稱前無須再加額外的冠詞：

　　例：人名：Jeremy Lin、Taylor Swift、Uncle Lin、Mr. Lin
　　　　地名/國名：Taipei、Hong Kong、China (Chinese)、Japan
　　　　　　　　　　(Japanese)、Germany (German)
　　　　街道：Roosevelt Rd.、Changchun St.、the Fifth Avenue
　　　　學校：National Taiwan University、Hsinchu Girls' High School
　　　　機構：Ministry of Education

b) 第二類：稱謂 + 姓：用獨一的稱謂＋姓氏，指稱獨一的個體

　　例：President Trump = the President of the US（現在的總統是 Trump）
　　　　Mayor Hou = the Mayer of New Taipei City
　　　　（現在的新北市長是姓侯 Hou）
　　　　➡ 職稱 + 姓氏
　　　　Uncle Sam = my uncle Sam ➡ 職呼 + 數字
　　　　World War II = the 2nd World War ➡ 特稱 + 數字

c) 第三類：the + 大寫一般名詞：指地球上獨一無二、眾人皆知的那一個

　　例：the Sun（太陽）、the Moon（月亮）、the Earth（地球）
　　　　➡ 將一般名詞大寫，標示專有性

在指涉強度與明確性上，[the + 一般名詞] 指涉明確，與**專有名詞**的效果類似。下圖顯示從 a 到 the 指涉強度階段變化，由小到大，從最廣泛、最

不明確的 something 到最明確的專有名詞 Sharon，其指涉範圍漸漸縮限變小（參考 Givón 1993）：

Do you see **something** there?　　　　　　　　明確性弱

　　　　　some animal there?

　　　　　a cat there?

　　　　　a black cat there?

　　　　　a black cat sitting on a rock at the corner there?

　　　　　a black cat with long whiskers sitting on the rock,

　　　　　licking her foot and wagging her tail at the corner

　　　　　there?

　　　　　THE cat there?

　　　　　MY cat there?　　　　　　　　　　　明確性強

　　　　　Sharon there?

? **(4) 使用 a 或 the 與時態有何關連呢？**

時態代表事件發生與否，和名詞的解讀有密切的關聯，請比較以下兩句：

John married <u>a rich woman</u>, but she was not beautiful.

➡ 確有其人

John would like to marry <u>a rich woman</u>, but he couldn't find <u>any</u>.

➡ 尚未確知

這兩句話中 "a rich woman" 的解讀不一樣，完全是受到時態的影響！確實發生的事必有其人，但尚未發生的事則有可能人物不定：

1）**確實發生的事（Real events）**：確實發生的事一定有確實的參與者，不管你知不知道，必然確有其人：

例：I met a friend. She's one of my best friends in elementary school.

　　➡ 說者的某個朋友，確有其人，但聽者可能不認識的人

　　I bought a car. It's a mini-van.

　　➡ 說者買了一輛車子，確實有這輛車，但聽者可能不知道哪一輛車。

「過去式」表明事件確實發生了，所以必然有確實的參與者，搭配的名詞必然具指涉性（referring nouns）。除了過去式，「現在完成」及「現在進行」也必然搭配確實存在的人物：

現在完成：I have met a Japanese. ➡ 一個確實存在的日本人

現在進行：I am meeting a reporter. ➡ 一個確實存在的記者

2）尚未發生的事（**Unreal events**）：既然事件本身都尚未發生，時間不定，當然人物也可能不確定：

例一：I want to buy a book.

　　➡ 可能一：一本說者確知的書 = a specific book

　　➡ 可能二： 一本說者也不確知的書 = any book

喜好動詞 want 只表達想要做的事，可是還沒發生，所以可能牽涉明確的個體（a specific one），但也可能是尚未確定的任何一個（any one）。即使時間座標改到過去，由於「想望喜好」動詞的語意特性，想做的事尚未發生，仍有可能搭配任何不確定的人物：

可能一：I wanted to buy a book, but I haven't found **it**.

　　➡ a specific one in mind（明確知道想要買哪一本書。）

可能二：I wanted to buy a book, but I haven't found **any**.

　　➡ any book（只是要買書，但不確定哪一本。）

例二：Jack decided to marry **a kind-hearted woman**.

可能一：Jack decided to marry a kind-hearted woman though he doesn't love **her**.

　　➡ Jack決定要娶一個心地善良的女人，但他並不愛她

　　➡ 他目前已有一個認識的對象。

可能二：Jack decided to marry a kind-hearted woman though he doesn't know **any**.

　　➡ Jack 要娶一個心地善良的女人，但是目前他還沒有找到，對象未定，仍在尋覓中

　　➡ **a kind-hearted woman** 只是一種他喜歡的類型。

? (5) 冠詞 the 的特異功能：萬一「我以為你知道，但你卻不知道」該怎麼辦呢？

狀況一：要是有好幾個人同名，專有名詞前也有可能加上 the

> A: You know what? I saw Fortuna on TV yesterday!
>
> B: Fortuna? Which one? You mean THE Fortuna we met last week?

這段對話中的 THE Fortuna 看似違反「人名前不加冠詞」的規則，但事實上是溝通時的變通，幫助語意更加明確，因為聽者不知道說者提到的 Fortuna 是誰？可能有好幾個叫 Fortuna 的人，所以為了進一步確認是哪一位，在 Fortuna 前加上 the，"The Fortuna you know!" 用來標記「對象的已知性」。

狀況二：「The + 專有名詞」表性質相同、最具其特點的那一位 （The ONE uniquely identifiable）

> 例：David is THE Picasso in his school.
>
> = David is the greatest painter in his school.

這裡用 The Picasso 不是指那位鼎鼎有名的大畫家 Picasso 本人，而是表示「像畢卡索一樣很會畫畫的人」，用來強調 David 是學校裡獨一無二很會畫畫的人，就像 Picasso 一樣。

本章對名詞的標記功能做了詳細的對照說明，和中文比起來，英文名詞的標記要求嚴謹明確，每一個介紹出場、具指涉對象的名詞，都要考量其是否個體化、單複數、聽者確知與否等區別，清楚標記名詞的語意特徵，因為「名詞出場，必有標記」！

4. 讀一段短文

Prince Harry and Meghan Markle reveal official engagement photos

By James Masters, CNN

Updated 1642 GMT (0042 HKT) December 22, 2017

Britain's **Prince Harry** and American actor **Meghan Markle** published **a set of official engagement photos** Thursday, **the latest** milestone on the road to their wedding next year.

> 註解：專有名詞是指特定對象專有的名稱，如人名或地名，一旦指名道姓後，
> 聽者就知道所指的特定對象是哪一個，毫無疑義，因此也就不需要冠詞
> 來做額外標記，如句中 *Prince Harry* 和 *Meghan Markle*。
> 他們因為要訂婚，出版了一套的官方訂婚照片，此處的 *a set of* 只是表
> 達數量，並不需要用定冠詞 *the* 來特別做標記，*photos* 用複數名詞表示
> 單獨個體不重要，指的是這些照片群體，無須細究是哪些照片。而 *the*
> *lastest milestone* 中的 *"the lastest"* 則為因為序數詞，屬於明確唯一指涉
> 對象，指的是最新的，是「你知我知」的範圍。

The couple, who announced their engagement last month, are due to marry on May 19 in **St. George's Chapel** at **Windsor Castle**, west of London.

> 註解：此句中 *The couple* 的定冠詞 *the* 用來代替修飾上文已提過的人事物:那
> 對要訂婚的新人，所以對聽者/讀者來說有共享的言談對話理解，指涉
> 對象明確，而且可辨識，也就是前面已經提過為「你知我知」的那個。
> *St. George's Chapel at Windsor Castle* 則為地名，專有名詞的地名僅
> 此一項，毫無疑義，因此也就不需要冠詞來做額外標記。

The photos, shot by **Alex Lubomirski,** were released **a day** after **the pair** joined **the Queen** and the rest of **the royal family** for Christmas lunch at **Buckingham Palace**.

> 註解：此句中 *Alex Lubomirski* 為專有名詞，一旦指名道姓後，聽者就知道所
> 指的特定對象是哪一個特定對象，毫無疑義，也就不需要冠詞來做額外
> 標記。*The photos* 及 *the pair* 的定冠詞 *the* 用來代替修飾此篇文章上文
> 已提過的人事物。*the Queen*、*the royal family* 用的 *the* 是在特定名詞
> 前。*Buckingham Palace* 為專有名詞的地名僅此一家，因此不需要冠詞
> 來做額外標記。而句中的 *a day* 在前文並未提及相關資訊，故僅用不定
> 冠詞

英文文法有道理！入門版

描述，後面則透過 *"after the pair joined the Queen and the rest of the royal family for Christmas lunch at Buckingham Palace"* 的形容詞子句來描述當天這對新人認識的場景。

The couple attended their first royal event together **in the city of Nottingham** earlier this month, and will spend their first Christmas as **an engaged couple** at the Queen's Sandringham estate.

註解：*The couple* 的定冠詞 *the* 用來代替修飾上文已提過的人事物：那對要訂婚的新人，所以對聽者、讀者來說有共享的言談對話理解，指涉對象明確，而且可辨識，也就是前面已經提過為「你知我知」的那個。
in the city of Nottingham 中的定冠詞 *the* 用在常識範圍內的「人或物」，所標記必然是「你知我知」的那個。
an engaged couple 中的 *an* 不定冠詞只是強調這對新人之後將會以一對已訂婚新人的身分在女王桑德林厄姆（*Sandringham*）莊園度過他們的第一個聖誕節。

From: http://edition.cnn.com/2017/12/21/europe/prince-harry-meghan-markle-official-photos-intl/index.html
(https://cnn.it/2PMYdS4)

5. 唱一首英文歌

A Dear John Letter

*Dear John

Oh! how I hate to write

Dear John

I must let you know tonight

That my love for you has gone

There's no reason to go on

And tonight I wed another

Dear John*

\<spoken\>

I was overseas in battle

When **the postman** came to me

He handed me **a letter**

And I was as happy as I could be

Cause the fighting was all over

And the battles they'd all be won

But then I opened up that letter

And it stated Dear John (*)

I was overseas in battle

When the postman came to me

He handed me a letter

"Won't you please send back my picture

 My husband wants it now"

歌詞資料來源及歌曲介紹：*https://goo.gl/UPyGq2*

說明：

When the postman came to me ➡ 此句說話者看見那位郵差所以指涉對象明確，故用 the postman。

He handed me a letter ➡ 但是說話者此時並不知道這位郵差要拿什麼信，只知道是一封信，所以用不定冠詞 a。

And I was as happy as I could be

Cause the fighting was all over ➡ 說話者在海外打仗，聽者知道他在海外打仗，所以告訴聽者這些戰爭已經結束了，故用定冠詞 the，表示「*你知我知*」的那個。

And the battles they'd all be won ➡ 說話者在海外打仗，聽者知道他在海外打仗，所以告訴聽者這些戰爭已經結束了，故用定冠詞 the，表示「*你知我知*」的那個。

But then I opened up that letter ➡ 但當說話者打開那位郵差拿給他的那封信時，此時說話者、聽者都知道是指哪封信，故用 that，表指涉對象明確。

6. 看一部影片

<u>VoiceTube</u>《看影片學英語》

Pride & Prejudice (1/10) Movie CLIP (2005)

1. Netherfield Park is let at last.

2. Do you not want to know who has taken it?

3. (Bennet) As you wish to tell me, my dear...

4. I doubt I have any choice in **the matter**. 這件事我別無選擇

5. Liddy, Kitty, what have I told you about listening **at the door**?
   Liddy、Kitty，跟妳們說過多少次不要在門口偷聽

6. Never mind that. There's **a Mr. Bingley...**
   不要緊，這次聽說是**Bingley**先生

7. arrived from **the North**. Perchance. 剛從北部過來的，這次開價

8. f5,000 **a year**. Really? 一年要五千法郎；真的嗎？

9. He's single. He's single.

10. Who's single? A Mr. Bingley, apparently.

11. And how can that possibly affect them?

12. Oh, Mr. Bennet, how can you be so tiresome?

13. You know he must marry one of them.

14. (Bennet) So that is his design in settling here.

15. You must go and visit him at once.

16. Good heavens. People.

17. For we may not visit if you do not, as you well know, Mr. Bennet.

18. Aren't you listening?

19. (Kitty) You must, Papa.

20. At once.

21. There's no need, I already have.

22. Have? When?

23. Oh, Mr. Bennet, how can you tease me so?

24. Have you no compassion for my poor nerves?

25. You mistake me, my dear.

26. I have **the highest respect** for them. 我可是很尊重我的女兒

27. They've been my constant companions...

28. these 20 years.

29. Is he amiable? Who?

30. Is he handsome?

31. He's sure to be handsome.

32. With £5,000 a year, it would not matter...

33. if he had warts and **a leer**. Who's got warts? 就算他身上長疣、眼睛沾到癩蝦蟆肉也不要緊

34. I will give my hearty consent...

35. to his marrying whichever of **the girls** he chooses. 無論他娶誰

36. So will he come to **the ball** tomorrow, Papa? 那他明天會出席舞會嗎，爸爸？

資料來源：*https://tw.voicetube.com/videos/1203?ref=movieclip (https://goo.gl/dNs1L3)*

說明：

4. I doubt I have any choice in **the matter**. 這件事我別無選擇
   ➡ 此句說者聽者都知道在談論那件事, 所以屬於「你知我知」的那個。

5. Liddy, Kitty, what have I told you about listening **at the door**?
   Liddy、Kitty，跟妳們說過多少次不要在門口偷聽
   ➡ 此句說者、聽者都知道在說的是哪個門，因為已經提醒過很多次不要在門口偷聽，所以屬於「*你知我知*」的那個。

6. Never mind that. There's **a Mr. Bingley**...
   不要緊，這次聽說是 **Bingley** 先生
   ➡ 此句說者是指有好幾個 **Mr. Bingley**，就是說明又來一個叫作 **Bingley** 的先生，沒有特定指哪一個 **Mr. Bingley**。

7. arrived from **the North**. Perchance.剛從北部過來的，這次開價
   ➡ 此句 the North 的定冠詞 the 用在表示方位 North 北方的名詞前面。

8. f5,000 **a year**. Really? 一年要五千法郎；真的嗎？➡ 此句 a year 指是某類的東西（a kind），只是傳達一年的數量概念

26 I have **the highest respect** for them. 我可是很尊重我的女兒
   ➡ 此句 **the highest** 的 **the** 是用在形容詞最高級的名詞前，屬於指涉對

象明確唯一，「*你知我知*」因為只有一個。

35. to his marrying whichever of **the girls** he chooses. 無論他娶誰

➡ 此句 **the girls he chooses** 是指他要娶的那些女孩們，是指說者聽者
知道的常識範圍內場景框架下的「*已知*」人物。

36. So will he come to **the ball** tomorrow, Papa? 那他明天會出席舞會嗎，爸
爸？

➡ 此句 **the ball** 是指他們明天要參加的舞會，是指說者、聽者知道的常識
範圍內場景框架下的「*已知*」事物。

 # 7. 做一點練習

Part 1：Write down a, an, the or x in the blanks.

1. Nobody lives on _____ Moon.

2. I like _____ red T-shirt over there better than _____ yellow one.

3. Judy's father works as _____ engineer in _____ big company in _____
   Taipei.

4. Jessica, do you still live in _____ Hong Kong?

5. I believe after _____ hour, you would have _____ whole afternoon
   free to get around _____ New York City.

6. Where's _____ USB drive Fortuna lent to you yesterday?

7. Ben has _____ terrible headache.

8. He didn't like _____ movie that you suggested.

9. _____ West has better national parks.

10. There is _____ dictionary in my schoolbag. _____ dictionary is very
    heavy.

11. _____ British Prime Minister lives in _____ Downing Street 10

12. My parents donated to a charity providing assistance to _____ elderly
    and _____ poor.

13. My brother lives next door to _____ Browns.

14. _____ phone on Daddy's desk belongs to Vicky.

15. A: Do you know where I left _____ car keys?

    B: Oh, I know. I just saw you put them on the dining table in _____
    kitchen this morning

16. That is _____ excellent novel. I like it a lot.

17. That is _____ most expensive hotel room I've ever heard of in my life.

18. My history teacher told me _____ Wright brothers invented _____ airplane.

19. Dr. Johnson visits many universities to educate students on _____ **AIDS**.

20. Henry had _____ heart attack. _____ heart attack weakened his heart seriously.

答案：

(1) the (2) the; the (3) an; a ; x (4) x (5) an; the ; x (6) the (7) a (8) the (9) The

(10) a ; The (11) The; x (12) the; the (13) the (14) The (15) the; the (16) an

(17) the (18) the; the (19) X (20) a; The

Part 2：克漏字

Once upon a time there was (1)_____ good and obedient girl who was loved by everyone and especially her grandmother who made her a red hood. (2)_____ girl loved wearing it, so she got (3)_____ nickname by it – Little Red Riding Hood. One day her mother told her that her grandma got ill and that she should visit and bring her some cakes and butter so that her grandma would get her strength back. Before she headed off to her grandma, she was warned that she has to follow (4)_____ path without making any turns.

Her mother also told her to act nicely at her grandma's and that she shouldn't roam around (5)_____ house and peek in every corner. Grandmother lived in another village, and (6)_____ Little Red Riding Hood had to go through (7)_____ forest to come to her house.

On her way to grandma, she intercepted (8)_____ wolf that immediately wanted to eat her. However, because they were in the forest filled with lumberjacks, he decided not to do so.

Since she had no clue that the wolf was (9)_____ dangerous animal she wasn't scared, and she started talking to him. The girl was naive, and (10)_____ wolf got her to talk about everything, starting from her ill grandma, what she was carrying to her house and (11)_____ location of the house. The wolf listened with (12)_____ interest and began plotting (13)_____ vicious plan. He couldn't be happier about eating (14)_____ girl and her grandma.

from https://www.bookreports.info/little-red-riding-hood-summary/ (https://goo.gl/7uwpoK)

答案：

(1) a (2) The (3) a (4) the (5) the (6) the (7) the (8) the (9) a (10) the (11) the
(12) X (13) a (14) the

Part 3：中英大不同

名詞標記：請根據本章所述道理分析 a、the、單數、複數之運用。

Humpty Dumpty	矮胖子
Humpty Dumpty sat on a wall. *Humpty Dumpty had a great fall.* *All the King's horses and all the King's men* *Could not put Humpty together again.*	矮胖子坐在牆上。 胖胖的胖子倒下了。 國王所有的馬和國王所有的人 都不能把矮胖子變回原來的樣子。

英文：

名詞前須有標記，標明單複數與[你知我知]否：Humpty Dumpty 為專有名詞，前面無須標記冠詞；"sat on a wall" 表示坐在一牆上，表數量，而且讀者不知道是哪一道牆；the King 是特定的人物，Humpty Dumpty 知道的國王，所以前用定冠詞 the 標記已知人物；"the King's horses / men" 是清楚標記為國王的馬和士兵，告知讀者是 [誰的] 馬和士兵，與 the King 有關且明確可知。

中文：沒有標記上要求，可以用單純名詞 [牆、馬、士兵]，其它語意由上下文推斷。

CHAPTER

5

什麼時候的事？

:

英文的動詞為什麼要加 ed？時態是怎麼回事？到底要如何區分現在、過去、未來和習慣？

)) 1. 你想說什麼？

如果小明說他看見一隻貓在追一隻狗，你一定會想知道這什麼時候發生的事？日常溝通時，當你聽到一件事情，一定想知道：什麼時候發生的？當你描述一件事情也要講清楚什麼時候發生的，這就是「事件的時間」（event time）。所以**「標記時間」**是溝通的首要任務之一！這就是英文時態的意義！

任何事情一定都牽涉到時間。如果把時間看成一條直線座標，那每件事一定都發生在時間座標的某一點上。通常我們會以說話當下的時間為基準，來判斷其它事件的時間順序是現在、過去或未來，或是一直都是如此？中文說：「我讀了三本書！」一定是在說話前就讀了，是過去發生的事；如果你說：「我想讀三本書！」一定還沒發生，是未來的事；要是當下正在讀呢？你會說：「我在讀這三本書！」

時間不同，就會有不同的標記方式；不同語言也用不同方式來標記。英語是用「動詞形式」來標記時間，因為動詞表達事件，所以用動詞的形式變化來表達事件在不同的時間發生，是最直接自然的方式。

所謂「動詞形式」（verb form）的變化，就是動詞本身會有形式上的改變：

English	Chinese
習慣：**She goes to school every day.**	她每天去上學。
過去：**She went to school yesterday.**	她昨天去上學。

英文的動詞形式會隨「事件時間」的改變而改變，但是中文的動詞形式保持不變。所以英文的動詞有「時態變化」，中文沒有！英文的標記原則是：「動詞一出場，時態必相隨！」

❓ **英文要分動詞時態，中文就不用分也可以溝通啊？！**

語言個性大不同，中英文都要表達事件發生的時間區隔，但是使用的標記方法不同：

Chinese	English
1. 我昨天「去」跳舞。 2. 我今天「去」跳舞。 3. 我明天「去」跳舞。 說明： 中文的動詞形式不變，不會隨時間改變，時間的標記要靠其他成分，如時間副詞「昨天」，或表「已發生」的「了」。	A. Where did you <u>go</u> yesterday? B. I <u>went</u> to a ball game. 說明： 英文的動詞隨時態改變，標記的特點就是「**動詞出場、時態相隨**」！動詞和時間同步出現。不管有沒有時間名詞出現，看到動詞過去式 went，就知道事件發生在過去！

 ## 2. 英文怎麼說？

英文有幾個『時段』的區別？如何搭配動詞時態？

根據 Givón（1993）的分析，英文動詞表達的時間概念，有四種：現在、過去、未來、及「事實習慣」。表達事件的時間，要以「現在」，就是「說話當下」的時間為基準：說話當下發生為現在，在之前發生為過去，之後發生為未來；若不管時間推移一直如此，則為習慣。「說話時間」確定後，才能決定事件發生在過去、現在、未來、或習慣。按照「事件時間」

（event time）和「說話時間」（speech time）的相對關係，英語將時間分為四個區塊，搭配四種動詞形式：

1）現在事件：發生在說話時間「同時」
　➡ 現在進行式 BE+V-ing：He is going to the party.
2）過去事件：發生在說話時間「之前」
　➡ 動詞過去式　　　　　：He went to the party.
3）未來事件：發生在說話時間「之後」
　➡ will + 動詞原形　　　：He will go to the party.
4）習慣事件：習慣性發生，無固定時間點
　➡ 動詞習慣式　　　　　：He goes to the party every Sunday.

➢**超簡原則1：動詞出場，時態相隨**

　　英文嚴格要求每一個動詞出場，都要清楚標記時間！時間標記的關鍵在於先釐清什麼是「現在」？現在就是就是「說話當下，以此為基準，就可判定四種不同的時間區塊：

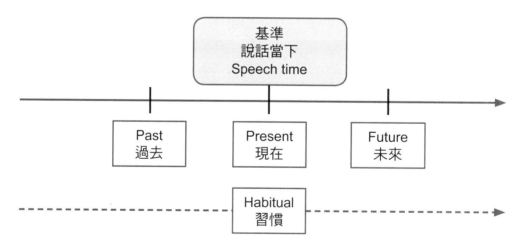

動詞的形式變化可清楚表達事件發生的時間，因此要養成在動詞上標記時間的習慣，選擇適當的動詞形式，用以標記「過去、未來、現在、習慣」四種不同的時段意義：

時段	形式變化	標記原則	時間意義
現在式	**A cat <u>loves</u> a dog.** **A cat <u>is chasing</u> a dog.**	動詞基本式：第三人稱 V+ s 動作動詞：進行 BE+V-ing	➡ 事件時間等於說話時間 ➡ 動作事件當下進行中
過去式	**A cat <u>chased</u> a dog.**	動詞 + ed	➡ 事件時間早於說話時間
未來式	**A cat <u>will</u> chase a dog.**	will + 動詞原形	➡ 事件時間晚於說話時間
習慣式	**A cat <u>chases</u> a dog.**	動詞基本式：第三人稱 V+ s	➡ 事件時間不固定/無定點（過去/現在/未來都適用）

　　基本上，英文的動詞形式直接表達時間上的區別，所以動詞隨著發生時間而改變：

1）現在式動詞：為動詞的基本形式，第三人稱主詞時要加「-s」；動作動詞的現在式則必然為進行貌：BE+V-ing。

2）過去式動詞：通常在動詞後加 -ed：walked、jumped。也有不規則的變化：went、ran、had。

3）習慣式動詞： 保持動詞基本形式，第三人稱主詞時要加「-s」；習慣式動作並不會變成進行貌。

　　重要的是：每次使用動詞，都要先搞清楚事件的時間區塊，以適當的形式清楚標記時間！

　　同樣的，疑問句或否定句要用到的「助動詞」，也要有清楚的時間標示：

➤疑問句：

時段	助動詞形式變化	例句
現在式	助動詞 **DO / DOES** 進行貌助動詞 **IS / ARE**	**Does** the cat like the dog? **Is** the cat chasing the dog?
過去式	助動詞 **DID**	**Did** the cat chase the dog?
未來式	助動詞 **WILL**	**Will** the cat chase the dog?
習慣式	助動詞 **DO/ DOES**	**Do** you go to school by bus every day?

➤否定句：

時段	助動詞形式變化	例句
現在式	助動詞 DO / DOES + **NOT** 進行貌助動詞 **IS / ARE + NOT**	The cat **doesn't** like the dog. The cat **isn't** chasing the dog.
過去式	助動詞 **DID + NOT**	The **cat didn't** chase the dog.
未來式	助動詞 **WILL +NOT**	**The cat won't** chase the dog.
習慣式	助動詞 **DO / DOES**	The cat **doesn't** usually chase the dog.

何謂「事實習慣式」？

如果只分三種時態（現在、過去、未來），會無法明確交代下列
兩句差別：

I eat apples. 我是吃蘋果的。 ➡ 習慣事實（習慣式）
I am eating apples. 我在吃蘋果。 ➡ 當下發生（現在式）

說明：

"I am eating apples." 為現在式，於說話當下發生，那 "I eat apples."

是何時發生的? 絕不是「現在」! 因為並非說話當下發生的動作,
而是一種「放諸四海」皆準的**真理**、**事實或習慣**,這就是習慣式。
請看下列例句:

例1:The sun rises in the East.
例2:Jessica goes to work on foot.
例3:Debby only eats two meals a day.

上述三個句子的事件時間上都沒有明確發生時間點,過去、現在、
未來都是如此,因此定義為「**事實習慣式**」。

所以英文有四種時間的區別:現在、過去、未來、習慣!

> **超簡原則 2:狀態、動作,形式有別**

如第二章所述,事件基本上分為「**動作**」與「**狀態**」。

表達「動作」的「動作動詞」,如 eat、go、hit、write,都表行為動
作,用於「現在式」時,必然成為「現在進行」,因為說話的當下發生的動
作必然在進行中。

表達「狀態」的就是「狀態動詞」,如:have、know、believe、
understand,不牽涉外在「動作」,不會隨時間而改變,屬於「**靜態語意**」,
不適用於「進行式」。

由於狀態、動作動詞的語意差異,和不同時間區塊搭配時,也會有形式
上的差異:

	狀態動詞(Stative V):know	動作動詞(Active V):write
Past 過去式	He **knew** the answer.	He **wrote** a novel.
Present 現在式	He **knows** the answer. (✕) He is knowing the answer. ➡ 沒有「現在進行式」用法	He is writing the letter. ➡ 必然為「現在進行式」

	狀態動詞（Stative V）：know	動作動詞（Active V）：write
Habitual 習慣式	He (always) knows the answer. ➡ 現在的事實或習慣	He (always) writes novels. ➡ 現在的事實或習慣

參考 Givón (1993:150-151)

❓ 「狀態動詞」和時態間有何關連呢？

　　狀態動詞的「現在式」與「習慣式」形式看起來一樣，是因為「狀態」本身「持久穩定」，現在存在的狀態可能持續了一段時間，與習慣事實有相同的屬性，語意相通。

　　💡搭配不同的時間副詞，可清楚區分「現在式」與「習慣式」兩種不同時段狀態：

1）He knows the answer right now.

　　➡ **present state 現在的狀態**：針對當下，他知道答案。

2）He always knows the answer.

　　➡ **habitual state 恆常的狀態**：他博學多聞，總是知道答案。

❓ 狀態動詞沒有「進行式」

　　狀態動詞是用來表達「狀態性事件」，如：have、know、like，帶有<u>靜態語意</u>，無法如動作動詞一樣，不會隨時間變化，沒有「進行」的可能，所以基本上是不會搭配「現在進行式」。少數的狀態動詞可用於進行貌，但語意必然已轉變，發展出「較為動態」的語意，而出現進行式：

　　例：have、be

Have：

I have a car. ➡ 表示擁有（**own**），➡ 不能用現在進行式，不能說（✕）I am having a car.

但是：

I'm having a great time. ➡ 表示享受（**enjoy**），轉為動態語意 ➡ 可以用現在進行式

I'm having a cup of coffee. ➡ 表示享受（**enjoy**），轉為動態語意 ➡ 可以用現在進行式

Be：

He is tall. ➡ BE 動詞表裝態連結，➡ 不能用現在進行式，不能說 (✕) He is being tall.

但是：

He is being ridiculous. ➡ 刻意的行為表現（**acting**），轉為動態語意 ➡ 可以用現在進行式

You are being a clown. ➡ 行為表現（**acting like**），轉為動態語意 ➡ 可以用現在進行式

❓ 「動作動詞」和時態間有何關連呢？

💡 動作動詞的現在式必然為現在進行式，不同於習慣式

動作發生於說話當下（現在）就是「現在進行式」： He is eating a guava. ➡ 當下正在吃芭樂

習慣性的動作 ≠ 現在進行的動作：He eats a guava. ➡ 表達一種習慣事實「他是吃芭樂的。」

因此，動作與狀態動詞會因為所表達的事件性質不同，因而造成不同時態搭配關係。

❓ 動詞的過去式為何有「不規則變化」？

動詞的時態變化可清楚標記事件時間！在英文裡，每個動詞都要有標記！表達過去式，大多數規則變化在動詞字尾加上「-ed」，但也有不規則的變化，如下表。不規則變化是隨歷史演變造成，不同歷史階段造成不同音韻變化並影響了動詞，雖然有點難記，但多用多看就容易記住了。

➤規則變化：**V + ed** ➡ 根據動詞字尾，有三種變化原則：

動詞 + ed	形式變化原則
walk + ed ➡ walk<u>ed</u> rain + ed ➡ rain<u>ed</u>	字尾為無聲子音 +ed ➡ /t/ 字尾為有聲子音或母音 +ed ➡ /d/
chase + ed ➡ chas(e)d	動詞字尾已有 -e ➡ 不需重複e
jog + ed ➡ jo<u>gg</u>ed	短母音加子音 ➡ 重複子音 再加 -ed 不重複子音會造成發音困擾 ➡ joged ➡ o 變長音？

➤不規則變化：有五種變化類型

	原形	過去式
無變化 形同、音同	set put cast	set put cast
形同、音不同	read	read
改變末尾子音	send lend spend	sent lent spent
改變母音子音	go say keep	went said kept

	原形	過去式
改變母音	see run sit give take know come begin find write	saw ran sat gave took knew came began found wrote

註：read /rid/ - read /rɛd/

➤**超簡原則3： 同形動詞如何辨識語意？**

　　動詞為形音義三者的組合，有些動詞形式相同，但語意不同，如下列例子：

lie 說謊	過去式 lied -- 過去分詞 lied -- 現在分詞 lying
	He lied to me about his age. ➡ lied to me對我「說謊」
lie 躺	過去式 lay -- 過去分詞 lain -- 現在分詞 lying
	He lay flat on the sofa.
	辨別步驟：第三人稱沒加-s ➡ 過去式 ➡ 無受詞 ➡ 不及物動詞「躺」
lay 擺放	過去式 laid -- 過去分詞 laid -- 現在分詞 laying
	He lays the book on the sofa.
	辨別步驟：第三人稱加-s ➡ 不是過去式 ➡ 有受詞 ➡ 及物動詞「擺放」

　　形式相同就會混淆，首先要將動詞形式變化記好，再搭配其他句子成分（明確情境、主題、時間、句子其他線索），才能斷定語意，例如："She is lying on the bed." ➡ 因為有 "on the bed"，lying的語意比較可能為「躺」（**lie on the bed**），而不是「說謊」！

❓ 未來式有幾種標記方式，溝通涵意有何不同?

💡 未來式有三種標記方式，溝通涵意各不同：

標記方式	例句	溝通語意
will (modal aux)	I will leave soon.	✓ 最正式 ✓ 確定性較高 ✓ 時間為最遠的未來 ✓ 說話當時決定要做的事 ➡ 表達個人主觀意願，will 原意為個人意願或遺囑。
be going to/ be gonna (complex aux)	I am going to leave soon.	✓ 較為口語 ✓ 確定性較低 ✓ 時間為較近的未來 ✓ 已經安排好未來將進行的事 ➡ be going to 是將 going 進行式的空間位移概念轉為時間上的移動，表近期要「去」做之事。

標記方式	例句	溝通語意
be V-ing (progressive aux)	I am leaving soon.	✓ 最為口語 ✓ 確定性很高 ✓ 時間為立即的未來 ✓ 已經安排好未來將進行的事 ➡ be V-ing 是藉由進行式表達未來要做的動作似乎已經在「進行中」為「立即要發生的事」。

參考 Givón (1993)

➢**超簡原則 4：未來距離可分遠近，will 語意最廣，可以表達「任何遠近的未來」；但「BE V-ing」是以進行貌表未來，只能表達「最近的未來」：**

近距離：**(O) I am leaving this afternoon.**	**立即要離開**
遠距離：**(??) I am leaving next year.**	**最好改成 (O) I will leave next year.**

 「BE V-ing」基本上是進行貌，但也可用於表示「立即」要發生的未來，這是一種概念的轉換： 把「即將發生的事」看做近到如同「正在進行中」！

3. 還能怎麼說？

(1) 時態和動詞語意有何關係？

前面提到動態動詞的現在式必然是正在進行中，相反的，靜態動詞卻不會出現進行式，因為沒有動態的改變。所以可說 "I saw a dog." 但不會說：(✕) I am seeing a dog.

然而，**Givón** (1993)[1] 提到有些狀態動詞可以加上進行貌「-ing」，而產生「動態化」的語意改變，舉下列三個動詞作說明：

---

1 參見 T. Givón (1993). *English Grammar: a function-based introduction.* Chapter 4, pp. 151-52.

➢知覺狀態動詞 see

例句	說明
I see her.	see 表「視覺狀態」，所以不能說： (✕) **I am seeing a bug now.**
I am seeing my boss first thing tomorrow.	此處 see 已轉為動態語意，意思為「拜訪」或「會面」，因此可以用 V-*ing* 的進行式！
He's seeing the guests right now.	

➢連接狀態動詞 be

例句	說明
Joe is tall.	**be** 表達「存在」狀態，所以不能說： (✕) **Joe is being tall.**
Joe is being stupid.	**be** 不是表達存在狀態，而是描述 **Joe** 暫時的「行為表現」，意思是平常 **Joe** 做事都很仔細，今天不知道怎麼了，做了件很愚蠢的事，所以才會用 "**He's being stupid.**"。

➢所有狀態動詞 have

例句	說明
Mary has long legs.	*have* 表達「擁有」，所以不能說： ***She is having long legs (x)**。
Mary was <u>having</u> dinner at 6 pm. **(吃)** 原來就有 "吃" 的意思。	*have* 加了 *-ing*，不再表達「擁有」，而是轉為動態語意：
Mary is <u>having</u> a baby. (懷孕) "have a baby" 的 have 原來是「生育」的意思	She's eating dinner. She's giving birth to the first baby. She's enjoying the time.
Mary was <u>having</u> a good time in Kenting. (享受) 原來是 "經歷" 的意思。	

(2) I'm lovin' it! 麥當勞叔叔的英文怪怪的？

　　love 是「心理狀態」動詞，表達「持久不變的狀態」，應該不能用進行式。但麥當勞的廣告詞怎麼說：I'm loving it! 麥當勞的英文錯了嗎？

I'm loving it!

　　這個廣告詞匠心獨具！ 故意將 love 的情感狀態轉變為「動作化」的用法，由「靜態」轉為「動態」（state to action），傳達出「愛就是要行動」的潛在訊息。廣告詞雖看似違反語法規則，卻是其獨到之處，靈活運用語言，語意創新：心動不如馬上行動！

(3) 如何表達過去的習慣？

💡表達「過去習慣」有兩種方式，但語意不同

❖**used to + V**：表達只存在於過去的習慣，現在不做了

　　例：She used to play the piano.

　　　➡ 以前彈鋼琴，但現在不彈了。

❖would + V：表達過去持續到現在的習慣

例：She would play the piano when feeling down.

➡ 每當感到消沉時，就會彈鋼琴。

這是過去的習慣，如今仍然有此可能；所以此處 would 帶有「可能性」。

❓ 同一句話裡可以有兩種時態嗎？

💡 一個句子裡有可能描述兩個時空不同的事件，舉下列說明：

例句	說明
1. **I guess** (that) his faith **helped** him face the challenge.	"I guess/ think"都是說話當下的想法或認知狀態，但想法的內容卻是關於過去發生的事件，所以 that 後名詞子句可以用過去式" **helped** him/ **came** from"。
2. **I think** (that) his talents **came** from his mother's side.	
3. I thought English was difficult, but it is not.	過去信念認為英文困難，但現在不認為。
4. I thought English is difficult and still do!	對事實認定，以前和現在都是一樣。

❓ 過去和未來可能在同一個句子裡嗎？英文如何說：他昨天說他明天會來？

💡 可有兩種說法，時間座標不同：

He said that he would come tomorrow.

➡ 向「過去」對齊，整句話投射在過去

He said that he will come tomorrow.

➡ 以「現在」為分野，過去說的，但明天還未到

英文在動詞上標記時間訊息，要完整表達一個事件，一定要養成標記時間的習慣。謹記：動詞出場，時態相隨！

Where <u>did</u> you go yesterday?

I <u>went</u> to the book fair!

 ## 4. 讀一段短文

看看這篇故事中有哪些動詞時態呢？

The Bull and the Goat

A BULL, escaping from a Lion, **hid** in a cave which some shepherds **had** recently **occupied.** As soon as he **entered,** a He-Goat **left** in the cave sharply **attacked** him with his horns. The Bull quietly **addressed** him, "Butt away as much as you **will.** I **have no fear** of you, but of the Lion. Let that monster go away and I **will** soon **let** you know what **is** the respective strength of a Goat and a Bull."

Moral: It **shows** an evil disposition to take advantage of a friend in distress.

http://www.aesopfables.com/cgi/aesop1.cgi?1&TheBullandtheGoat

(https://goo.gl/rvuZ4q)

註解：

此故事為描述「說話以前」發生的事情，因此用「過去式」為時間主軸：

A BULL, escaping from a Lion, **hid** in a cave which some shepherds **had** recently **occupied.** As soon as he **entered,** a He-Goat **left** in the cave sharply **attacked** him with his horns.

如為直接引述說出的話，則要「原音重現」，回歸「說話當下」，也就是當時的「現在」：

The Bull quietly addressed him: "Butt away as much as you will. I **have** no fear of you, but of the Lion..."

以說話當下為基準，在過去已經發生的事，就要用「過去完成式」：

A BULL, escaping from a Lion, <u>hid</u> in a cave which some shepherds
　　　　　　　　　　　　　　　　　　　　過去式

had recently **occupied.**
　過去完成式

說話之後才會發生的事，屬於未來時間，就用「未來式」：

The Bull quietly addressed him, "Butt away as much as you **will**. I have no fear of you, but of the Lion..."

而最後一句的寓言，屬於「事實習慣式」：

Moral: It **shows** an evil disposition to take advantage of a friend in distress.

此為以「事實式」表達一種真理的「永久事實真相」。

5. 唱一首英文歌

Bad Day （Daniel Powter）

Music Video: https://goo.gl/PY5bV6

Where is the moment we needed the most (1)

You kick up the leaves and the magic is lost

They tell me your blue skies fade to grey

They tell me your passion's gone away

And I don't need no carrying on

You stand in the line just to hit a new low (2)

You're faking a smile with the coffee to go

You tell me your life's been way off line (3)

You're falling to pieces every time

And I don't need no carrying on

Cause you had a bad day (4)

You're taking one down

You sing a sad song just to turn it around

You say you don't know

You tell me, don't lie

You work at a smile and you go for a ride

You had a bad day

The camera don't lie

You're coming back down and you really don't mind

You had a bad day

You had a bad day

Well you need a blue sky holiday

The point is they laugh at what you say

And I don't need no carrying on

You had a bad day

You're taking one down

You sing a sad song just to turn it around

You say you don't know

You tell me, don't lie

You work at a smile and you go for a ride

You had a bad day

The camera don't lie

You're coming back down and you really don't mind

You had a bad day

(Oh.. Holiday..)

Sometimes the system goes on the blink (5)

And the whole thing turns out wrong

You might not make it back

And you know that you could be well oh that strong(6)

And I'm not wrong

So where is the passion when you need it the most

Oh you and I

You kick up the leaves and the magic is lost

Cause you had a bad day

You're taking one down

You sing a sad song just to turn it around

You say you don't know

You tell me don't lie

You work at a smile and you go for a ride

You had a bad day

You've seen what you like

And how does it feel for one more time

You had a bad day

You had a bad day

Had a bad day

Had a bad day

Had a bad day

Had a bad day

Had a bad day

Lyrics from: https://goo.gl/tuU8T5

註解：

1. Where is the moment we needed the most

   回到說話當下，我們[之前最需要]的時刻[現在在哪]？所以用現在式 "Where is the moment?" 而 needed 則為說話當下以前發生的事件，所以用過去式。

2. You **stand in the line** just to hit a new low

   You're faking a smile with the coffee to go

   回到說話當下，看到你站在隊伍中，你不禁又沮喪起來，我看到當時的你正裝著笑臉，你端著咖啡離開了，所以 "**stand in the line**" 為現在式，

"**You're faking a smile**" 為現在進行式。

3. You tell me **your life's been way off line**

   You**'re falling to pieces** every time

   And I **don't need** no carrying on

   回到說話當下，在說話當下以前，你告訴你的生活一蹋糊塗，所以 "your life's been way off line" 為現在完成式的 "has been"。"You**'re falling to pieces** every time" 強調每一次我看到你時當時你在進行的動作。"And I **don't need** no carrying on" 是說我看你這樣我也不必堅持下去，need 為描述需要跟偏好的狀態動詞，不能用現在進行式，這裡指現在式，針對眼前的狀態，說者也不必堅持下去。

4. Cause you **had** a bad day

   You**'re taking** one down

   這是說：在說話當下以前，因為你過了倒楣的一天，所以用過去式 **had**，造成你現在正心情低落，所以用 "You**'re taking**" 現在進行式。

5. Sometimes the system **goes** on the blink

   And the whole thing **turns** out wrong

   這裡說：在說話當下，表達有時整個系統會停擺，一切都會不對勁，表示是一種「事實習慣」，所以用現在式 **goes/ turns**。

6. And you **know** that you **could** be well oh that strong

   And I**'m** not wrong

   而你知道你可以……堅強起來！這表示在說話當下的知道的事情，所以用現在式 **know**，知道的內容是表是可能語意，所以用 could，接著又回到說話當下，認為：我現在沒說錯吧！"I**'m** not wrong."

6. 看一部影片

VoiceTube《看影片學英語》

Minions Official Trailer #1 (2015) - Despicable Me Prequel HD

from: https://tw.voicetube.com/videos/51091 (https://goo.gl/xJXk27)

Minions. Minions **have been** on this planet far longer than we have.

They **go** by many names: Dave, Carl, well that one **is** Norbit, he's an idiot.

They all **share** the same goal: to serve the most despicable master around.

- Banana! Gnam gnam!

Finding a master was easy; keeping a master, that's where things **got** tricky.

Oh...

But nonetheless they **kept** on looking.

speaking their language

Without a master they **had** no purpose, they **became** aimless and depressed.

If this went on much longer they would surely perish.

But then one minion **stepped** forward.

Kevin **felt** pride he **was going to** be the one to find his tribe the biggest baddest villain to self.

Stuart felt... hungry mostly... he was going to be the one to eat this banana.

And Bob, Bob **was frightened of** the journey ahead.

註解：

此故事為描述「說話以前」發生的事情，因此用「過去式」為時間主軸：

Finding a master was easy; keeping a master, that's where things **got** tricky.

But nonetheless they **kept** on looking.

Without a master they **had** no purpose, they **became** aimless and depressed.

But then one minion **stepped** forward.

Kevin **felt** pride he **was going to** be the one to find his tribe the biggest baddest villain to self.

And Bob, Bob **was frightened of** the journey ahead.

如為直接引述說出的話，則要「原音重現」，回歸「說話當下」，也就是當

時的「現在」：

They **go** by many names: Dave, Carl, well that one **is** Norbit, he's an idiot.

They all **share** the same goal: to serve the most despicable master around.

 ## 7. 做一點練習

Part 1：請填入正確動詞時態

Sick

（By Shel Silverstein）

"I cannot go to school today,"

(1)_____(say) little Peggy Ann McKay.

"I have the measles and the mumps,

A gash, a rash and purple bumps.

My mouth is wet, my throat (2)_____(be) dry,

I'm (3)_____(go) blind in my right eye.

My tonsils are as big as rocks,

I've (4)_____(count) sixteen chicken pox

And there (5)_____(be) one more--that's seventeen,

And don't you think my face (6)_____(look) green?

My leg is cut--my eyes (7)_____(be) blue--

It might be instamatic flu.

I (8)_____(cough) and sneeze and gasp and choke,

I'm sure that my left leg is broke--

My hip (9)_____(hurt) when I move my chin,

My belly button's caving in,

My back is wrenched, my ankle's sprained,

My appendix pains each time it (10)_____(rain).

My nose is cold, my toes are numb.

I have a sliver in my thumb.

My neck is stiff, my voice is weak,

I hardly (11)_____(whisper) when I speak.

My tongue is (12)_____(fill) up my mouth,

I think my hair is (13)_____(fall) out.

My elbow's bent, my spine ain't straight,

My temperature is one-o-eight.

My brain is shrunk, I cannot hear,

There (14) _____(be) a hole inside my ear.

I (15)_____(have) a hangnail, and my heart is--what?

What's that? What's that you say?

You say today is...Saturday?

G'bye, I'm (16)_____(go) out to play!"

Source: https://www.familyfriendpoems.com/poem/sick-by-shel-silverstein
(https://bit.ly/2PPNRAP)

答案：

(1) said (2) is (3) going (4) counted (5) is (6) looks (7) are (8) cough (9) hurts

(10) rains (11) whisper (12) filling (13) falling (14) is (15) have (16) going

Part 2：中英大不同

請就以下中英對照分析此詩句所用的事件發生時間。

泰戈爾經典英文詩句

Once we dreamt that we were strangers. We wake up to find that we were dear to each other.	有一次，我們夢見大家都是不相識的。 我們醒了，卻知道我們原是相親相愛的。

說明：

英文：動詞形式有別，以標記時間：Once we **dreamt** that we **were** strangers.➡ 表示發生在過去

We **wake up** to find that we **were** dear to each other.➡ wake up 是現在式，回到說話當下，然後發先之前是 we **were** dear to each other。

中文：中文動詞形式不變，不能直接表達時間，需要加上：醒了、原是，才能表達動詞發生時間。

資料來源：*http://f1f6lai.blogspot.tw/2013/09/blog-post_2990.html*
(https://goo.gl/aDeLCe)
泰戈爾經典英文詩句

CHAPTER

6

事件的進展如何？

🗣 1. 你想說什麼？

單元1 事件的樣貌：進展狀態

　　英語的標記特點之一就是：「動詞出場，時態相隨」。所謂「時態」，包含「時間」和「時貌」兩個部份。事件發生的「時間」可藉由不同的時段標記來表達（過去、現在、未來、習慣式）；但是事件進展的「樣貌」，究竟是單純完整的事件，或是正在進行的事件，還是已經完成的事件，又該怎麼表達呢？是三種不同的事件樣貌，表達三種描述事件的觀點，因此稱為「時貌」。這三種事件樣貌，可用三幅圖來說明：哆啦A夢 5:30 PM 在找大雄（正在進行），然後 6:00 PM 找到他了（簡單完整），在 6:30 PM 看電視之前已經找到了（之前完成）：

Doraemon was looking for Nobita.	Doraemon found Nobita.	Doraemon had found Nobita.
5:30 PM	6:00 PM	6:30 PM

　　這些事件都發生說話之前，所以時間標記都是過去；但是，事件呈現的樣貌卻不同：「尋找」是正在進行中 "I was looking for him."，「發現」則可視為簡單完整的事件 "I found Nobita."，而相對而言，看電視之前已經「找著」了 "I had found him."。所以描述事件有三種可能的樣貌：

簡單完整：I **did** my homework at 5:30 PM.
正在進行：I **was** doing my homework at 5:30 PM.
之前完成：I **had** done my homework by 5:30 PM.

這三種樣貌可搭配不同事件發生的時間，形成完整的時態標記。下圖描述大雄和哆啦A夢整個晚上所做的事情（說話時間為 7 PM），請看看有哪些時態（時間 + 樣貌）的組合？

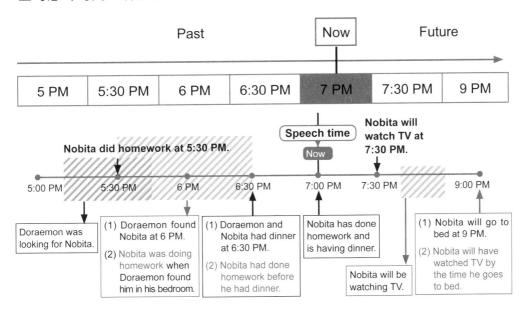

再讀讀以下這段對話，不同的時態（時間 + 樣貌）標記所表達的意思有何不同？

情境對話

Shizuka: Do you have the time, Giant?

Giant: Yes, it's 7 PM.

Shizuka: Why did Doraemon look so tired? What did he do this evening?

Giant: He **was looking for** Nobita at 5 PM.

Shizuka: Did he find Nobita?

Giant: Yes, he finally **found** him in his bedroom at 6 PM.

Shizuka: What was Nobita doing when Doraemon found him in his bedroom?

Giant: He **was still doing** the difficult math homework until he **had** dinner at 6:30 PM.

Shizuka: Thank God. I think he **has done** his homework by now. What will he do after dinner?

Giant: He **will be watching** TV at 7:30 pm until he **goes** to bed at 9
　　　 PM.

Shizuka: So, he **will have watched** TV by the time he **goes** to bed.

Giant: Exactly!

　　由上圖及對話得知，不同的「時、態」表達事件發生在不同的時間，呈現不同的樣貌。簡單來說，「時、態」所傳達的就是「時點」與「觀點」的結合。若要充分了解「時、態」的語意，就需要先了解什麼是「時點」與「觀點」。

單元2 時態就是「時點」與「觀點」的結合

什麼是「時點」？什麼是「觀點」？

時點（Tense）：事件發生的時間點（客觀事實）
觀點（Aspect）：描述事件樣貌的觀點（主觀選擇）

　　我們用大雄在傍晚 7 點前後所進行的四件事，來進一步說明「時點」和「觀點」如何連結：

Past 1	Past 2	Present	Future 1	Future 2
Homework	Dinner	Speech Time 說話時間	TV	Bed
5:00 PM	6:00 PM	7:00 PM	8:00 PM	9:00 PM

　　要準確表達大雄在 5:00 PM 到 9:00 PM 所做的事情，一定要在動詞上標記兩個「點」：一個是「時點」，另一個是「觀點」。

時點	(1)「時點」（Tense）就是以「說話時間」（Speech Time）來看待事件發生的時間點到底是落在哪一個時段（現在、過去、未來、或習慣）： 現在：時點落在「說話時間」當下 過去：時點落在「說話時間」之前 未來：時點落在「說話時間」之後 習慣：時點不確定，可落在任何時段 「說話時間」是 7:00 PM，那麼大雄在 7:00 PM 說話當下所做的事都落在「現在」：Nobita is home. He is doing his homework now. 說話之前 5:00 PM 和 6:00 PM 分別做的兩件事（寫作業和吃晚餐），「時點」就是落在「過去」：He did his homework and ate dinner. 說話之後，8:00 PM 和 9:00 PM 會發生的兩件事（看電視和睡覺），「時點」落在「未來」：He will watch TV at 8 PM and go to bed at 9 PM. 如果大雄每天都是 8:00 PM 看電視，就沒有明確的時點，卻又包含過去、現在、和未來，這就是習慣式：He always watches TV at 8 PM.
觀點	(2)「觀點」（Aspect）就是對事件進行的樣貌加以說明（簡單、進行、或完成），是說話者選擇描述事情的角度或方式，意即主「觀」的切入「點」。「觀點」要搭配「時點」才能完整描述一個事件。 例 1. 「時點」為過去的前提下，描述大雄寫作業這件事的樣貌，有三個不同的「觀點」可以選擇：

163

觀點	過去 + 簡單貌	把寫作業這件事看成單純、完整、獨立的事件 viewing the event as a whole，就是「過去簡單式」
		Nobita **did** his homework at 5:00 PM.
	過去 + 進行貌	把寫作業這件事看成正在發生進行中的事件 simultaneously ongoing，就是「過去進行式」
		Nobita **was doing** his homework when Doraemon found him at 5:00 PM.
	過去 + 完成貌	把寫作業這件事看成在「過去某個時點」（吃晚餐6:00 PM）之前完成的動作 completed by a past time，就是「過去完成式」。
		Nobita **had done** his homework before he **had** dinner.

若是沒有言明「過去某個時點」，通常就是以「說話當下」為基準，時點就落在「現在」，現在之前完成的就是現在完成式：

完成貌 + 現在	把寫作業這件事看成是在「說話時間」（7:00 PM）之前完成的動作（completed by now），就是「現在完成式」
	Nobita **has done** homework by now.

[例2] 在未來的時點下，描述大雄要看電視這件事，哆啦A夢也有三個不同的「觀點」可以選擇：

未來 + 簡單貌	把看電視這件事看成在時間上單純、完整、獨立的事件，就是「未來簡單式」
	Nobita **will watch** TV at 7:30 PM.
未來 + 進行貌	把看電視這件事看成未來正在發生進行中的事件，就是「未來進行式」
	Nobita **will be watching** TV until he **goes** to bed.
未來 + 完成貌	把看電視這件事看成是會在「未來某時點」之前完成的動作，就是「未來完成式」
	Nobita **will have watched** TV by the time he goes to bed.

以上描述事件的觀點又可稱為「時貌」（aspect），三種時貌與四個時點結合就產生12種時態組合：

時點 （Tense） + 時貌 （Aspect）	現在簡單：I see an apple. 現在進行：I am eating an apple. 現在完成：I have eaten an apple. 過去簡單：I ate an apple. 過去進行：I was eating an apple. 過去完成：I had eaten an apple before I ate dinner. 未來簡單：I will eat an apple. 未來進行：I will be eating an apple when I watch TV. 未來完成：I will have eaten an apple before I watch TV. 習慣簡單：I eat an apple every day. 習慣進行：I am always eating an apple at 7 AM. 習慣完成：I have always eaten an apple before I go to school.

單元3 不同的時態標記傳達不同的語意

從上節可以得知同一個事件可有三種不同的觀點，每個觀點又可配合四個不同的時點就至少有 12 種不同的標記方式，而每一種時態組合所表達的語意究竟有何不同？我們來一一探討觀點（或時貌）的溝通意義：

觀點	時態組合	表達的意涵
簡單貌 （整體）	現在／過去／未來／習慣＋簡單貌 (1) He gets up at 5:00 AM. (2) He got up at 5:00 AM. (3) He will get up at 5:00 AM. (4) He would get up at 5:00 AM. 　　He always gets up at 5 AM.	簡單貌有三個語意的特性： 1. 表達遠距離「全景式」的觀點。拉遠距離（zoom out），看到整體。

165

觀點	時態組合	表達的意涵
簡單貌 （整體）	現在／過去／未來／習慣 + 簡單貌 (1) He gets up at 5:00 AM. (2) He got up at 5:00 AM. (3) He will get up at 5:00 AM. (4) He would get up at 5:00 AM. or He always gets up at 5 AM.	2. 單純地將事件視為一個單一的整體（describing the event as a whole）。 3. 簡單貌只「簡單」表達某個時點所發生的事，並不細究事件的進行狀態，所以只有簡單的「時點」標記。
進行貌	現在／過去／未來／習慣 + 進行貌 (1) He is doing an experiment. (2) He was doing an experiment when the phone rang. (3) He will be doing an experiment. (4) He would be doing an experiment.	進行貌有三個語意的特性： 1. 表達近距離「聚焦式」的觀點。拉近距離（zoom in）看到事件內部。 2. 表達事件正在進行狀態中（ongoing），不見頭也不見尾，只見進行中。 例：He is doing an experiment. 3. 表達與某個時點同時進行的共時性（simultaneity）。 例：He was doing an experiment when the phone rang.

觀點	時態組合	表達的意涵
完成貌	現在／過去／未來／習慣 + 完成貌 (1) He has done his work by now. (2) He had played baseball before he did his work. (3) He will have done his work by the time he goes to bed.	完成貌有三個語意的特性： 1. 表達事件「在某時點之前」完成的概念，這個時點就是「參照點」： ✓ 現在完成：在「現在參照點」之前完成 ✓ 過去完成：在「過去參照點」之前完成 ✓ 未來完成：在「未來參照點」之前完成 2. 並非表達事件本身的時間，而是強調與參照點之間的關聯。 3. 完成式表達<u>動作</u>在參照點「之前」完成結束了，但若是<u>狀態</u>，則有可能延續到參照點： I have read the book. (finished) I have been a student. (I am still a student.)

 ## 2. 英文怎麼說？

形式上，相較於簡單貌僅標記事件的時點，「進行」與「完成」兩種時貌需加上額外標記：

➢ 進行貌： Be + V-ing
➢ 完成貌： have / has / had + PP（過去分詞）。

不同的標記形式是為了傳達不同的語意，接下來就進一步分析這兩種「時貌觀點」所呈現的形式和意義的搭配。

1. 進行貌 Be + V-ing 表達近距離的「聚焦式」的觀點（zoom in）：

「進行貌」就像進行曲，強調動作「正在發生中」（on-going），不管什麼時候開始也不管什麼時候結束，只看到這個動作「一直在進行中」。這是一種近距離、特寫式的觀點（zoom-in），好像眼睛貼近事件來看，不見頭尾，只看見當中這一段「進行中」的樣貌。

搭配的形式用 BE 動詞 + V-ing，如同動作「處於」進行狀態 ➡ BE in the state of happening。

2. 進行貌的四種形式：

這種「聚焦特寫式」觀點，假如放在不同的時間區段，讓「時點」和「觀點」結合就可表達四個時段下的進行貌，形式上主要的區別在 BE 動詞上：

名稱與意義	形式	例句
過去進行式： 說話之前某時點上共時進行	was / were + V-ing	He **was negotiating** with his boss before now.
現在進行式： 說話當下正在發生	am / is / are + V-ing	He **is negotiating** with his boss now.
未來進行式： 說話之後某時上共時進行	will be + V-ing	He **will be negotiating** with his boss after now.
習慣進行式： **通常習慣性**在某時點進行	would be + V-ing	He **would be negotiating** with his boss every day.

3. 簡單式與進行式之不同：

(1) 我們用以下的疑問句來看看簡單式和進行式的不同：

簡單貌	Nobita: What did Mr. Chen do at 9 AM yesterday? Doraemon: He **invigilated** during the biology exam at 9 AM yesterday.
	簡單貌選擇用最簡單的觀點，將監考這件事描述為一個單純的「整體」事件。
進行貌	Nobita: What was Mr. Chen doing at 9 AM yesterday? Doraemon: He **was invigilating** the biology exam at 9 AM yesterday.
	進行貌是一種「聚焦式」的特寫，說話者不在乎什麼時候開始監考也不在意什麼時候結束，重點強調 9 點時陳先生正在監考，因此 V-ing 的標記形式就帶有「共時進行、正在發生」的意涵（simultaneously ongoing）。

(2) 最後再用一個實例來說明各個時段下進行式與簡單式的不同。假設現在我們說話的時間（Speech Time）是14:00，當下（14:00）大雄正在和同學辯論西歐國家是否要接納敘利亞難民，在這之前（11:00）他看了 CNN 新聞，之後（18:00）他要寫一篇社論探討難民的議題：

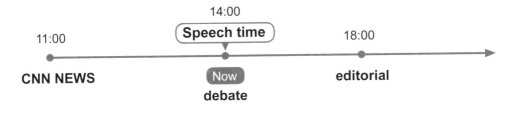

Past	Present	Future
11:00	14:00 Speech Time	18:00
CNN news	debate	editorial

(3) 在不同時段下，配合不同「時點」的標記要求，可以用「簡單」或

「進行」的「觀點」來表達所做的事，就會出現五種不同標記的可能：

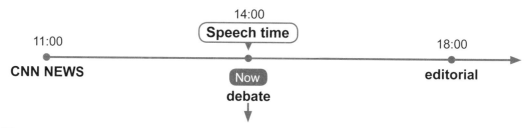

Past	Present	Future
11:00	14:00 Speech Time	18:00
[過去簡單式] Nobita **watched** CNN news at 11 AM.	[現在簡單式] 動作若是發生當下，必然在進行中	[未來簡單式] Nobita **will write** an editorial on the refugees issue at 6 PM.
[過去進行式] Nobita **was watching** CNN news at 11 AM.	[現在進行式] Nobita and his classmates **are debating** whether Syrian refugees should be accepted by the host countries.	[未來進行式] Nobita **will be writing** an editorial on the refugees issue at 6 PM.

單元2 完成貌的形意搭配

1. 完成貌 have / has / had + PP 表達「在參照點之前」完成的觀點

何謂「參照點」？

參照點就是以什麼時間為基準點來看事件是否已完成。完成貌是一種相對的概念，要決定完成與否，一定要先有一個參照時間，譬如事件是從早上 10 點到下午 5 點，若在中午 12 點看，就還沒有完成，但從下午 5 點看就已經完成了。所以完成與否是由參照點來決定。由此看來，完成貌牽涉兩個時間點：一個是事件本身的時間，一個是參照時間。完成貌表達的就是事件時間與參照點之間的相對關係。由於參照時間不同，因此有三種可能：現在（之前）完成、過去（之前）完成、未來（之前）完成。

形式上，必須用助動詞 have / has / had + PP（過去分詞），助動詞幫助標記參照時間是現在、過去、或未來，過去分詞 PP 則清楚表達完成狀態。

Past 1	Past 2	Present	Future 1	Future 2
Homework	Dinner	Speech Time 說話時間	Watch TV	Go to bed
5:00 PM	6:00 PM	7:00 PM	8:00 PM	9:00 PM

再拿大雄晚上發生的事件為例，要認定一個事件是否完成，必須先定出「參照時間」，在參照時間前做完的才算完成。如果把哆啦A夢說話當下 7:00 PM 當作是參照時間，那麼大雄在此參照點前完成了兩個事件（做作業和吃晚餐）就可用「現在（之前）完成」來表達：

He has done his homework.

He has eaten dinner.

如果我們用過去的時點 6:00 PM 當作是參照時間，那麼大雄在此前做作業這個事件就是「過去（之前）完成」：

He had done his homework before dinner.

同樣地，參照時間如果是未來時點 9:00 PM，大雄在此前看電視這個事件就變成「未來（之前）完成」：

He will have done his homework before 9 PM.

小結：「參照點」定義清楚後，才能決定事件是否完成。完成貌所表達的是事件在參照點「之前」就已達成的概念，如下圖所示：

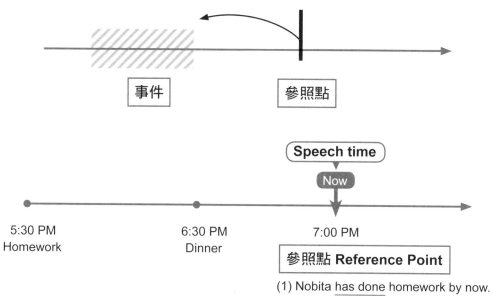

(1) Nobita has done homework by now.
(2) Nobita has had dinner by now.

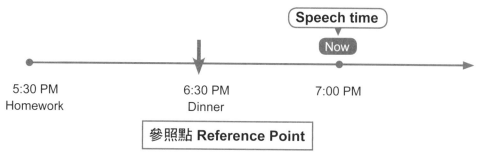

Nobita had done homework before he had dinner.

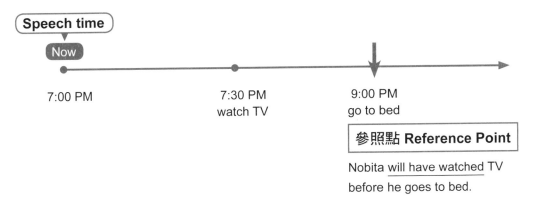

Nobita will have watched TV before he goes to bed.

2. 「現在完成式」其實是「過去」所發生的事件，為什麼要稱為「現在完成」？

釐清上述「參照點」的概念後，就不難理解，「現在完成式」的「現在」是指「參照時間」，而不是事件本身發生的時間，參照時間是「現在」，是在「現在之前」完成的，所以「現在完成式」應理解為「現在之前完成」。

3. 完成貌的四種形式：

(1) 完成貌牽涉至少兩個時間點，一個是作為觀點基準的參照點（可能是現在、過去、未來的某一點）；另一個是事件本身的時間點（必然在參考點之前）。依照參考點的不同，會有四種形式的出現。

意義	形式	例句
在「現在」之前完成 completed by now	現在完成 have / has + PP	She **has wired** the money to my account by now.
在「過去」之前完成 completed by a past time	過去完成 had + PP	She **had wired** the money to my account before she left Taiwan.
在「未來」之前完成 completed by a future time	未來完成 will have + PP	She **will have wired** the money to my account by the time she goes to Japan.
習慣性的在某一點之前完成 completed by a future time	習慣完成 would (always) have + PP	She **would have wired** the money to my account by the 6th of each month.

(2) 現在再舉一個例子來說明這四者的不同，若時間座標上依序有四個事件，完成式的觀點就是將兩個事件關連起來，以參照點為基準來強調另一事件已完成。

Past 1	Past 2	Present	Future 1	Future 2
May 1	May 2	May 3	May 4	May 5
campaign	protest	Speech Time	poll	referendum

2.1 現在完成式：以**說話當下（Speech Time）**為參照點，之前所發生的事在「現在之前」已經完成，意即 "completed by now"。

Past 1	Past 2	Present
May 1	May 2	May 3 參照點
campaign	protest	Speech Time

(1) They **have initiated** a campaign against the proposed building development in the area (by now).
(2) They **have protested** against the government's arrogance and indifference (by now).

2.2 過去完成式：以**過去某個時間點（Past 2）**為參照點，強調之前還有一個更早的事件（Past 1）已完成，意即 "completed by a past time"。

Past 1	Past 2	Present
May 1	May 2 參照點	May 3
campaign	protest	Speech Time

(1) They **had initiated** a campaign against the proposed building development in the area <u>before</u> the protest against the government's arrogance and indifference.

(2) They **had initiated** a campaign against the proposed building development in the area <u>by the time</u> they **protested** against the government's arrogance and indifference.

(3) They **had initiated** a campaign against the proposed building development in the area <u>prior to</u> protesting against the government's arrogance and indifference.

　　由以上的過去完成式例句可得知，過去完成式常和過去式併用，原因就在「完成式」需要一個過去的「參照點」：過去式所標記的事件（protest）剛好作為過去的「參照點」。有了過去的參照點，才能表達「過去完成式」，亦即動作在「過去之前」就早已完成了。這也就是為什麼老師常提醒學生，過去完成式要和過去式併用的原因。

　　2.3 未來完成式：以**未來的某件事**（Future 2）為參照點，另一個未來將發生的事件（Future 1）將會在其之前完成，意即 "completed by a future time"。

Present	Future 1	Future 2
May 3	May 4	May 5 參照點
Speech Time	poll	referendum

(1) They **will have conducted** a poll to find out what people think of the proposed building development <u>by the time</u> they hold a referendum to decide whether to unseat their government or not.

(2) They **will have conducted** a poll to find out what people think of the proposed building development <u>prior to</u> a referendum on the issue of unseating their government.

(3) They **will have conducted** a poll to find out what people think of the proposed building development <u>before</u> holding a referendum to decide whether to unseat their government or not.

3. 還能怎麼説？

究竟該選擇進行還是完成？

英語時態標記的特點就是：「動詞出場，時態相隨」，除了時點（事件發生的時間）以外，觀點（事件的樣貌）也要交代清楚，因此「觀點紀實，面面俱到」。但到底該選擇進行還是完成，必須先深入瞭解兩者所表達的溝通功能。

單元1 進行貌的標記特色與溝通功能

(1) 進行貌的三種語意特性：進行貌與簡單貌的對照

前面已說明進行式就是表達「正在進行中」（on-going），簡單式（整體式）是把事件視為完整單一的整體，兩者觀點是非常不同的：

進行貌	When Aaron entered the conference room, Peter **was raving** at his opponents.
簡單貌	When Aaron entered the conference room, Peter **raved** at his opponents.

以下是進行貌與簡單貌的詳細對照。根據 Givón (1993) 的說法，進行貌的標記 V-ing，表達三種語意特性：

	進行貌	簡單貌
1	◆持續發生（on-going） 相對於中止或結束（terminated），進行式 "was raving" 表達動作正在發生中，並且持續進行著，未中止亦未結束。	◆單一整體性（as a whole） 簡單式將 raved 視為完整單一的整體，發生於某一點或某一段時間，不分始末。

進行貌	簡單貌
2 ◆近距離、特寫式的視角（zoom in） 進行式表達近距離、特寫式的觀點（zoom in）。說話者採取「貼近」式的描述，以封閉的觀測角度，「放大」Peter 正在對他的對手咆哮的動作。	◆遠距離、全景式的視野（zoom out）
3 ◆共時性（simultaneous） 相較於「時序性」（sequential），進行式表達同時進行的共時性，"raving at his opponents" 正好和背景事件 "Aaron entered the conference room" 同時發生，彼此重疊，並非先後孤立。	

(2) 與進行式相關的動詞：

進行貌的概念將動作「放大明察」，細究其內部進行狀態，表達時間上持續存在。這樣的語意恰好符合一些動詞補語的需要。例如，感官動詞的補語可以用進行貌來表達「看到、聽到」的同時正在發生進行的動作事件，就像是描述交通事故當時的情況：

進行貌：I saw a car <u>coming</u> to me.

➡ coming 表達「看到」當下正在發生進行的事

➡ 我看到一輛車當時正朝我衝來。

簡單貌：I saw a car <u>come</u> to me.

➡ come 只單純表達「看到」一個整體事件

➡ 我看到一輛車朝我衝來。

此外，有些動詞與時間密切相關，如「開始（start / begin）、結束（stop / finish）、持續（continue / keep）」等動詞也需要用到進行貌。Givón 將所有具備 V-ing 形式的用法串連起來，延伸出三種特定的事件類型：重複進行（continue / keep）、開始進行（start / begin）、以及中止進行（stop / finish），這三種事件都與進行貌有關，分別說明如下：

◆重複進行（continue / keep）
動詞 continue 和 keep 的涵義有一再持續重複某個動作的意思。既然是持續發生的，其後的動作當然是在進行中，所以要用進行貌 V-ing 標記。然而，因動作本身語意不同，重複進行的意思可能是短時間內持續發生，或間隔很久卻屢次發生：

The man **kept bragging** on and on about his glorious past.
➡ 短時間內不間斷的重複動作（一直在談論光榮的過去）

The girl **continued dancing** for two hours.
➡ 短時間內不間斷的重複動作（持續跳舞兩小時）

The athlete **kept spraining** his ankle.
➡ 長時間中有間斷但重複發生的動作（表示常扭傷腳踝）

英文文法有道理！入門版

◆開始進行（start / begin）

表示開始的動詞（start / begin），可接進行貌，表達動作的確開始進行了：

The man **started fixing** my bike.

➡ 開始一直修理腳踏車

◆中止進行（stop / finish）

停止本來一直進行的事情，已經進行的事才能終止，所以動詞 stop、finish、quit 等動詞後面用 V-ing。

The man **stopped mowing** the lawn and took a rest.

➡ 結束單次的 mowing 動作

The man stopped mowing lawns.（lawns 為複數！）

➡ 結束多年的 mowing 習慣，也就是說不再割草了。

(3) V-ing 和 to-V 在語意上的不同：

以上這些接 V-ing 的動詞後面也可以接不定詞 to-V，但語意不同：V-ing 是表達「動作持續的進行中」，而不定詞則表達「目的」或「接下來」要做的事，時間上允許一個間斷或間隔（gap）。

They continued playing basketball for three hours.

➡ 沒有間斷地連續打了三小時的籃球

They continued to play basketball after class.

➡ 下課後，繼續打球

They went on playing basketball.

➡ 之前一直在打球，沒有間斷地繼續打

They went on to play basketball.

➡ 做完某事後才又去打球

They stopped drinking water.

➡ 停止喝水

They stopped to drink water.

➡ 停止之前所做的某件事後去喝水

They remembered doing the laundry.

➡ 記得已經洗了衣服

They remembered to do the laundry.

➡ 記得要去洗衣服

They forgot taking pills.

➡ 忘了已經吃了藥

They forgot to take pills.

➡ 忘了要吃藥

They started speaking English.

➡ 開始講起英文

They started to speak English, but they stopped.

➡ 準備要開始講英文了，但卻突然停止

(4) 進行貌的使用與分布

4.1 分詞構句中的進行貌：

　　一般的分詞構句常使用進行貌，表示「共時發生」的主動關係。這和敘述結構分為前景焦點（foreground）與背景說明（background）有關。作為前景的主要事件（主要句子）會有清楚的時間標記（過去、現在、未來或習慣），而作背景的次要事件則可用進行貌，表示同一時間發生的「共時」事件。

The student did his homework, **listening to** classical music.

The student did his homework while **listening to** classical music.

主要子句中帶有過去式標記的動作，用來說明主要內容，表達前景焦點 "The student did his homework"；而進行中的現在（主動）分詞是附屬子句，交代「共時發生」的背景事件 "listening to classical music"。

4.2 動名詞的進行貌：

進行貌 V-ing 表動作「進行」，進行的動作必然「存在」，必然出現於時間座標中。因此動名詞也可用 V-ing 的形式，因為「進行」的動作就像名詞一樣在時間中「存在」。表示「開始／結束／享受／感謝」等類的動詞要求進行貌的補語，表達如同名詞般存在或進行的動作。

He began studying math. ➡ 已開始做的事必然存在

He stopped studying math. ➡ 可以停止的事必然先存在

He enjoyed reading novels. ➡ 可享受的事必然先存在

He devoted his energies to writing poems.

➡ 投入的「對象」是名詞性的

4.3 具有「時效性」的進行貌：

進行式雖表達「持續」進行，ongoing 的事件通常與某個時間點重疊，但是只適用於「有限的」一段時間內，很難長久不變一直進行。以下兩個問答一個用進行式，一個用習慣式，兩者含意完全不同。

Kate: What does Peter do for a living?

John: He is working at a café.

➡ 進行式表達 Peter 目前在咖啡廳工作而已，只是目前進行的工作。

Kate: What does Peter do for a living?

John: He works at a café.

➡ 習慣式表達 Peter 長期在咖啡廳工作，是較穩定長久的工作。

The old lady is watering her plants now.

➡ 進行貌表達此刻正在發生，老婦人正在澆花。

The old lady waters her plants every day.

➡ 習慣貌表達一種每天都如此的習慣，老婦人習慣每天澆花。

4.4 習慣性的進行貌：

有些動作是習慣性的進行，在重複出現的條件下經常發生。因此進行貌也可用於表達「某情況下重複進行的習慣」，我們比較以下兩個句子。

片刻進行：She **is playing** an online game right now.

➡ 此刻正在玩線上遊戲

習慣性進行：Whenever I came in, she **would be playing** an online game.

➡ 屢次重複發生

單元2 完成貌的標記特色與溝通功能

(1) 完成貌的四個語意特色：

完成貌是一種相對複雜的觀點，牽涉到事件間前後參照的關係。根據 Givón (1993)，完成貌的語意很豐富，同時包括了四個特色：**前時性**（**anteriority**）、**達成性**（**perfectivity**）、**逆序性**（**counter-sequentiality**）以及**相關性**（**relevance**）。以下將詳細說明：

1

「前時性」指的是「在參考時間之前」：

這是完成貌最重要的概念，每次使用完成貌，都要將「事件」、「參照時間」和「說話時間」三者關聯起來，「事件」必然在「參照時間」之前發生。

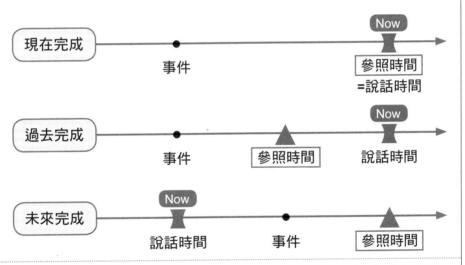

2

「達成性」指的是在參考時間之前，強調某一事件已經結束或完成了。請看下例：

Ms. Lee: Why are you absent-minded in class?

Peter: I've already read what you taught.

➡ Peter 在說話前，已經讀過 Ms. Lee 所教的東西了。

3

「逆序性」指的是不依照實際發生的先後順序來陳述一連串的事件。請看下例：

若三個事件實際出現的順序是 (1) ➡ (2) ➡ (3)，則依照「發生順序」來陳述，也會有一樣的「陳述順序」➡ (1)、(2)、(3)

He found a job, worked hard for 10 years, and studied abroad in 2017.
      (1)   (2)   (3)

➡ 最後發生的先說，"found a job" 發生早於 "studied abroad"。

但使用完成式，則「陳述順序」可以不依照「發生順序」：

He studied broad in 2017, and had found a job and worked hard for 10 years.
     (3)   (1)   (2)

4

「相關性」是指完成式經由「參照點」將兩個事件「關聯起來」。這種時間上的關聯又依照動作、狀態本質上的不同，而有不一樣的解讀：(1) 動作沒有延續性，不會與參照點重疊；(2) 狀態有延續性，在時間上可持續到參照點。

(1) 動作沒有延續性，不會與參照點重疊
The former employee <u>has filed</u> a lawsuit against the company claiming unfair dismissal.
➡ 現在之前已經完成了提出訴訟的動作（已結束）。
➡ 這位員工曾對公司提出訴訟，在參照點前動作已結束。
(2) 狀態有延續性，可持續到參照時間
The woman has been an accountant.
➡ 現在之前已經是 "an accountant"，狀態已開始並持續到現在。
➡ 因為狀態具有持續性，她現在仍是會計師。
(3) 若要表達完成的「動作」一直持續到參照點，就要用「完成進行」

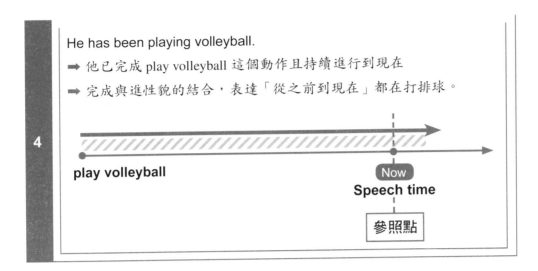

He has been playing volleyball.

➡ 他已完成 play volleyball 這個動作且持續進行到現在

➡ 完成與進性貌的結合，表達「從之前到現在」都在打排球。

play volleyball
Now
Speech time
參照點

(2) been to 與 gone to 的正確用法：

為什麼 been to 是指曾經去過，而 gone to 是指已經去了某地方？這其實是現在完成式的「完成語意」與「動詞語意」結合後的結果。只要清楚理解「現在完成式」的意涵與動詞本身的語意，就能分辨了。

Has/ have gone to	Has/ have been to
動詞go是動作，是指從一點「**移動**」向另一點，並且一定是遠離原先所在之處 "away from the speaker"。因此要表達完成「離開原地、移動到另一處」的動作，必須用 "gone to"： He has gone to Japan. ➡ 既然已移動到日本，人當然就在日本。 ➡ 他去了日本。	Be動詞表存在狀態，與地點合用時的基本含意是「**處於**」某地，例如："I am at Hsinchu." 就是我「處在」新竹。若要表達「曾經處於某地」，就要用 "been to"： He has been to Japan. ➡ 曾經處於「人在日本」的狀態。 ➡ 他去過日本。

(3) since 與 for 的正確用法：

3.1 用 for 的語意：

小時候老師會跟我們說 for 要跟完成式連用，基本上這是一個不正確的觀念。其實 for 並不是「完成式」所專用的，而是指這個事件本身持續了一段時間（for a duration）。比如說我從 2010 年搬到臺北，到目前 2017 年為

止在臺北住了 7 年，時間座標上的概念如下：

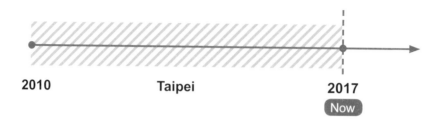

這可以有兩種不同的表達方式，代表兩種不同的觀點：

I **lived** in Taipei for seven years.
簡單貌：單純陳述「過去一段時間」所發生的整體事件

I **have lived** in Taipei for seven years.
完成貌：強調「到目前為止」所發生的事情

3.2 用 since 的語意：

也有老師會說 since 常和完成式連用，強調事件的「起點」，所以很多人誤以為完成式是標記「開始」，而非「完結」，這也是一種誤解。since 和完成式連用，的確是標記「起點」，但仍是在相對於「參照點」的前提，所以，since 是強調從「起點」至「參照點」為止，所完成的動作或狀態。

I **have lived** in Taipei for seven years **since 2010**.
➡ 從 2010 起到參照點「現在」之前已經住了7年

I **have lived** in Taipei for seven years **until now**.
➡ 從 2010 至目前為止都住在臺北。

3.3 過去完成的語意要求：

有了以上對 for 和 since 的瞭解，我們可以將「過去完成」加入考量。

如果 2010 年搬來臺北以前，我在新竹住了 20 年，而 2010 年又剛好買了一台新車：

過去完成需要有過去的參照點：參照點為 2010 年，說話時間為 2017年。

Hsinchu　　Taipei

1990　　2010　　2017 Now
I bought a new car.

I had lived in Hsinchu for 20 years before 2010. ← 參照點是2010年

I had lived in Hsinchu for 20 years before I bought a new car in 2010.

I had lived in Hsinchu for 20 years since 1990. ← 參照點仍是2010年

I had lived in Hsinchu for 20 years till I bought a new car in 2010.

I had lived in Hsinchu for 20 years since 1990 till I bought a new car in 2010.

(4) 什麼時候不適合使用「完成貌＋for」：

有些動詞因為是瞬間完成，瞬間發生的變化，不會延續一段時間，所以不太適合使用「完成式＋for 一段時間」。例如：die / stand up / sit down / break / feel 等等。

他已經死了10年。

(??)He has died for ten years.

➡ 死了10年是指死的狀態（dead），而不是死的動作變化（die）

建議改為以下兩個較合理的句子：

(1) He has been dead for ten years.

(2) It has been ten years since he died.

結論：動詞出場，時態相隨。每次使用動詞，除了時間的標記（過去、現在、未來習慣），也要考量時貌的表達（簡單、進行、完成）。充分了解時態的形意搭配原則就是掌握動詞標記的關鍵！

187

"My boyfriend, John, and I **have been** together for about six months. My 16th birthday **was coming** up and I was so excited because my previous birthdays **had been** bad. Of course I was crushed when he told me his family **was going** away to Florida that weekend! While he was gone, my sister took me to the mall to get my mind off it. The whole time I kept **texting** him how much I missed him. I really started to get bummed out and we **had shopped** all day, so she decided to take me home. On the way, my sister said she wanted to stop at her boyfriend's house to say hi. When we walked in my friends all screamed, "Surprise!" I was happy about the party but still upset because John wasn't there. Then my sister told me to go to the closet to get my presents. I walked over and opened the door, and there stood John with a big red ribbon on his shirt! It turns out he **had planned** the whole party just so I could finally have an amazing birthday. I couldn't have asked for a better day, or a better boyfriend!"

http://www.seventeen.com/love/dating-advice/advice/a9286/love-stories-present-perfect/

(https://bit.ly/2PQLbTL)

註解：

完成式：

● **have been**[1]：兩人一起的狀態已開始並持續到現在已經六個月了。

● **had shopped**[5] 與 **had planned**[6]：過去完成式常和過去式併用，**had shopped**[5] 以過去為「參照點」，動作在過去式（started to get bummed out）之前就早已完成了，也就是購物一整天後，筆者才開始覺得難過（get bummed out）。**had planned**[6] 則是在 "I could finally have..." 之前就完成的動作。

進行式：

● **was coming**[2] 與 **was going**[3]：BE V-ing 是以進行貌表未來，表達「最近的未來」**was coming**[2] 指生日就要到了。而 **was going**[3] 指「最近的未來」且計畫好的。

kept texting[4]：動詞 keep 有一再持續重複某個動作的意思，其後的動作是在進行中，所以要用進行貌 V-ing 標記。

Where Have All the Flowers Gone

(By Peter Seeger)

Where **have** all the flowers **gone**, long time passing?

Where **have** all the flowers **gone**, long time ago?

Where **have** all the flowers **gone**?

Gone to young girls, every one!

When will they ever learn, when will they ever learn?

Where **have** all the young girls **gone**, long time passing?

Where **have** all the young girls **gone**, long time ago?

Where **have** all the young girls **gone**?

Gone to young men, every one!

When will they ever learn, when will they ever learn?

Where **have** all the young men **gone**, long time passing?

Where **have** all the young men **gone**, long time ago?

Where **have** all the young men **gone**?

Gone to soldiers, every one!

When will they ever learn, when will they ever learn?

And where **have** all the soldiers **gone**, long time passing?

Where **have** all the soldiers **gone**, a long time ago?

Where **have** all the soldiers **gone**?

Gone to graveyards, every one!

When will they ever learn, when will they ever learn?

And where **have** all the graveyards **gone**, long time passing?

> Where **have** all the graveyards **gone**, long time ago?
>
> Where **have** all the graveyards **gone**?
>
> **Gone to** flowers, every one!
>
> When will they ever learn, oh when will they ever learn?
>
> *https://www.youtube.com/watch?v=T1tqtvxG8O4 (https://bit.ly/2PI30UO)*

 6. 看一部影片

https://www.youtube.com/watch?v=mWfDrPeBDl8

(https://bit.ly/2PIU6q8)

 7. 做一點練習

Part 1：克漏字

(A) happened	(B) can produce	(C) cured	(D) thinks	(E) was doing
(F) would come	(G) have	(H) had happened	(I) had left	(J) being captured

    When I found some children catching butterflies one sultry August afternoon, I was reminded of an incident in my own childhood. When I was a boy of twelve in Rio de Janeiro, something happened to me that __1__ me forever of wanting to put any wild creature in a cage. We lived on the edge of a wood, and every evening at dusk the mockingbirds __2__ and perch in the trees and sing. There is not a musical instrument made by man that __3__ a more beautiful sound than the song of the mockingbird. Therefore, I decided that I would catch a young bird and keep it in a cage and that way have my own private musician.

    Luckily, I finally succeeded in catching one and put it in a cage. At first, in its fright at __4__, the bird fluttered about the cage, but eventually it settled down in its new home. I felt very pleased with myself and looked forward to some beautiful singing from my tiny musician.

    I __5__ the cage out on our back porch and, on the second day of the bird's captivity, my new pet's mother flew to the cage with food in her bill. The baby bird gulped down everything she brought to it. I was pleased to see this. Certainly the mother knew better than I how to feed her offspring.

However, the following morning when I went to see how my captive __6__, I discovered it on the floor of the cage, dead. I was confused! What had happened? I had taken excellent care of my little bird, or so I thought.

Anderson, the renowned ornithologist, __7__ to be visiting my father at the time and, hearing me feel sorry for the fate of my bird, explained what __8__. "A mother mockingbird, finding her young in a cage, will sometimes bring it poisonous berries. She __9__ it better for her young to die than to live in captivity." Never since then __10__ I caught any living creature and put it in a cage. After all, all living creatures have a right to live free.

克漏字解答

1. (C) 2. (F) 3. (B) 4. (J) 5. (I) 6. (E) 7. (A) 8. (H) 9. (D) 10. (G)

註解：1. cure of 與 2. in its fright at 後面要加動名詞，因為前為介系詞。3. had left 為過去完成式，以 flew to 為過去參照點，在小鳥媽媽飛去餵食前，筆者先把鳥籠放在前廊。4. 鳥類學家跟他解釋為過去參照點，發生了什麼事則發生更早之前，故用過去完成式（what had happened）。5. 為倒裝句，原句應為："I have never caught any living creatures since then."。

Part 2：文法選擇題

1. There were some students on the court. They _____ basketball with their friends.

   (A) have played　(B) were playing　(C) play　(D) will play

2. The old couple _____ care of the naughty boy for a month. They hope his parents can come to take him home.

   (A) takes　(B) will take　(C) have taken　(D) are taking

3. Everyone was relieved to learn that the police _____ the murderer.

   (A) were eventually catching　　(B) had eventually caught

   (C) eventually catch　　(D) have eventually caught

4. He _____ Taipei by the time you arrive here.

   (A) had left　(B) has left　(C) is leaving　(D) will have left

5. It's almost 3:30 am now, but Terry _____ in his room for the exam tomorrow.

   (A) is still studying　　(B) has still studied

   (C) still studies　　(D) will still have studied

6. When the TV show started, they _____ lunch at an eatery.

   (A) were eating   (B) eat   (C) will be eating   (D) have eaten

7. She _____ in Taipei for 20 years before she had a baby.

   (A) is living   (B) will have lived   (C) had lived   (D) lives

8. She always _____ up at 5:30 when she studied at junior high school in Hsinchu.

   (A) got   (B) gets   (C) had gotten   (D) is getting

選擇題解答

1. (B) 2. (C) 3. (B) 4. (D) 5. (A) 6. (A) 7. (C) 8. (A)

> 註解：1. 前一句已有過去式，後面用過去進行代表共時進行。2. 後面的時間為 "for a month" 因此用現在完成代表到現在為止已照顧一個月。3.警察逮捕殺人犯後，大家才鬆了一口氣（Everyone was relieved to learn...），所以逮捕的動作比較早發生，因此答案為 "had eventually caught"。4. 未來你還沒到達前，他「早就」離開。比未來的參照點，發生的更早，所以用未來完成 "will have left"。5. 前面有時間 now，因此式共時進行，用進行式。6. started 為過去式，因此後面一樣要過去時點的當下，用過去進行式。7. 除了有 "for 20 years" 外還有一個過去參照點 "had a baby"，因此要用過去完成式，表達生孩子前就住在台北 20 年了。8. 雖有 always 代表習慣但是後面時間參照點是過去式，因此是過去的習慣，指以前常 5 點半起床。

Part 3：時點與觀點的搭配

　　本章介紹了「時間」搭配「觀點」的標記方式，請就以下這段《湯姆歷險記》*Adventures of Tom Sawyer* 的對話（湯姆的阿姨在尋找湯姆）觀察文章中出現的時態與觀點的選擇：

"TOM!"

No answer.

"TOM!"

No answer.

"What's gone with that boy, I wonder? You TOM!"

No answer.

The old lady **pulled** her spectacles down and **looked** over them about the room; then she **put** them up and looked out under them. She seldom or never looked through them for so small a thing as a boy; they **were** her state pair, the pride of her heart, and **were** built for "style," not service—she **could have seen** through a pair of stove-lids just as well. She **looked** perplexed for a moment, and then said, not fiercely, but still loud enough for the furniture to hear:

"Well, I lay if I **get hold of** you I'll—"

She did not finish, for by this time she **was bending down** and punching under the bed with the broom, and so she needed breath to punctuate the punches with. She resurrected nothing but the cat.

"I never did see the beat of that boy!"

She went to the open door and stood in it and looked out among the tomato vines and "jimpson" weeds that constituted the garden. No Tom. So she lifted up her voice at an angle calculated for distance and shouted:

"Y-o-u-u TOM!"

There was a slight noise behind her and she turned just in time to seize a small boy by the slack of his roundabout and arrest his flight.

"There! I might have thought of that closet. What **have you been doing** in there?"

"Nothing."

"Nothing! Look at your hands. And look at your mouth. What **is** that truck?"

"I don't know, aunt."

"Well, I know. It's jam—that's what it is. Forty times I**'ve said** if you **didn't let** that jam alone I**'d skin** you. Hand me that switch."

The switch hovered in the air—the peril was desperate—

"My! **Look** behind you, aunt!"

The old lady whirled round, and snatched her skirts out of danger. The lad fled on the instant, scrambled up the high board-fence, and disappeared over it.

註解：1. could have + PP 指可能在過去發生但沒發生，意指那位女士如果把鍋蓋當眼鏡也是看的到的。2. 這個時候她正在彎下腰⋯⋯。3. have been doing 為現在完成進行式，意思指「到現在為止前，你都在做什麼？」4.

I've said if you didn't let... I'd skin you：I've said（我說過），是表達現在之前已經說過，後面的 "if you didn't let...I'd skin you" 則是間接引句，所以時態是過去式，意思是如果你拿了果醬，我就要剝你的皮。5. "My! Look behind you, aunt!" 有引號為直接引句，所以用當時所用的時式，且為祈使句，「阿姨看一下後面」。

英文文法有道理！入門版

CHAPTER

7

辨明真假
事實與假設

單元1 真實發生了還是但願如此？

想想看下圖所發生的事件和對話，看看能否分辨說話者所說的到底是真是假：

「真實」情況

情境一：

Shizuka: Look! Giant **is** chasing Nobita. What **happened**?

Doraemon: He **failed** to catch a pitch, and it **irritated** Giant.

Shizuka: Oh, my God! Giant **punched** Nobita in his face.

Doraemon: Yes, he **did**. Nobita **got** purple bruises on his face and around his eyes.

標記方式：**使用符合該事件確實發生的時態。事件的時間與真實性有關，之前發生的（過去式），已經完成的（現在或過去完成）或正在發生的（現在或過去進行貌）都是「確實」發生的事。但是未來式只是推測，並未實際發生。

「假設」情況

情境一：有可能發生的假設或願望

Shizuka: I **hope** Nobita **will play** better next time.

If he **practices** more, he **will be** better in catching.

Doraemon: **Maybe** he **won't get** into this kind of trouble **if** he **is** more

careful in catching the ball.

I **guess** Giant **can** find someone else to play with him.

標記方式：

(1) 使用「非事實」的時態

未來式表未來 ➡ He will practice more.

習慣式表可能 ➡ If he practices more, he will be better.

(2) 條件子句加上假設標記 ➡ if、unless、when、on the condition

(3) 使用表達可能性的副詞➡ maybe、perhaps、possibly…

(4) 使用情態助動詞表示「非真」 ➡ can、may、must、will、shall、
could、might、should、would

(5) 藉由動詞語意來表示真假 ➡ guess、wish、promise

情境二：不可能實現的假設或願望 (與事實不符的假設)

Shizuka: I **wish** I **was** not here.

I **wish** I **had** not **seen** the game.

I **wish** Nobita **could have run** faster, and then Giant **would
not have punched** him in his face.

Doraemon: If Nobita **had practiced** more, he **would have caught** a
ball.

If he **had caught** a pitch, he **would not have irritated**
Giant.

標記方式：

使用與事實不同的時態標記。既然與事實不符，句子的時態就要和正常時態有所區別：

(1) 與現在事實不符，就用過去式 ➡ I wish I <u>was</u> not here.

與過去事實不符，就用過去完成式 ➡ I wish I <u>had</u> not <u>seen</u> the game.

(2) 當時可能發生卻沒發生的遺憾，用「情態助動詞 + 完成式」

➡ He <u>could have run</u> faster. He <u>would have caught</u> a ball.

情態助動詞表示「非真」➡ could、might、would、must、could、might、should、would

完成式表達「之前」的時間點 ➡ He would <u>have</u> not <u>irritated</u> Giant.

　　由以上兩個不同情境的對話得知，事件的「真實與否」是英文溝通上一大重點。人們想知道說話者所說的是否為真，說話者也有義務要清楚標記事件是不是確實發生。如果要表示時間座標上真實發生的事，則需維持與該事件相符的標記時態；若表示非真實或假設狀態，則需加上假設或條件標記，在時態的標記上也要有所不同。因為「真實」與「假設」這兩種情況在溝通上有不同的意義，英文對兩者採取不同的處理原則及標記方式；唯有如此，才能將兩者區分開來，讓聽者可以清楚分辨，說話者說的到底是確實發生的事情，還是他的希望，亦或是發呆時做的白日夢。

單元2 「假設」有兩種：有可能實現和不可能實現的

白日夢有兩種

1. 對未來的期望或未來有可能發生的事：

I hope that Nobita will practice more and become a better player.

He **won't get into** this kind of trouble if he **is** more careful when catching the ball.

➡ 希望以後大雄多練習，就會有進步。假如以後他小心一點，或許就不會再遇到這種麻煩了，這句話抱持著「希望」，未來有可能發生。

2. 對過去的悵惘或不可逆轉的願望：

[Non-fact] If Nobita **had caught** a pitch, he **would not have irritated** Giant.

➡ 大雄當時沒有接到球；如果有接到球，那他就不會把胖虎惹毛了。

[Fact] Nobita didn't catch a pitch, so he irritated Giant.

2. 英文怎麼說？

單元1 非事實的標記方式

不是真實發生的事一定在標記上有所區別。「非事實」的標記至少有以下五種方式：

(1) 情態助動詞表達「非事實」：

英文的情態助動詞包括 can、may、must、will、shall、could、might、should、would，說話者只是表達個人主觀的「期望值」，對「可能性」或「責任義務」的判斷，但這些判斷都未確實發生，所以屬於「非事實」，例如：

◆He **can** fly a plane backwards.
➡ 他有能力把飛機向後飛，但不是「確實」在開飛機。
◆He **may** apply for a job with the local newspaper.
➡ 他可能申請當地報社的工作，但只是表達一種可能性。
◆You **must** reject this absurd idea.
➡ 你一定要拒絕這荒謬的想法，就代表這件事尚未做。

(2) 使用未來式表達「非事實」：

非事實	如果是未來才出現的事件，因為尚未發生，就屬於「非事實」： ◆She **will vacuum** the carpets. ➡ 尚未發生 ◆She **would vacuum** the carpets if she had time. ➡ 尚未發生 ◆She **will have vacuumed** the carpet by the time her mother gets home. ➡ 尚未發生
事實	如果是「現在或過去進行式」、「過去簡單式」或「現在或過去完成式」的事件都是「確實發生的」： ◆She **is vacuuming** the carpets. ➡ 確實發生中 ◆She **vacuumed** the carpets two days ago. ➡ 確實發生過 ◆She **has vacuumed** the carpets. ➡ 確實已發生

(3) 使用動詞語意來表示事件的真假：

　　有些動詞可以表達訊息的來源，本身的語意就足以表達事件的真實性，例如：

暗示尚未成真的動詞	**guess、wish、promise、think** ◆I **guess** she booked a table for two at 7:00 PM. ➡ 猜測而已，不能當真。 ◆I **wish** I won the scholarship. ➡ 但願如此就好了，只是白日夢。 ◆I **promise** I will help you. ➡ 承諾將會幫你，但尚未發生。 ◆I **think** he explained the theories about how marine life moves about the reef. ➡ 想想而已，沒有根據。
表達親眼見、親耳聞的動詞	**see、hear** ◆I **saw** that she was washing her car. ➡ 眼見為憑，真實的事件。

(4) 使用情態副詞來表達真假：

使用情態副詞會影響句子的真實性。副詞比時態更具影響力，即使是過去式，加了 maybe、perhaps、probably 等具有猜測意味的副詞，會改變這句話的真實及確定性：

◆**Maybe** you should hire a bodyguard.

　➡ 可能該請位保鏢，但不確定。

◆I wonder if **perhaps** I offended him somehow.

　➡ 猜測可能冒犯他了，但不確定。

◆Archaeologists think the temple was **probably** built in the 3rd century AD. ➡ 這個廟可能在西元 3 世紀蓋的，不過只是考古學家想想而已，除了沒有證據以外，也無法確定。

(5) 使用條件／假設句來表示真假的關聯：

前面提及白日夢有兩種，一般條件句是指「有可能」的假設，對「未來」抱持希望；假設句是「不可能或不可逆轉」的條件，對「過去」的追悔。無論哪一種，都是在講「非真事件」，所以在動詞時態標記上，必須和「真實事件」的標記明顯不同。以下是不同假設的對照：

1	未來可能出現的條件 ➡ 以沒有特定時間標記的「習慣式」表達「可能的條件」，以「未來式」表達「未來結果」。 If Nobita **fails** the test tomorrow, his mom **will be** very angry.
2	違反現在的事實的假設 ➡ 以「過去式」標記。 If the Japanese princess **were** a man, she **could succeed** to the throne.
3	違反過去事實的假設 ➡ 以「過去完成式」標記。 If you **had told** me your situation earlier, I **would have had** more sympathy for you.

總結：

確實發生的事件（realized）		未發生的非事實（non-realized）
1	It rained hard last night. ➡ 昨晚確實有下大雨。	The ground is wet. It **must** have rained hard last night. [標記方式：**使用情態助動詞**] ➡ 只是推測昨晚一定下大雨，並沒有確實的證據。
2	習慣事實 They always took a bus to the airport and never ran into a blizzard. ➡ 他們以往都是搭公車去機場，也從沒遇過暴風雪。	If they **run into** a blizzard tomorrow, they **will be stranded** at the airport. [標記方式：**使用條件句表示可能情況**] ➡ 未來可能出現的條件，用沒有特定時間的習慣式表達。
3	Jason published short stories and novels. ➡ Jason 確實在過去出版過短篇故事和小說。	Jason **will publish** short stories and novels. [標記方式：**使用未來式**] ➡ 未來可能出版短篇故事和小說。
4	She **bought** a raffle ticket and **won** $5,000. ➡ 她的確買了彩券並贏得五千塊美元。 ➡ 「過去式」標記過去確實發生的事。	**She wishes** she **had bought** a raffle ticket and won $5,000. [標記方式：**藉由動詞語意來表示真假**] ➡ She wishes 如果當時有買彩券就太好了，可惜無從追悔。 ➡ 違反過去的事實，以「過去完成式」標記。
5	She saw a cat. ➡ 事實（certain and real）	**Perhaps**, she saw a cat. [標記方式：**使用表可能性的副詞**] ➡ 非事實（uncertain and not real）

確實發生的事件（realized）		未發生的非事實（non-realized）
6	He is a boy. ➡ [現在事實] 他就是個男生。	If he **were** a girl, he **would wear** a skirt. [標記方式：**使用假設句來表示真假的關聯**] ➡ 違反現在事實，假如是女的才會穿裙子。
7	We took a chemistry exam yesterday afternoon. ➡ [過去事實] 我們昨天下午考化學。	If we **had not taken** a chemistry exam yesterday afternoon, we **could have played** basketball with you. [標記方式：**使用假設句來表示真假的關聯**] ➡ 違反過去事實，假如昨天下午沒有考化學，早就可以跟你們打籃球了。

單元2 如何區別「條件句」與「假設語氣」？

上節已提到假設分為「有可能」與「不可能」實踐的。所謂的條件句是對「未知」可能的預設，時間投射在未來；假設語氣則是投射在「已知」的反事實，時間向過去推移。以下再次定義兩者的不同：

◆ 條件句（有可能的假設）

定義：條件句是指在「未來」有可能發生的事情，但不能確定是否成真，標記上以沒有特定時間標記的「習慣式（現在式）」表達「可能的條件」，以「未來式」表達「未來結果」。

例句：

If Jason **works** harder, he **will gain** promotion to a senior position.

If our company's profits **slump** in the next fiscal year, it **will direst** its less profitable business operations.

I hope everything **goes** well.

◆ 假設語氣（不可能的假設）

定義：假設語氣就是「事與願違」的假設。在「與事實相反」的假設前提下，提出「與事實相反」的結果。

既然與事實相違，在**動詞時態**上就要與事實有所區別。英文選擇用時間上的「錯亂」（將時態倒退）來標示假設或講反話：

1. 「**現在**」的事： 時間倒退 ➡ 動詞用 過去式
2. 「**過去**」的事： 時間倒退 ➡ 動詞用 過去完成式

與事實相反的假設

違反 現在 事實 ➡ 以 過去式 標記

1

現在事實：I **am** not a bird.

違反現在事實：**I wish I** was / were a bird.（*were*是形式固定的用法）

現在事實：I **am** not a bird, so I **don't fly** in the sky.

假設語氣：**If I** were **a bird, I** could fly **in the sky.**

與事實相反的假設

現在事實：She **doesn't have** money now, so she **doesn't buy** this book.

假設語氣：**If she** $\boxed{\text{had}}$ **money now, she** $\boxed{\text{could buy}}$ **this book.**

1

現在事實：The problem is not solved.

假設語氣（事與願違情況）：The problem $\boxed{\text{would be solved}}$ if you $\boxed{\text{could tell}}$ me that earlier.

➡ 要是你 $\boxed{現在}$ 早點告訴我，問題可能解決了。

違反 $\boxed{過去}$ 事實 ➡ 以 $\boxed{過去完成式}$ 標記

2

過去事實：Aaron **didn't study** hard last year.

違反過去事實：**I wish** Aaron $\boxed{\text{had studied}}$ hard last year.

過去事實：Aaron **didn't study** hard last year.

假設語氣：違反事實的假設下, 違反事實的結果：

If Aaron $\boxed{\text{had studied}}$ **hard,** he $\boxed{\text{would have entered}}$ college.

過去事實：Some politicians **accepted** bribes last year, so they **were sentenced to** ten years' imprisonment.

假設語氣：違反事實的假設下，違反事實的結果：

If those politicians $\boxed{\text{had not accepted}}$ bribed last year, they $\boxed{\text{would not have been sentenced to}}$ ten years' imprisonment.

從以上的例句得知，投射在過去的反事實，都有固定的標記形式：

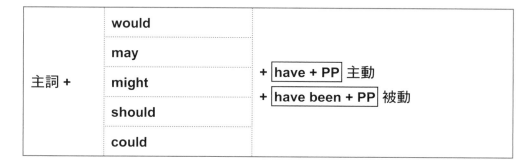

	would	
	may	
主詞 +	might	+ have + PP 主動
	should	+ have been + PP 被動
	could	

這種標記方式結合兩種特別的語意：

(1) 使用表示「非真實」的「情態助詞」（may、might、would、could、should）指出句中所述為「非事實」。

(2) 動詞時態上則使用「完成式」表示事情應該發生於現在之前（anteriority）。

單元3 any 的用法

一般人認為 any 只能用在否定句或疑問句，但這種說法不完整也不完全正確。我們由以下的對話中看看 any 還可以用在哪些情境，並仔細觀察

any 所帶出來的句子是表達真實或非真實。

情境一：

Doraemon: You look so sad. Are you OK?

Nobita: I failed my math exam again. Do you have **any** idea about how to improve it?

Doraemon: I don't have **any** idea, but I think you can ask Aaron for advice. He is a math expert.

Nobita: Good idea. Aaron is a nice man. I think he **will** do **anything** to help me.

情境二：

Dear Nobita,

Mom's birthday is coming, and we are going to give her a birthday party next Tuesday evening. **If** you have **any** suggestion for the party, please let me know. I will appreciate **any** input from you.

By the way, don't lock the door that evening because **anyone** may come to our party.

Best,

Doraemon

情境三：

Dear Nobita,

Someone came to see me and told me **something** bad about your grandfather. He was hospitalized for a heart attack last night. I don't know what I'd do **if anything** terrible happens to him. I will leave home to take care of your grandfather, and I won't come back until next Wednesday. If you are worried that you won't have **anything** to eat, please rest assured that I have made some cookies and marinated chicken breasts for you and Doraemon. You may take **any** of these when you are hungry.

Love,

Mom

說明：

Any 可能出現的句式：

疑問句：Do you have **any** idea about how to improve it?

否定句：I don't have **any** idea.

未來式：I think he **will** do **anything** for me.

條件句：**If** you have **any** idea for what I could buy Mom, please let me know.

I don't know what I'd do **if anything** happened to him.

情態句：You may take **any** of these when you are hungry.

非事實狀態：By the way, don't lock the door that evening because **anyone** may come to our party.

Any 不可能出現的句式：

已發生的事實：(×) He did anything.

(×) Anyone came to the party.

總結：

(1) 從上述句子得知一個共通點，any 指出現在「非事實」的句子，因為是尚未實際發生的事，事件參與者就有可能不確定，有可能是任何人或任何事，所以都可以和 any 合用。情人說："I will do anything for you!" 可能只是空話一句，尚未兌現；最好是 "I did everything for you!"，千萬別說：(×) I did anything for you!

(2) 但對已實際發生的事，參與者是確定的，例如：大雄的外公的確生病住院，媽媽才會說 "something about your grandfather"，而不會是：(×) anything bad happened to your grandfather。

(3) 從這些句子可推論出，any 的使用不僅限於疑問句和否定句，而是可以出現在前述所有「非事實」句式中，這包括情態、祈使、未來、條件、承諾等句式。

(4) some 和 any 有何不同：

some	any
使用時機	使用時機
(a) 真實事件	(a) 非真實事件
➡Something bad happened.	➡Anything bad will happen.
(b) 具有指涉性或有特定對象，雖然不是我們可指認的人、事、物，但是指涉確定的某人、某事、某物，只是不曉得是誰罷了。	(b) 沒有指涉性或有特定對象，參與者未定，「誰」都有可能參與其中。因為事情尚未發生，人物也就尚未確定，任何人都有機會。
➡Somebody came here.	➡Anybody may come here.

 ## 3. 還能怎麼說？

單元1 時態與情態

事件的時間與真實性息息相關：

(1) 之前發生的（過去式），已經完成的（完成貌）或正在發生的（進行）都是「確實」發生的事：

過去發生了（過去式）	Nobita **washed** his car.
事件已完成（完成式）	Nobita **has washed** his car.（現在完成） Nobita **had washed** his car before dinner.（過去完成）
現在發生中（進行式）	Nobita **is washing** his car now.（現在進行） Nobita **was washing** his car at 6 PM.（過去進行）

(2) 未來式只是推測，並「未實際」發生；習慣式在時間標座上，因為沒有對應的「時點」或「實點」，無法落實，所以也可以用「非真」的情態助動詞 would 來表達：

未來可能發生（未來式）	Nobita will wash his car.
時間上不確定（習慣式）	Nobita washes his car. Nobita would wash his car.

「習慣」是否屬實？

習慣式所表達的事件，表面上看似不變的事實（fact），但其實只是一種傾向（tendency）或陳述（statement），而並未在時間座標確實出現：

Aaron sips coffee.

➡ 但確實喝了嗎？

Aaron exercises for 20 minutes every morning.

➡ 但他今早真的有運動 20 分鐘嗎？

習慣式因為沒有對應的時間點，所以也可以用非真實的情態助動詞來表達：

Aaron **would** sip coffee.

➡ 習慣傾向 ➡ 加了情態助動詞 ➡ 非真實事件

Aaron **would** exercise for 20 minutes every morning.

➡ 習慣傾向 ➡ 加了情態助動詞 ➡ 非真實事件

單元2 動詞與情態

前面提過動詞語意可表達「訊息來源」，表達事件的真偽，例如：

非真實或不確定	**I believe** [Peter is fighting with John]. ➡ 只是相信這件事，但不代表有這個事實
	I suppose [the CEO will be forced to resign.] ➡ 純屬臆測，沒有證據

真實或確定	I **saw** [a girl dancing with her father]. ➡ 眼見為憑，確有其事
	I **heard** [a wolf howling in the dead silence of the night]. ➡ 親耳聽見，狼真的在吼叫

　　除了感官動詞 "see、hear" 以外，還有一些追悔動詞 "**regret、recall、apologize**" 和形容詞 "**sorry**" 本身也含有強烈的預設前提（presupposition），當遇到這些動詞或形容詞的時候，我們早已預設追悔的事件必然已發生。

◆I **regret** that [I betrayed my best friend].
　　➡ 後悔背叛摯友一事必然已發生
◆I **recall** that [I owed her $10,000].
　　➡ 想起欠人一萬元的事必然曾經發生
◆I **apologized** profusely for [having criticized him].
　　➡ 再三道歉的原因必然先發生了
◆I am **sorry** that [I took advantage of you]. ➡ 抱歉的事必然已做了

單元3 預設事件的標記方式

　　如果我問你："Have you stopped smoking?" 此問句中已包含了一個不可撼動的預設前提："You smoked."
　　◆Have you stopped abusing your cat?
　　　➡ 預設前提：你一直有虐貓的事實
　　◆Have you finished reading this journal?
　　　➡ 預設前提：你已讀了這篇期刊

　　此外，還有多種語法句式含有預設前提：
1）WH- 問句

◆What did you say last night?
　　➡ 預設前提：You said something last night. 你昨晚說了一些話

◆Who broke the vase?

　⇒ 預設前提：Someone broke the vase. 一定有人打破花瓶

◆When did you start learning French?

　⇒ 預設前提：You started learning French. 你已開始學法文

◆Why did he tell a lie? ⇒ 預設前提：He told a lie. 他說謊了

2）關係子句

◆I saw the girl you dated last year.

　⇒ 預設前提：You dated a girl last year.

◆The man who came to see you called again.

　⇒ 預設前提：a man came.

◆The book I bought yesterday was lost.

　⇒ 預設前提：I bought a book.

3）名詞子句

◆His moving out is devastating to her.

　⇒ 預設前提：He moved out.

◆Your filing a lawsuit may not be wise.

　⇒ 預設前提：You filed a lawsuit.

◆I couldn't forgive their lying to me.

　⇒ 預設前提：They lied to me.

單元4 may 和 might 的不同（直接 vs. 委婉）

　很多人認為 might 是 may 的過去式，所以如果要表示過去的可能性或非事實，助動詞改用 might 就可以了；也有人覺得 might 所表達的可能性比 may 小，但這些講法都有問題，我們看看以下的句子來釐清原有的觀念：

(1) may / might、will / would、can / could 的確可以用來表達時間上的區別：

They **are** not sure if she **may / will / can** complete the mission.

➡ 時間是現在，表示他們現在無法確定她現在是否可以完成任務。

They **were** not sure if she **might / would / could** complete the mission.

➡ 時間在過去，表示他們過去無法確定她過去是否可以完成任務。

(2) 然而，同一時間上的同一事件，可以用 may 或 might 表達兩種不同情態，例如，我們在同一個時間點上要表達她有可能完成任務，使用不同的情態助動詞會有不同的含意：

She **may** complete the mission.

➡ 語氣上較直接爽快（straightforward），直接表達出說話者的猜測或推論。

She **might** complete the mission.

➡ 語氣上較委婉保留（reserved），說話者對事件的肯定度比較沒有那麼高。

(3) 事實上，如果要表達「未來的可能性」或是對「過去的推測（過去可能……）」，情態助動詞後面的動詞形式才是關鍵：

	未來的可能或不確定 may / might + V-base	過去的可能或不確定 may / might + have + PP
語氣上較 直接爽快	He **may notice** a monkey stealing their food.	He **may have noticed** a monkey stealing their food.
語氣上較 委婉保留	He **might notice** a monkey stealing their food.	He **might have noticed** a monkey stealing their food

單元5 must / can 的用法

情態助動詞表達主觀的判斷，判斷有兩種：對「可能性」的判斷及對「好壞度」的判斷。大多情態助動詞都可表達這兩種語意：

must 的兩種語意：

好壞度	必須、應該 （= have to）	You must study hard. 你必須用功。 All passengers must fasten seat belts. 所有乘客都必須繫上安全帶。
可能性	一定、必然	He must be busy. 他一定很忙。 You must be upset. 你一定很難過。

should 的兩種語意：

責任好壞	應該要	He should take care of his family. （他該做什麼？）應該要照顧家人。
是非可能	應該是	He should be home by now. （他人在哪？）應該在家。

may 的兩種語意：

許可的態度	You may go now.
可能性的推敲	He may be right.

can 的兩種語意：

能力判斷	She can play the piano. (= She is able to play the piano.)
許可的態度	She can leave now. (= She is allowed to leave.)
可能性的推敲	She can be wrong. (= It is likely that she is wrong.)

有些文法書說這兩個附屬連接詞用法相同，都是表示「條件」，真的是如此嗎？來看看以下的句子，就知道用法並不相同：

Given that [she has inherited a big fortune from her father], she doesn't need to worry about her future life.

➡ For the fact that she has inherited a big fortune from her father, she doesn't need [not worry about her future life.

在這個句子裡面，「她已繼承爸爸的財產」是一件確定的事，是一個「已知的」事實。Given that在這裡表示「有鑑於、考慮到（considering）」這個「已知的」事實，她不用再擔心以後的生活了。

Providing that [she inherits a big fortune from her father], she will not worry about her future life.

➡ On the condition that she inherits a big fortune from her father, she will not worry about her future life.

這個句子的 Providing that 所帶出的並不是一件確定的事實，只是一種可能的條件（on the condition that），一個「未知的」假設，只有在這個條件成立的狀況下（有辦法繼承爸爸的財產），她以後才不需擔心未來的生活。

結論：

(1) "given that..." 是表示「有鑑於、考慮到 （considering）」一個「已知的」事實；

(2) "providing that..." 則用來表示未知的假設或條件，意思為「如果（if...）」。

Given that she had two months to finish this job, she hasn't made much progress.

➡ Since she had two months to finish this job, she hasn't made much progress.

反正還有兩個月可以完成這份工作，她在工作上就沒有什麼進展了。

Providing that she has two months to finish this job, she will make more progress.

➡ If she has two months / more time to finish this job, she will make more progress.

假如她有多一點時間完成這份工作，她就會做得更好。

單元7 hope 和 wish 的不同（人間可能 vs. 聽天由命）

如果把 hope 和 wish 翻譯成中文，都有「希望」的意思，但是兩字並非可以通用，因為當我們對希望的事情有不同的態度或者對事情有不同的認定，那就有不同的用法。先看看以下的句子，我們就可以看出兩字的差異性：

情境一：

Giant: Happy Chinese New Year!

Nobita: Happy Chinese New Year! **Wish** you and your family a joyful, healthy, prosperous and happiest new year ahead!

Giant: Thank you! What is your new year's resolution?

Nobita: I **hope** I can get an offer of admission to University of Columbia.

Giant: Wow, I envy you. I **wish** I could study abroad. I regret that I didn't devote more time to my study. If I had studied harder, I could go with you. Will you find a job there after graduation?

Nobita: Yes, I will. I **hope** I will get a well-paid job in the States.

Giant: Good for you. Anyway, I **wish** you good luck.

由以上的對話中，hope 和 wish 的意思都是希望，但是在英文裡面卻有不同的使用時機。

(1) hope 是單純由自身出發、針對未來懷抱的喜好、努力可及的「人間事」，在人世間可能實現的「夢想」，只要努力付出就有可能達成。

例如：

[希望] I **hope** I can get an offer of admission to University of Colombia.

➡ 人間可能發生的事情，只要肯努力就有可能申請到哥倫比亞大學。

[希望] I **hope** I will get a well-paid job in the States.

➡ 這裡的 hope 是對未來懷抱希望，也是人世間可能實現的夢想，只要努力或許就可以在美國找到高薪的工作。

(2) wish 則是謙卑的祈求許願，認定此事可能超出個人能力範圍，帶有些許「聽天由命」的意味，能不能如願以償，並不完全能夠操之在己。所以生日時我們許願是 "birthday wishes"，而非 hopes。此外，wish 也用在與事實相反的假設句中，表示事情已發生且事與願違。

例如：

[祈願] **Wish** you and your family a joyful, healthy, prosperous and happiest new year ahead!

[祈願] I **wish** you good luck.

➡ 當大雄和胖虎相互給予對方祝福的時候，發出的「祈願」不是光憑他們的能力就可做到的，這是上帝才能給予的恩典，所以不用 hope，而用 wish。

[事與願違] I **wish** I could study abroad. I regret that I didn't devote more time to my study. If I had studied harder, I could go with you.

➡ 這句是與現在事實相反的假設句，心中帶有遺憾，如果以前有認真讀書，現在或許就可以跟大雄出國念書了。因為出國念書這件事對胖虎來說只是個白日夢，非真實的事情，所以只能用 wish，不用 hope。

結論：

(1) 人間可能的事，憑藉自己的力量可以改變現狀就用 hope。

例句：

I hope tomorrow is a sunny day.

She hopes she will win the scholarship.

We hope John can visit us next summer.

Nobita hopes he will land a job in Canada.

(2) 上帝決定的事，超出人掌控範圍的願望就用 wish。

例句：

I wish tomorrow is a sunny day.

I wish you a happy anniversary.

I wish you all the best.

We wish you a merry Christmas and a happy New Year!

 ## 4. 讀一段短文

Three Days to See

I have often thought it would be a blessing if each human being were stricken blind and deaf for a few days at some time during his or her early adult life. Darkness would make this person more grateful for sight; silence would teach this individual the joys of sound.

Recently, I was visited by a very good friend of mine. I asked her what she had observed from a long walk in the woods. "Nothing in particular," she replied. **Had I not been accustomed to such responses, I might have** suspected her words, for long ago I became convinced that the seeing sees little.

How was it possible to walk for an hour through the woods and see nothing worthy of note? I, who cannot see, find hundreds of things to interest me through just touch. I feel the delicate symmetry of a leaf. In spring, I touch the branches of trees hopefully in search of a bud, the first sign of awakening nature after her winter's sleep. Occasionally, if I am very fortunate, I place my hand gently on a small tree and feel the happy quiver of a bird in full song.

It is human, perhaps, to appreciate little that which we have and to long for that which we don't have, but it is a great pity that in the world of light, the gift of sight is used only as a mere convenience, rather than as a means of adding fullness to life. If, by some miracle, I were granted three seeing days, I should divide the period into three parts.

On the first day, I should want to see the people whose kindness, gentleness, and companionship have made my life worth living. First, I should like to gaze long upon the face of my dear teacher, Mrs. Anne Sullivan Macy, who came to me when I was a child and opened the world to me. I should want not merely to see the outline of her face, so that I could cherish it in my memory, but to study that face and find in it the living evidence of the sympathetic tenderness and patience with which she accomplished the difficult task of my education. I should like to see in her eyes that strength of character which has enabled her to stand firm in the face of the plight and that compassion for all humanity which she has revealed to me so often.

On the second day of sight, I should devote my time to a hasty glimpse of the world, past and present, through museums. I should try to investigate the soul of man through his art. The whole magnificent world of painting would be opened to me, from the Italian Primitives, with their serene religious devotion, to the Moderns, with their feverish visions. I should look deep into the canvases of Raphael and Leonardo da Vinci. I should want to feast my eyes upon the warm colors of Veronese. Oh, there is so much rich meaning and beauty in the art of the ages for you who have eyes to see!

On my third and last day of sight, I should spend this day in the workday world of the present, so that the city could become a destination of mine. From Fifth Avenue, I would make a tour of the city—to Park Avenue, to the slums, to factories, to the parks where children play. My eye would strive to touch and hold closely each thing its gaze rested upon. Some sights would be pleasant, filling the heart with happiness; some would be miserably pathetic. To the latter, I would not shut my eyes, for they, too are part of life. To close the eye on them is to close the heart and mind.

I can give one warning to those who see: Use your eyes **as if tomorrow you would be stricken blind**. And the same method can be applied to other senses. Hear the music of voices, the song of a bird, the vigorous strains of an orchestra, **as if you would be stricken deaf tomorrow**. Touch each object you want to touch **as if tomorrow your tactile sense would fail**. Smell the fragrance of flowers, taste with enjoyment each scrap of food, **as if tomorrow you could never smell or taste again**. Make the most of every sense glory in all the aspects of pleasure and beauty which the world reveals to you through the several means of contact which nature provides. But of all the senses, I am sure that sight must be the most delightful.

註解:1.「如果每個人都能在他們早期成人階段,有一段眼盲失聰的機會,那是一種恩賜」。"it would be...if each human being were stricken..." 這裡使用與現在事實相反的假設。2. 這是倒裝句,原句為:"If I hadn't been accustomed to..., I might have suspected her..."。"the seeing see little" 意思是能看到的人,通常看到的不完全。3. "if, by some miracle, I were..., I should..." 「如果(奇蹟發生)我有三天能看到東西,我會……」,筆者看不到,所以用與現在事實相反的假設句。4.「善用你的眼睛,就好像(as if)明天就看不到一樣」。as if 之後用 would,表達想像但不太會發生的事,因為筆者是說給看的到的人聽。

 ## 5. 唱一首英文歌

If I Were A Boy
(by Beyoncé)

If I were a boy
Even just for a day
I'd roll outta bed in the morning
And throw on what I wanted and go
Drink beer with the guys
And chase after girls
I'd kick it with who I wanted
And I'd never get confronted for it.
'Cause they'd stick up for me.

If I were a boy
I think I could understand
How it feels to love a girl
I swear I'd be a better man.
I'd listen to her
'Cause I know how it hurts
When you lose the one you wanted
'Cause he's taken you for granted
And everything you had got destroyed.

https://www.youtube.com/watch?v=AWpsOqh8q0M

(https://bit.ly/2PIfjjY)

註解：1. "If I were a boy, I'd roll out of bed...and throw on what I wanted and go drink..." 為 "If I were..., I would..."的句型。與現在事實相反，因為唱歌的人為女生。2. "If I were a boy, (I think) I could ..."，could = would be able to。3. 前面也是接 "If I were a boy" 所以後面是 " (I swear) I would be a better man, I would listen to her."。

 ## 6. 看一部影片

If You Were the President...

https://www.youtube.com/watch?v=UPg0eGBpmg0

(https://bit.ly/2PVPwVs)

Obama　　**Trump**

7. 做一點練習

Part 1：選擇題

_____ 1. He should be very grateful if you _____ that thing for him now.

(A) would have done　(B) will do　(C) would do　(D) do

_____ 2. If Peter were diligent, he _____ now.

(A) may be able to get the job

(B) might have won the first prize

(C) would not be in distress

(D) is certain to be successful

_____ 3. His son passed away two years ago. If he were alive now, he _____ in the six grade.

(A) will be　(B) is　(C) was　(D) would be

_____ 4. _____ he honest, I would trust him.

(A) Were　(B) Was　(C) Would　(D) Is

_____ 5. It finally stops raining now. If it _____, I should have to stay here for the nights.

(A) is still raining　　　　(B) was still raining

(C) were still raining　　　(D) rains

_____ 6. If I _____ to take this examination now, I could sleep at home.

(A) don't need　(B) hadn't needed　(C) didn't need　(D) need

選擇題答案：

1. (C)　2. (C)　3. (D)　4. (A)　5. (C)　6. (C)

> 註解：第 1、2 題：「她看起來/動作、說話好像她……」可判斷與現在事實相
> 反，只是一種想像，故選擇 "were" 過去式動詞。第 3、4 題："It
> seems...as if...yesterday." 跟 "The man told me...as if he...two days ago."
> 都有表過去的時間副詞，也有 "as if" 所以判斷為與過去事實相反假設，
> 故答案為「had + PP」。5.「她叫的好像……」，判斷為假設句，as
> though = as if。7.「他的行為舉止好像他比我們所有的人好」，語意判
> 斷說話者不認為是事實且有 "as if"，得知與現在事實相反，故選過去式
> 動詞 were。

222

Part 2：翻譯題

1. 假如我有足夠的錢，我就能買這棟房子。

_____

_____

2. 假如 Mary 是一隻鳥，她就能飛去你那邊。

_____

_____

3. 假如你們沒有做這件事，也就不會被人嘲笑。

_____

_____

4. 假如 Peter 沒有買這本書，他可能會後悔。

_____

_____

5. 假如他是你，他會選擇去美國玩。

_____

_____

6. 假如我沒有生病，今天就能和你去。

_____

_____

答案：

1. If I had enough money, I could buy this house.

2. If Mary were a bird, she could fly to you.

3. If you did not do this thing, you would not be laughed at.

4. If Peter did not buy this book, he might feel regret.

5. If he were you, he would choose to visit America.

6. If I were not sick, I could go with you today.

Part 3：選擇題

_____ 1. If you _____ me, I could have succeeded last year.

   (A) have helped   (B) helped   (C) did help   (D) had helped

_____ 2. Had Peter studied hardier, he _____ to National Taiwan University two years ago.

   (A) would be admitted   (B) could admit

   (C) would have admitted   (D) could have been admitted

_____ 3. If she _____ such an extravagant girl, I would have married her.

   (A) were not   (B) wouldn't   (C) has been   (D) hadn't been

_____ 4. Had you told him the truth, he _____ some suggestions.

   (A) might make   (B) would make

   (C) might have made   (D) had made

_____ 5. If they had not sent for the doctor then, their brother _____.

   (A) might have died   (B) may die   (C) died   (D) had died

_____ 6. If you _____ him last night, he should not have caught the train.

   (A) didn't remind   (B) hadn't reminded

   (C) reminded   (D) might have reminded

選擇題答案：

1. (D) 2. (D) 3. (D) 4. (C) 5. (A) 6. (B)

> 註解：1. 後半句為 "could have + PP." 又有 "last year" 因此可判斷為與過去事實相反，因此選擇 "had + PP."。2. 倒裝句，原句為：If Peter had studied hardier, he..."，後面又有 "two years ago"，因此也是與過去事實相反假設，解題與第 1 題同。

Part 4：翻譯題

1. 要是他現在在這裡，那有多好啊！

_____

_____

2. 要是現在我們能遇見阿姨，那有多好啊！

_____

_____

3. 但願我現在有很多錢。

_____

_____

4. 去年要是我買了這棟房子有多好啊！

_____

_____

5. 要是我的錢昨晚沒被偷那有多好啊！

_____

_____

6. 昨晚要是你能找到這家餐館那有多好啊！

_____

_____

翻譯題答案：

1. I wish (that) he were here now.

2. We wish (that) we could meet our aunt now.

3. I wish (that) I had a lot of money now.

4. I wish (that) I had bought this house last year.

5. I wish (that) my money had not been stolen last night.

6. I wish (that) you could have found that restaurant last night.

選擇題：

_____ 1. She looks as if she _____ ill.

     (A) is   (B) was   (C) be   (D) were

_____ 2. She acts and talks as if she _____ a queen now.

     (A) is   (B) were   (C) be   (D) has

_____ 3. It seems as if he _____ the work the day before yesterday.

     (A) finished   (B) were finished   (C) had finished   (D) finishes

_____ 4. The man told me about the incident as if he _____ it with his own eyes two days ago.

     (A) saw   (B) had seen   (C) had been seen   (D) were seen

_____ 5. She shouted and cried _____ she were out of her mind.

     (A) as though   (B) as like   (C) as to   (D) so as to

_____ 6. He talks as though _____ a doctor.

     (A) he were   (B) he is   (C) he was   (D) he has

_____ 7. He behaves as if he _____ better than all of us.

     (A) is   (B) were   (C) was   (D) be

_____ 8. He talked yesterday as though he _____ this work the day before yesterday.

     (A) could finish   (B) can finish

     (C) could be finished   (D) could have finished

_____ 9. He looked as if he _____ the whole thing.

     (A) had understood   (B) understands

     (C) will understand   (D) was understanding

選擇題答案：

1. (D)   2. (B)   3. (C)   4. (B)   5. (A)   6. (A)   7. (B)   8. (D)   9. (A)

翻譯題：

1. 他對日本很了解，好像他以前曾經去過那裡似的。

_____

_____

2. 他講得好像他是個國王似的。

_____

_____

英文文法有道理！入門版

3. 他們把這個男生當死人對待。

_____

_____

4. 他講得好像他可能活不久了

_____

_____

翻譯題答案：

1. He knows much about Japan as if he had been there before.

2. He talks as if he were a king.

3. (1) They treat the boy as if he were dead.

    = They treat the boy as if he were a dead person.

  (2) They treated the boy as if he had been dead.

    = They treated the boy as if he had been a dead person.

4. He talks as if he might not live long.

CHAPTER

8

誰該負責？
主動與被動

:

1. 你想說什麼？

　　一個動作的發生，一定有發出動作的人，有時也會有一個受動作影響的人。發出動作的人是握有主控權的一方，是事件的負責人；被動作影響的一方則是被事件影響的對象。其實每一個及物事件中，都會有這兩種角色，例如：

The cat chased the dog.
➡ 做出追的動作的對象是追狗的貓；受影響者是被追的狗。

John built the house. ➡ 負責人是 John；被造的物品是 the house。

　　舉例來說，在打人的事件中，一定有「打人的」，也有「被打的」，一方是事件的「主導者」，一方是「受害者」。打人這事件可以從「主導者」的角度來描述，也可以從「受害者」的角度來描述：

> 師 發生甚麼事？
>
> 生 女生打男生！　➡ 以「主導者」為主詞
>
> 　　男生被打了！　➡ 以「受害者」為主詞

　　這兩種不同的描述角度就是「主動」和「被動」最大的區別。在描述這個打人事件時，兩個角色帶出兩種可能，主詞和動詞也因此形成兩種關係：

　　造成事件發生的負責人作主詞 ➡ 主動句型 ➡ The girl hit the boy.
　　被事件影響的受害人作主詞 ➡ 被動句型 ➡ The boy was hit.

2. 英文怎麼說？

單元1 被動句的標記方式

　　在英文裡「主動句」和「被動句」在動詞形式上有明顯的差異：

主動句：The dog <u>chased</u> the boy. ➡ V_{tense}

被動句：The boy <u>was chased</u> (by the dog). ➡ BE + V_{pp}（過去分詞）

　　「狗追男孩」還是「男孩被狗追」在英文的動詞上要有清楚的標記。「主動句」用一般動詞，「被動句」要用 BE 動詞加過去分詞（BE + V_{pp}）。

　　為何被動句的主要動詞要用 BE 動詞，而不是一般動詞呢？這是因為被動句表達的是動作發生造成的「結果狀態」，而 Be 動詞作為主要動詞，本來就是表達狀態連結。舉例來說，"He is happy." 這個句子就是以 BE 動詞表達「他很快樂」的狀態。

　　我們可以從下列句子觀察到主動句和被動句的差異：

I made him leave.（我逼他離開）

➡ 主要動詞為 make，強調我「逼迫」他離開這個動作

He was made to leave.（他被迫離開）

➡ 主要動詞為 BE 動詞，強調「逼迫」發生後，他「被迫離開」的「結果狀態」。

　　總而言之，因為「被動句」其實是表達動作的「結果狀態」，所以要用表示狀態的 BE 動詞！

231

單元2 被動句是將「主題焦點」放在「被處置、受影響」的一方

我們在說話或寫作的時候通常使用主動句，因人很自然會以「主動做事」的一方為切入點，來描述事件的發生。主動句的主語焦點通常放在「造成事件」的主控者身上。

主動句：主詞=主控者

<u>John</u> broke the window.

<u>The architect</u> built the house.

<u>The police</u> sent the victim to the hospital.

但被動句剛好相反，是將焦點放在「被處置、受影響」一方。在此情況下，主要焦點放在「受影響者」，故其重要性高於「主控者」，甚至「主控者」都可以省略。

被動句：主詞＝受影響者

<u>The window</u> was broken.

<u>The house</u> was built in 1990.

<u>The victim</u> was sent to the hospital.

單元3 被動句有哪些溝通特點？

就溝通功能而言，被動句的使用表達了以下四個特點：

(1) 主控者的重要性降低 ➡ 受影響者的重要性提高

主控者重要性降低或不需要出現時，句子便可以「受影響者」為主語。有幾種情境會傾向使用被動句：

主控者不詳	A man was injured in the robbery. ➡ 只曉得發生了這件事，但不曉得確切的主控者是誰。
主控者已經提過	The protesters went on strike and soon the whole plaza was packed. ➡ 示威者進行遊行罷工，使得廣場上擠滿了人，示威者就是主導者，不需再提一次。

主控者不需言明	The food is being cooked in the kitchen. ➡ 如果沒有特殊情況，食物一定是廚師在廚房裡烹調的。	
主控者相當於所有「路人甲乙丙丁」：	It is known that the risk of cognitive decline increases with advancing age. ➡ It 這個虛主詞，代表 that 後面的內容。此句在闡述一個事實，因此 know 的主控者可說是所有人。	
主控者刻意被隱藏，以推卸責任	Mistakes were made regarding the status of the refugees from Syria. ➡ 事情的真相可能是「移民局官員將難民資料搞錯了」，但這個句子只做出部分描述，另外一部分的資訊則被隱藏起來了。	

(2) 維持連貫的主題焦點 ➡ 主題剛好是受影響者

有時我們使用被動句是為了承接之前提過的主題，維持上下文的連貫性：

I have a dog whose name is Spark. He likes cats but is always chased by them.

➡ 在這個例子中，我的狗 Spark 為主題焦點，為了持續聚焦在同一個主題上，第二個句子以被動句呈現，好讓 Spark 繼續作為主詞。如果第二句為主動句的話，句子主詞勢必改變，使得主題不連貫，無法緊密連接前文。

(3) 描述動作造成的結果狀態 ➡ 動作狀態化：Be 動詞 + 過去分詞

一般而言，主動句是描述「動作」，但被動句則是描述動作發生造成的「狀態」。為了描述動作發生後的「狀態」，被動句要用表示狀態的 BE 動詞為主要動詞。若要表達「動態式」的被動，我們可以用 get 來取代 Be，這樣的用法會賦予句子不同的動感：

動態事件 John got killed in the accident.

➡ 結果狀態 He was killed in an accident.

用 got 可表達「動態化」的被動事件，強調事件的出現，但用 was 則是結果狀態的描述。

233

(4) 淡化人的主動性 ➡ 強化事實結果的客觀性

如果我們希望以觀察到的事物為主題，強調「被發現」的事實，被動句可以隱藏個人的主觀性與操控性，彰顯敘事立論的客觀性：

It is found that the English behave differently from the Chinese.

單元4 英文的被動式，就是中文的「被」字句嗎？

英文的每一個句子都有主動、被動之分，每說一句話都要考慮主詞和動詞的關係，若是被動的關係，一定要有被動的標記。但是中文的被動句卻不一定有「被」：

中文的被動句不一定有「被」：

報紙送來了。　➡ 報紙是「被」送來的
功課寫完了。　➡ 功課是「被」寫完的

在中文裡，「被」這個字最早只用於悲慘、受害（adversity）的情況：被打、被殺、被罵，但在英文翻譯文學影響下，亦逐漸用於描述「人」處於非自主狀況下受到的影響：被褒揚、被提名、被選上、被肯定等好事。若是「物」受影響，只有不受歡迎（undesirable）的情況會用「被」，如：電腦被偷、車子被砸，表示受損狀況。其他一般「用物」情況可用「主題＋評論」的句式，不需用「被」字來標記。

報紙送了。➡ The newspaper was delivered.
房子賣了。➡ The house was sold.

以上的被動關係在中文裡「全無標記」，但英文的標記法則要求「釐清責任、分辨角色」，只要是「被動關係」就一定要有「被動形式」的標記：

主動句 S主導者 + V + O	被動句 S受控者 + BE + V$_{pp}$
I bought a pen. （我買了一枝筆）	**The pen** was bought. （筆買了）

主動句 S_{主導者} + V + O	被動句 S_{受控者} + BE + V_{pp}
Mom prepared dinner for me. （媽媽為我做晚餐）	**Dinner** was prepared for me. （晚餐準備好了）
She sent a book to him. （她送了一本書給他）	**The book** was sent to him. （書送給他了）

筆不會自己買、晚餐不會自己準備、書也不會自己送，因此當這些角色出現在主語位置時，英文都必須用被動式來表達。

文法小撇步：每個句子都注意，主動被動標清楚！

英文句子結構嚴謹，每個句子主詞和動詞的關係都必須要釐清！因此，英文的每個子句都必須標示為主動或被動。這種「責任清楚」的標記原則可以從中英文的對照看出，所以，千萬不要因為中文沒有「被」，就忘了要釐清主詞和動詞的關係！

 3. 還能怎麼說？

單元1 如何區別「現在分詞」和「過去分詞」？

「分詞」是動詞的一種形式，基本上分為「現在分詞」和「過去分詞」，通常和 BE 動詞合用，作為修飾語：

現在分詞 V-ing：The book is <u>interesting</u>. ➡ 表達主動語意
過去分詞 V-en：The book is <u>broken</u>. ➡ 表達被動語意

「現在分詞」和「過去分詞」這樣的名稱有時會造成誤解，其實這兩者的區別並不是在於發生在「現在」還是「過去」，而是在表達「主動」和「被動」的區別。現在分詞就是「主動分詞」，表達主動的語意；過去分詞就是「被動分詞」，表達被動的語意，請比較以下的分詞構句：

主動句： I helped my mom and I washed the dishes.

主動分詞： Helping my mom, I washed the dishes.
為了幫媽媽的忙，我洗了碗。

⬇

被動句： I was helped by my mom and I washed the dishes.

⬇

被動分詞： Helped by my mom, I washed the dishes.
在媽媽的幫忙下，我洗了碗。

完整的句子可以被簡化為分詞，有一個很重要的條件，那就是要有相同的主詞，分詞的主詞要和主要子句的主詞一致：

主動分詞 V-ing	Teaching at a high school, **she** became more outgoing. 在高中教書，她變得比較活潑。 (X) Teaching at a high school, **her job** is secure. ➡ 這個句子將 "her job" 當作主要子句的主詞，也就成為 "teaching at high school" 的主詞。但是從事 teaching 的人是 she 而不是 "her job"，故分詞 "teaching at high school" 的主詞應該是 she。
被動分詞 V-en	Taught by a good teacher, she made progress in English. 被一位老師教導，她的英文進步了。 (X) Taught by a good teacher, her English improved. ➡ 這個句子將 "her English" 當作主要子句的主詞，也就成為 "taught by a good teacher" 的主詞。但是被教的人是 she 而不是 "her English"，故分詞 "taught by a good teacher" 的主詞應該是 she。

以上的分詞又稱為「簡單分詞」，單純表達主語相同的關聯。然而，分

詞構句也可將時間的先後帶入，用完成貌來強調「之前」已經發生，稱為「完成分詞」，形式上用 Having + V-pp：

完成分詞 Having V-en	主動：Having worked for 20 years, he retired this year. 在工作了 20 年後，他退休了。 被動：Having been fired by his company, the man disappeared. 在被公司解雇後，他就失蹤了。

單元2 分詞作為形容詞

現在分詞和過去分詞都可以做形容詞，但兩者的差別卻常常搞混。其實，兩者的差異仍是在主動和被動的區別：現在分詞帶有主動「使得……」的意味。過去分詞則含有被動「受到……」的意味：

a heart-breaking experience（現在分詞作形容詞 ➡ 主動）
➡ 一段令人心碎的經歷
a health-threatened man（過去分詞作形容詞 ➡ 被動）
➡ 一個健康受到威脅的人

總而言之，不管分詞出現的位子在哪，現在分詞（present participle）的形式都是用來表達主動的關係，過去分詞（past participle）的形式則都是用來表達被動的關係。

單元3 誰是情緒的主導者？

以英文的邏輯來看，人是理性的動物，情緒上的變化並不是自己「主動選擇」的，而是受到外界刺激影響被挑起的。情緒的主導者其實是外界的刺激，而不是人本身。

既然引發情緒的元兇是外界的刺激，英文大多數情緒動詞就以「刺激物」為主語，由主控者的角度出發，人反而變成「受控」的一方。人產生情

237

緒變化是被影響，被挑起，語意角色上成了「接受者」，只能作情緒動詞的受詞。這就是為什麼英文會說 "English interests me." 或 "I am interested in English."

下列的情緒動詞也是依循相同的邏輯運作：

I am excited by the news. ➡ The news is exciting.

I was frightened by the picture. ➡ The picture is frightening.

單元4 「他被分手了」有何意涵？

受到英文被動句型的影響，中文的「被」字句逐漸用於描述「人」處於非自主狀況下受到的影響，故出現「她被離婚」或「他被分手了」等新穎用法。此處加入「被」字可用來表達「非自願」或「不受歡迎」的結果狀態，與英文被動句的功能相仿。由於英文翻譯作品的影響，中文的「被」字句用得愈來愈多，但語意上有其特別含意，並不等同英文的被動句！

他們離婚了 ➡ They are divorced.（彼此分開）

他們「被」離婚了 ➡ They are forced to get divorced.（強迫分開）

結論：英文每一個句子都有主、被動之分，都要清楚標記主詞和動詞間語意關係! 請記住文法小撇步：**主動或被動，句句標清楚！**

4. 讀一段短文

Elegy for the King and Queen

His early life unfolded like something coauthored by Dickens and Darwin. As an infant he was taken from his mother – he almost certainly saw her die trying to protect him – then sold in an orange crate for $25 and a thumbprint.

He was carried across an ocean, installed inside a cage, taught to depend on the imperfect love of strangers. He charmed Jane Goodall, threw dirt at the mayor of Tampa, learned to blow kisses and smoke cigarettes, whatever it took to entertain the masses. Although he was afforded the sexual privileges conferred by rank, he never chose a mate. He had no interest in females of his own kind. He preferred blonds in tank tops.

He reigned through the death of one zoo and the birth of another. He proved himself a benevolent leader who knew how to keep the peace and observe the social formalities. He was a good listener. He was loyal and forgiving. Looking into his brown eyes, his keepers had no doubt he possessed a soul.

註解：1. "he was taken from....then sold..." 為被動句他被帶離開媽媽並被賣掉。2. "Looking into his brown eyes, his keepers had no doubt he possessed a soul." 前半段為分詞構句，分詞的主詞與後面 "his keepers" 同，意思為飼養他的人看過他的眼睛後，都覺得他是有靈魂的動物。

5. 唱一首英文歌

Love You Like a Love Song

(By Selena Gomez)

It's been said and done
Every beautiful thought's been already sung
And I guess right now here's another one
So your melody will play on and on, with the best of 'em
You are beautiful, like a dream come alive, incredible
A sinful, miracle, lyrical
You've saved my life again
And I want you to know baby
I, I love you like a love song, baby
I, I love you like a love song, baby
I, I love you like a love song, baby
And I keep hitting re-peat-peat-peat-peat-peat-peat
Constantly, boy you play through my mind like a symphony
There's no way to describe what you do to me
You just do to me, what you do
And it feels like I've been rescued
I've been set free
I am hypnotized by your destiny
You are magical, lyrical, beautiful
You are and I want you to know baby

https://www.youtube.com/watch?v=EgT_us6AsDg (https://bit.ly/2PGvTk7)

239

註解：1. " It has been said and done (that) every beautiful thought has been already sung." 這裡用現在完成表示一直以來，意思為美麗的事物都已經唱頌過了，大家都這麼說也這麼做。2. "I've been rescued, I've been set free, I am hypnotized..." 前兩句是現在完成被動式，我已經被救贖、我已經被釋放、我被你的命運迷住了。

 ## 6. 看一部影片

Dear John opening scene

https://www.youtube.com/watch?v=yifLIpMNPFU

(https://bit.ly/2PNB4yT)

Passive voice in TV series

https://www.youtube.com/watch?v=-SYAtZw4sqY

(https://bit.ly/2zS4qRR)

Mr. Passive Voice

https://www.youtube.com/watch?v=yKUNYp_Bc0g

(https://bit.ly/2zPwx4i)

 ## 7. 做一點練習

Part 1：選擇題

_____1. Harry Potter and the Goblet of Fire _____ by J K Rowling

  (A) was written   (B) written   (C) wrote

_____2. Over a million dollars in cash _____ from the Bank of East Asia in Central.

  (A) have stolen   (B) have been stolen

_____3. Thieves _____ over a million dollars in cash from the Bank of East Asia in Central.

  (A) stolen   (B) were stolen   (C) have stolen   (D) was been stolen

_____4. I'll have to come by bus as my car _____.

   (A) is repairing   (B) is being repaired

_____5. The meeting _____ until the end of the month.

  (A) has postponed   (B) has been postponed   (C) is been postponed

---

_____ 6. In Hong Kong, many shops _____ at around nine in the morning.

(A) are opened　　(B) open

_____ 7. Helmets must _____ past this point.

(A) wear　　(B) are worn　　(C) be worn

選擇題答案：

1. (A)　2. (B)　3. (C)　4. (B)　5. (B)　6. (A) or (B)　7. (C)

註解：第 1、2 題：主詞「哈利波特」跟「超過一百萬的現金」是被寫及被偷，故用被動式，第 1 題為過去被動，第 2 題為現在完成式的被動。3. 主詞為小偷，所以不能用被動，(A) 為分詞因此也不可選，故答案選 " have stolen" 偷了。4. 我的車是「被修」所以不能選 (A)，(B) 加上 being 則是強調狀態。6. open 營業，及物與不及物皆是，所以兩個答案都可以。例：The coffee shop opens at 9am. / He opens his coffee shop at 9am. 7. 主詞為 helmets 安全帽，後面有助動詞，所以答案為原形動詞的被動。

Part 2：改寫題

請將下列句子改寫為被動句

1. The supermarket has replaced the old shelves.

_____

2. Chileans were growing grapes over a thousand years ago.

_____

3. People speak English all over the world.

_____

4. The police didn't find the missing girl last weekend.

_____

5. Tourists don't visit this museum very often.

_____

6. Workers are building a new park in town.

_____

改寫題答案：

1. The old shelves have been replaced by the supermarket.

2. Grapes were being grown by Chileans over a thousand years ago.

3. English is spoken (by people) all over the world.

4. The missing girl was not found by the police last weekend.

5. This museum is not visited (by tourists) very often.

6. A new park is being built in town.

Part 3：填空題

請看提示填入被動式

1. The authorities decided that the meeting _____ next Wednesday. (hold)

2. The goods _____ to our house in the Midlands every Friday. (transport)

3. The larger portrait _____ by a well-known Flemish artist.(paint)

4. When I arrived I _____ a note by one of the delegates. (hand)

5. For the past few days I had to work in Jack's office because mine _____ at the moment. (renovate)

6. I'll have to stay at home because our new furniture _____. (deliver)

填空題答案：

1. will be held 2. are transported 3. was painted 4. was handed

5. is being renovated 6. will be delivered

Part 4：改寫題

請將下列句子改寫為被動句

1. When did they translate this book into English?

_____

2. Some dangerous looking men were following me the whole evening.

_____

3. The cleaning lady has watered the plants.

_____

4. Have they delivered the new music system yet?

_____

5. They have never opened the door before.

_____

6. We will remove any vehicles found parked in front of these gates.

_____

改寫題答案：

1. When was this book translated into English?

2. I was followed by some dangerous looking men the whole evening.

3. The plants have been watered by the cleaning lady.

4. Has the new music system been delivered yet?

5. The door has never been opened before.

6. Any vehicles found parked in front of these gates will be removed.

改寫題：

請將下列句子改寫為被動句

7. He had written three books before 1867.

_____

8. By this time tomorrow we will have signed the deal.

_____

9. The traffic might have delayed Jimmy.

_____

10. I had cleaned all the windows before the storm.

_____

11. Somebody has drunk all the milk!

_____

12. Somebody must have taken my wallet.

_____

改寫題答案：

7. Three books had been written by him before 1867.

8. By this time tomorrow the deal will have been signed.

9. Jimmy might have been delayed by the traffic.

10. All the windows had been cleaned before the storm.

11. All the milk has been drunk!

12. My wallet must have been taken.

Part 5：克漏字

A. was obliged to	B. are believed to have been	C. was brought
D. is not known	E. are thought to be	F. was packed
G. is thought to have been	H. was seen	I. were made to
J. is known to have experienced		

A plane carrying 15 members of the government to a conference in Brussels ___1.___ a small scale fire earlier this morning. The plane ___2.___ about 20 minutes into its journey when the fire occurred in the luggage department. It ___3.___ how the plane caught fire, but early eyewitness reports confirm that a trail of smoke ___4.___ coming from the undercarriage. The fire ___5.___ rapidly under control, but the pilot ___6.___ make an emergency landing. Five people ___7.___ treated for shock. The plane ___8.___ with businesspeople flying to Belgium.

All 209 passengers ___9.___ stay behind for questioning after landing at a military airport in northern France. Police ___10.___ treating the incident suspicious.

克漏字答案：

1. J   2. G   3. D   4. H   5. C   6. A   7. B   8. F   9. I   10. E

註解：3. It 這個虛主詞，代表 that 後面的內容。此句在闡述一個事實（how the plane caught fire），因此 know 的主控者可說是所有人，事實不為人知故答案為 "is not known'。6. oblige 為迫使的意思，意思為駕駛不得不迫降，用被動式。9. "were made to..." 是被要求留下來問問題的意思。10. "Police are thought to be..." 沒有出現主詞，代表無須言明，是大家都這麼認為。使用被動式也有比較客觀的含意。

英文文法有道理！入門版

CHAPTER

9

在哪裡發生的？
介系詞該怎麼用？

♀))) 1. 你想說什麼？

我們在描述事件時，如果想要表明事件發生的地點，就必須用介系詞帶出地點：

> 孩子們在 後院裡／餐廳前／街上 玩耍。

介系詞最直觀的用法是用來描述空間方位，例如：上、下、前、後、裡、外等。但這些詞也可以用在時間的描述上，例如我們可以說：他的位子在我的「之前」，也可以說聖誕節在新年「之前」。位子是空間的概念，聖誕節卻是時間的概念，這種「空間」和「時間」相互連結的例子隨處可見。請再看以下對話：

> 小明 期末考快要到了。
>
> 小華 時間過的真快，希望暑假快點來！
>
> 小美 時間不停的走，想追也追不上！

對話中的動詞「到、過、來、走、追」原本都是表達空間移動，時間不會真的「來到」你家，但是這些空間動詞都被用來描述「時間」。這是因為「時間」是抽象的，很難理解，除非借用具體的「空間」詞彙來描述，才比較容易理解。

除此之外，空間概念也可以延伸來表達抽象的概念，例如：

> 我一直把你放在心上。
> 她的倩影在我的腦海中徘徊不去。

在接下來的章節中，我們會深入探討介系詞的原型概念和延伸用法，來分析何時該使用哪個介系詞。

2. 英文怎麼說？

單元1 介系詞的涵義與標記方式

　　介系詞（preposition）這個字可以拆為兩個部分：「pre + position」，意即放在地點位置（position）之前（pre-）的詞。顧名思義，英文的介系詞一定出現在地點名詞之前，用來標記「地點方位」，如：on the table、in the box、at the shop、behind the car 等。

　　既然是用來標記地點位置，每一個介系詞的基本核心語意必然是空間上的概念。這些空間概念也可以延伸至其他範疇，用來表達時間概念或抽象概念。

　　總結來說，介系詞在標記上有兩個特點：

(1) 介系詞既是地點方位的前置詞（pre-position），後面一定要接名詞
　　➡ P + NP（Noun Phrase，名詞片語）

(2) 介系詞的核心語意為具體的空間概念，此空間概念可協助我們理解描述其他非空間或抽象概念。

單元2　in、at、on 的基本空間概念

　　in、at、on 是英文中最常見的三個介系詞，這三個介系詞各自有其專屬的空間概念，如下表所示：

介系詞	空間原型	概念圖像	例子
in	在空間範圍內	空間容器（**container**）	in a city in a box in a room
at	在空間定點	空間實點（**point**）	at the bus stop at the entrance at the shop

介系詞	空間原型	概念圖像	例子
on	在空間接觸面上	空間平面（**surface**）	on the floor on the table on the road

如上圖示，"on、in、at" 表達三種最基本的空間概念：on 在接觸面上（on a surface）、in 在範圍內（in a boundary）、at 在定點（at a spot）。

➢ in vs. at

何時該使用 in 和 at 是學生最常碰到的問題之一。有些老師會教 in 後面要接大範圍，at 後面要接小範圍，但這個說法並不正確。因為這兩者有時可接同一個處所地點，例如：

I am in the park.
I am at the park.

這兩個句子因為使用不同的介系詞，表達的語意也不盡相同。"in the park" 表達的是 in 的概念：「在公園這個範圍之內」，"at the park" 表達的是 at 的概念：「就在公園這個定點」。由於 in 和 at 的空間概念不盡相同，其後常用的空間名詞也不盡相同，in 通常接一個三度立體空間，作為明確的範疇邊際（a boundary），at 後面通常接一個地理位置，作為明確的處所地點（a spot）：

I saw the dog in the car. ➡ 在一個範疇之內 ＝ in a boundary
I saw the dog at the corner. ➡ 在一個定點 ＝ at a spot

➢ on vs. in

「我看見一隻鳥在樹上」應該說 "I saw a bird on the tree." 還是 "I saw a bird in the tree." 呢？

按照「形義」搭配原則，這兩句話的形式既然不一樣，語意就不一樣。in 的語意仍是 "in a boundary"，是「包含於某範疇內」的概念，on 則是 "on a surface"「在接觸表面上」的意思。所以如果我們把樹當作一個「涵蓋範疇」，就可說 "a bird in the tree"，若把樹當作是一個「接觸表面」，則可說 "a bird on the tree"。

單元3 介系詞空間概念可延伸，用於時間或抽象概念

　　介系詞的基本空間概念，可以延伸到其他的生活範疇，而產生看起來不一樣的語意。從認知層面來看，空間關係較為具體，可以幫助我們理解時間和其他抽象概念。而「時空轉換」就是介系詞語意多樣的來源。

➤ 介系詞如何用於標示時間

　　英文裡不同的時間單位要與不同的介系詞連用，如幾點幾分用 at，星期幾用 on，月份和年份用 in。要理解該用哪些介系詞來標記不同時間類型，就必須從各介系詞的核心概念出發：

(1) in 的空間原型為「在範圍內」，故在時間概念中可用來標示一段「時間上的範圍」，而年、月的基本功用就是表示長短不同的「時間範疇」：

in the afternoon

in March

in 1994

除了固定的時間範疇外，in 還可用於標示任何「一段時間範疇之內」的概念：I finished the homework in an hour. ➡ 一個小時之內完成的

(2) on 的核心概念為「在接觸面上」，故可用來標示時間上的接觸面，有「在明確時日上」的含意。而「日期」的存在意義就是提供一個可以置放事件的接觸面，方便談話者確認事件發生的時間：

on Monday

on Monday afternoon

on March 17

(3) at 的核心概念為「在定點」，故在時間概念中可用來標示時間軸上的一個「定點」。此定點為一個可以明確指出的「時間點」：

at 5:30 pm

at 7 o'clock

at noon

> ### ➤ 介系詞如何用於標示抽象概念

(1) in 的空間原型為「在範圍內」，故在抽象概念中也是用於表達「涵蓋於內」的語意：

a lady in red ➡ 被紅色包覆

in love ➡ 被愛包覆

interested in English ➡ 興趣範圍內

(2) on 的核心概念為「在接觸面上」，故可抽象概念中可用來標示某一主題或焦點的「面向」：

The paper is on linguistics. ➡ 研究主題

spending money on books ➡ 花費方面

(3) at 的核心概念為「在定點」，故在抽象概念中可用來表達能力的「定點」或情緒的「定位」：

good at music ➡ 專長點

amazed at his change ➡ 訝異點

look at him ➡ 視覺點

單元4 使用介系詞 to 來標示「行動的趨向目標」

介系詞 to 主要是標記由 A 點往 B 點移動的空間位移，有明確的方向性，後面接的大多是「空間標的」，用以表示路徑位移的終點，例如：I went to the park.。然而經由時空轉換的認知機制，其後的空間目標可變成時間上的目標，"I look forward to seeing you."。進一步，可接任何具有「目標對象」含意的人或物，"I wrote a letter to him."。再進一步，可延伸至非實體的結果或理想趨向：

空間趨向：I go to the supermarket every day. ➡ 超市是要前往的目的地

時間趨向：It's a quarter to five. ➡ 五點鐘是一個時間標的

人物趨向：I gave the book to Jim. ➡ give的致贈對象

結果趨向：I was moved to tears. ➡ 感動的終極結果

夢想趨向：I live up to my dream. ➡ 生活的目標方向

在這些多樣的延伸用法中，to 的核心語意仍然保持不變：標示行動的趨向目標。

➤ 如何區分介系詞 to 和不定詞 to？

介系詞 to 後面接名詞（如：to the party），不定詞 to 後面接動詞短語（如：to walk），兩者功能看起來不太一樣。但其實這兩個 to 的根源是相通的：空間上要前往的「目標地點」可轉換為時間上要從事的「目標事件」，意即接下來要去做的事。介系詞 to 和不定詞 to 皆表達「趨向目標」。只是介系詞 to 用於空間位移，其目標是一個實體（名詞）；而不定詞 to 用於時間上的位移，標記尚未發生的未來事件。

I went to his house. ➡ I went to tell him what happened.
空間上要到達的目標 ➡ 時間上要達到的目的（＝接下來要做的事）

➤ 「這是給你的」究竟是 "for you" 還是 "to you"？

To 是源於空間位移的「方向標的」，用來標記「授予對象」，即「接收者」；for 則是標記受益關係中的「受益者」，這兩種角色的對照如下：

I sent a birthday card to my mom. ➡ to a goal
I baked a birthday cake for my mom. ➡ for a beneficiary

To 的核心語意為目標方向（goal），所以從 A 轉移到 B 的「對象」要用to。但 for 不是空間關係，而是角色關係，主要功能是在表達「為誰的好處」，標記事件的「受益者」（beneficiary）。

學生會分不清楚 to 和 for，是因為換成中文，都可能變成「給」：
The book was sold to you.
➡ 我把書「賣給你」，你是我賣書的目標對象。
I bought the book for you.
➡ 我把書「買給你」，書是為你買的，所以你就變成買的受益者。

對中文來說，「目標」跟「受益者」這兩種關係，都合併在「給」這個詞裡，但英文選擇藉由 to 和 for 兩種不同的形式來區分這兩種不同的概念。

251

　　如上所述，介系詞核心語意都是最具體、最容易理解的空間概念，經過時空轉換後，發展出不同的延伸用法。接下來我們將以一些常用介系詞為例，示範如何透過掌握核心語意來理解介系詞的多樣延伸用法：

From	Toward	Along	Past	Opposite
In / inside	At	Behind	In front of	Above
On	Up	Down	Next to / by / beside	Against
Near	Off	Out of	Through	Across
Between	Round / around	Among	under	below
opposite	onto	into	from-to	over

➢ **over and beyond**

Over 的基本語意是 above 和 across 的意思，就像下圖所表示的概念：

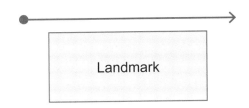

over 牽涉到物體移動的路徑（path），這個路徑是 "above and across a landmark"。

但路徑和地標都有延伸變化的可能，造就 over 的多重語意：

The plane flew over the mountain. ➡ 飛機飛越這座山

Sam lives over the hill. ➡ 指的是路徑最終的端點（翻過山丘的另一頭）

The painting is hung over the fireplace.
➡ 畫懸掛在火爐上方（靜態的關係）

The tablecloth is over the table. ➡ 桌巾覆蓋在桌面上

The guards were all over the place.
➡ 這裡四處都是警衛（路徑的概念就變成點狀的分佈）

I searched all over the place.
➡ 我找遍了這個地方（路徑也可變成連續的線狀延伸）

Over 的空間概念也可以延伸做其他抽象用法：

The play is over. ➡ 結束了 ➡ 沿用路徑終點的概念

I can't get over with it. ➡ 克服、渡過 ➡ 也是路徑延伸通過的意思

Beyond 的基本語意為「高於」，意即比某物還要高遠的地方，可延伸為「越過」的含意, 其空間概念如下圖所示（從高於到超過）：

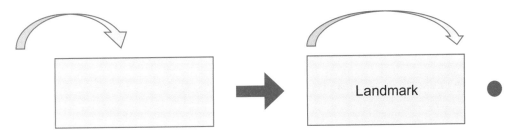

在使用上，beyond+NP（參考點）通常用於描述超越參考點之上或之外的語意：

Beyond this pasture, there's a river and some small mountains.

➡ 放牧場再過去是一條河和幾座小山

The dog came to the front door, but not beyond.

➡ 狗走到前門，但沒有再向前走

Beyond 的基本空間語意「高於／過於」，通過時空轉換，可轉為表達時間概念上的「遲於、晚於」：

Don't stay there beyond the visiting hours. ➡ 待在那兒別超過會客時間

再延伸至抽象概念中，beyond 可以用來表達「超出」數量、水準、限度，或是「超出」理解能力：

Golf is a great game for people beyond the age of 65.

➡ 高爾夫球對 65 歲以上的人而言是很棒的運動

Her beauty is beyond description.

➡ 她的美麗超過言語所能形容的程度，亦即她的美難以言喻

She has intelligence beyond the ordinary. ➡ 她聰明過人

With so many new words, this passage is beyond me.

➡ 這段文章生詞太多，對我而言實在太難了（超越我能理解的程度）

➤ Across and through

Across 的基本概念是「穿越平面」，through 的基本概念則是「通過隧道」：

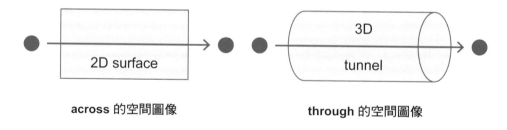

across 的空間圖像　　　　　through 的空間圖像

We walked across the street. ➡ 我們穿越馬路

因為 across 的核心概念為「橫越」，故可延伸為某物在參考點的「另一側」：

He stared at the Englishman across the table.

➡ 他盯著坐在桌子對面的那個英國人看（他的視線橫越桌面，盯著另一邊的英國人）

There's a bus stop just across the road. ➡ 馬路的另一側有個公車站

此外，「橫越」這個路徑概念也可以在抽象概念中延伸為「遍及各處」之意：

The TV series became popular across the country.

➡ 這部電視連續劇在全國各地廣受歡迎（這部電視劇的魅力橫掃全國）

Through 這個介係詞的空間概念則是強調「從這一點穿過一個實體」：

The train went through the tunnel. ➡ 火車穿過隧道

The wind whistled through tiny cracks in the wall. ➡ 風穿過牆上的隙縫

在時間概念中，through 可以延伸為「穿越時間範圍」，表達「從……開始至終」或「在……整個期間」之意：

He stayed there through the summer. ➡ 他在那裡住了一整個夏天

I'll be staying at camp for five days, Monday through Friday.

➡ 從星期一到星期五都會在營地

在抽象概念中，through 的「穿越」之意可以延伸為「透過某人或某物」或「憑藉」之意：

She got the position through her older brother.

➡ 她透過她哥哥獲得那個工作

We learned it through experience.

➡ 透過經驗的累積，我們學會了這件事

➤ **Under、below、beneath**

Under, below, beneath 皆可表示「在某物體的下方」，那麼這三者的語意有何不同呢？

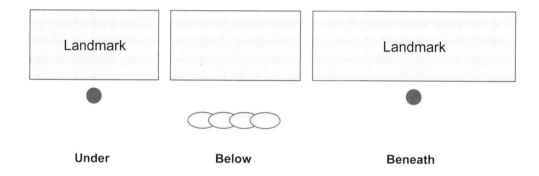

Under	**Below**	**Beneath**

　　Under 和 Below 的空間概念相近，皆為「位置低於參考物」（A is lower than B），但語意又不完全一樣: under表示「上下」位關係（在……下方）；below則表示「高低」關係（低於……）：The apple is under the table. ➡ 在桌子下方 The apple is below the table. ➡ 位置低於桌子

　　空間上兩者似乎都傳達「蘋果在桌子下方」的意思。

　　不過在非空間的語意上，below 和 under 仍有些許不同：under 通常指目標物在參考物的正下方。因為 under 是在「在參考物正下方」，所以我們可以用這個介系詞來表達「某個東西被另一個東西遮蓋隱藏住了」；

The cat is under the bed. ➡ 貓在床鋪下方（正下方）

　　　　　　　　　　　➡ (?)The cat is below the bed.

　　　　　　　　　　　➡ 我們比較不說：(?)貓低於床鋪

I hid the key under a rock.

　　　　　　　　　　➡ The key is under a rock. 鑰匙在石頭下（遮蓋住）

　　　　　　　　　　➡ (?)The key is below the table. 鑰匙低於石頭(?)

I'm under the blanket.　➡ 被子蓋住了我，我在被子底下

　　　　　　　　　　➡ (?)I'm below the blanket. 我低於被子(?)

　　不同於 under，below 表示「高低」相對位置，指出物件的相對位置低於參考物。舉例來說：

Moles are animals that live underground. Therefore, wherever a mole moves, it is always below the trees. ➡ 鼴鼠住在地底下，所以鼴鼠無論在地底下移動到何處，牠的相對位置一定比樹木低

The fish swims below the surface of the water. ➡ 魚在水面之下游動

這兩種不同的核心概念可以延伸到其他「非空間」的領域。舉例來說，under 的空間概念為「定點的正下方」，故我們可以用 under 來表示「數字或年齡小於某個數值」（less than/ younger than）：

You have to be under 18 to get an allowance.

➡ 年齡小於「18 歲」這個數值定點

We finished the project in under a year and a half.

➡ 時間少於「一年半」這個數值定點

The bag was just under 10 kilos, so I was able to bring it on the plane.

➡ 重量沒超過「10 公斤」這個數值定點

We were able to raise just under fifteen thousand dollars.

➡ 金額少於「15,000」這個數值定點

相對的，below 的空間概念涉及水平高低，可以延伸用於度量衡（measurement）的高低關係，表示在「水平、標準」之下：

It is 10 degrees below zero. ➡ 現在是零下十度

We're at 150 feet below sea level. ➡ 我們在海平面下 150 英尺處

His grades are below average. ➡ 他的成績低於平均水平

Below the poverty line ➡ 貧窮線之下

Below 除了表達「空間」位置的高低，也可以用來表示「非空間」位置的高低，如職位、地位等低於另一人：

His position in the company is below hers. ➡ 他在公司裡職位比她低

有趣的是，職位的高低也可轉換成權利結構的上下關係：

He is under her. 他在她以下 ➡ His position is lower than hers.

Beneath 的空間概念強調目標物在面積較大的「覆蓋面」之下，例如：

Much of that water remains hidden beneath the surface of Mars in the form of water ice.

➡ 水結凍成冰，隱藏在火星表層之下

They slept outside beneath the stars. ➡ 他們露宿在繁星之下

因為 beneath 傳達「在覆蓋面之下」的意象，所以也具有「在某物覆蓋

257

之下」之意。例如：We huddled together for warmth beneath the blankets.

Beneath 「在覆蓋面之下」的空間概念可以延伸用來表達非空間的能力或地位在他人認覆蓋之下：

He is beneath his brother intellectually. ➡ 他在智力方面不如他兄弟

He considered that job beneath him. ➡ 他認為做那個工作有失他的身分

> **Below and above**

如上所述，below 的空間概念為「相對位置在某物之下」，above 則是 below 的反義詞，其空間概念為「相對位置在某物之上」。

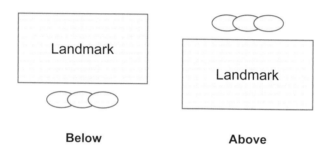

Below　　　　　**Above**

The moon is now above the trees. ➡ 月亮正位於樹梢之上

Can you raise your hand above your head? ➡ 將手舉高過頭頂

正如同 below，above 可以延伸用於衡量概念（measurement），表示「在某種水平、水平面、標準之上」：

Mexico City is 2,240 meters above sea level.

Temperatures above 25 degrees are rare in this part of the world.

His performance is above average.

雖然我們通常會使用 over 作為 under 的反義詞，表示「超過某數值」（more than），例如：

She is over 2 meters tall.

He weighs over 100 kilograms.

There were over 40 people at the party.

I've been waiting for over an hour.

不過表示年齡則是一項例外，over 和 above 皆可用來表示「年齡在……之上」（older than）：

The movie is suitable for children over/ above 13 years old. ➡ 這部電影適合13歲以上的孩童觀賞

> **Into and onto**

Into 的空間概念是「進入內部」，帶有三度空間（container）的含意；onto 的空間概念則是「到上面」，仍是接觸面（surface）的含意，如下圖所示：

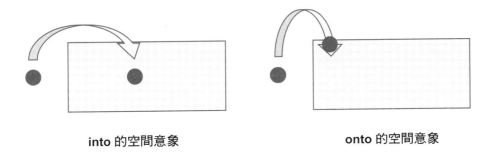

into 的空間意象   onto 的空間意象

The man walked into the house in the dark. ➡ 摸黑進入房間
The cat jumped onto the chair. ➡ 貓跳到椅子上

Into 的空間概念也可以延伸至時間領域，表示時間推移「進入到某時間範圍」：He worked late into the night. ➡ 他工作到深夜

Into 也可以用來表達事物的轉變，「進入」一種新的狀態中；或是用來表示某人「投入」某個領域：

All the buildings had been turned into hospitals.
➡ 所有大樓都改成了醫院。
She is really into yoga. ➡ 她很喜歡瑜珈

Onto 的核心語意為「到上面」，在抽象概念中可以想像為「踩到某個重要的東西」，意即「發現／做了某件重要的事」：

When the crowd responded to the show so positively, we realized we were onto something.

259

➡ 群眾的正面回饋，讓我們領悟自己做了一件挺了不起的事

I think you could be onto something here.

➡ 你有可能發現了一件了不得的大事

文法小撇步：總結來說，介系詞具有「時空轉換」及「認知轉換」的特性，其核心語意為空間概念，經過時空轉換後，可延伸至時間或其他抽象領域，每一次的延伸與轉換，就構成一個新的語意。

 ## 3. 還能怎麼說？

單元1 用於標示一段時間的 in 和 for 有何不同？

前一章節提到 in 可用於標示任何「一段時間範疇之內」的概念，如：

I finished the homework in an hour. ➡ 一個小時之內完成的

另一介系詞 for 似乎也可表示「一段時間」，如：

I have stayed here for three days. ➡ 在這待了三天

那麼 in 和 for 在標記一段時間上究竟有何不同？ in 的空間原型是「在範圍內」，強調「界限範疇」（boundary）；而 for 則是標記「一段持續的時間」，強調「持續時程」（duration）：

He will be here in 5 minutes. ➡ 5 分鐘之內會到這（界限範圍）

He will be here for 5 minutes. ➡ 會待在這 5 分鐘（持續時間）

單元2 誰是介系詞片語的修飾對象？

介系詞片語（Prepositional Phrase）就是介系詞加名詞所組成的單位（P + NP），基本上是用來標示處所地點或空間關係，可跟在名詞後面，當作名詞的修飾語，指出人或物的所在地：

A pot on the table

A girl in the room

不過當句子中有好幾個參與者時，到底介系詞片語會修飾誰呢？舉例來說，"I saw a dog in the car." 有三種可能的解讀方式：

可能一：I was in the car.

可能二：The dog was in the car.

可能三：Both the dog and I were in the car.

這種語意上的曖昧不明是因為介系詞片語不一定會和其修飾對象緊緊相連。

如此一來，介系詞片語的出現可能會讓一個句子的意思產生多種可能性。從形義搭配的角度來看，這種現象是因為介系詞片語與修飾對象間之間的解讀有著「一對多」的關係，如上述例子所示。

不過在現實生活中，介系詞片語造成的歧義通常不會造成溝通困難，這是因為日常生活中的對話都是在情境（context）中發生，上下文的情境往往使我們選擇最有可能的解讀。

➢ 介系詞片語的延伸角色

正如同介系詞可以從空間概念延伸發展出不同語意，介系詞片語和不同的名詞合用也可以形成不同的角色功能。例如，with 本來是表達空間上同時存在的「相伴」關係，但也可延伸出其他語意：

a man with long hair ➡ 擁有（長頭髮）

He wrote the letter with caution. ➡ 態度（小心翼翼）

I opened the can with a knife. ➡ 工具（用刀）

後兩句的介系詞片語是用來說明動作的態度或方式，等同於副詞（修飾動詞或形容詞）的功能，也可改用對應的副詞：

He wrote the letter cautiously. (= with caution) ➡ 小心翼翼的態度

He made the tool manually. (= with hands) ➡ 用手工的方式

單元3 介系詞和介副詞有何不同？

介系詞是「介詞」，介詞是「介於」名詞間，後面一定要有名詞；介副

詞是「副詞」，用來修飾動詞，位置可變動。所以，介系詞一定要跟著名詞走，介副詞卻可以自由移動。

介系詞跟著名詞走：

He turned to <u>his boss for help</u>. ➡ 後面要接名詞！

He turned to.（✕）➡ 文法錯誤，後面一定要有名詞！

介副詞可自由移動：

I turned on <u>the computer</u>. ➡ 放在名詞前，強調名詞訊息

I turned it on. ➡ 放在代名詞後，強調on

The computer is on. ➡ 單獨出現，表結果狀態

介副詞表達既像副詞又像介系詞的兩種語意，既標記動詞相關的副詞語意，也標記名詞的空間狀態。但基本上，因為是副詞，所以可以單獨出現，表示結果狀態。

以下的對照，介系詞不能脫離名詞單獨出現，但是介副詞可以：

I put the book on the table. ➡ The book is on?（✕）➡ 無此說法，介系詞必須接名詞，「on the table」是一個詞組

I turned on the microphone. ➡ The microphone is on. ➡ 表示「麥可風打開了」的結果狀態

He took his shoes off the car. ➡ The shoes are off the car. ➡ 鞋子被帶離車子，「off the car」是一個詞組

He took off his shoes. ➡ The shoes are off. ➡ 表示「鞋子脫掉了」的結果狀態

單元4 相同的動詞與介系詞搭配，為何會產生不同語意？

He <u>took off</u> the jacket. ➡ 脫掉夾克

The airplane <u>took off</u>. ➡ 飛機起飛

The airplane <u>was taken off</u> the runway. ➡ 被拖離跑道

這三句的動詞都一樣，但是語意不同，這是因為句子是不同成份組合產生的。上面三種用法除了動詞外，句子裡還有其他元素可以幫助我們釐清語意。所以，「飛機」作主詞時的動詞語意，和飛機作受詞時當然不一樣。

同樣，"put out" 是「拿出來」，還是「撲滅」也要考慮周邊的語意成分：

The TV show put out one episode each week. ➡ The show is on each week. ➡ 上演了

He put out the fire. ➡ The fire is out. ➡ 撲滅了

從「形意搭配」的角度來看，"put out" 的語意仍有 put 和 out 結合的軌跡："put something out" 是「拿出來」，out 與動詞分離，所以保持了副詞 out 原始的語意；對照 "put out the fire"，put out 為一個不可分離的詞組，又和 fire 合用，自然和「拿出來」的語意不同：

Put the fire out! ➡ 把火拿出來

Put out the fire! ➡ 把火熄滅

單元5 介系詞與情緒狀態

情緒狀態的後面為何要用不同的介系詞？我們還是必須回到介系詞的核心概念來理解：

I'm afraid of math. afraid of 後的受詞表「成因內含」。

I'm interested in math. interested 的介系詞 in 意表「沈浸其中」。

I'm amazed at his math ability. amazed at 後的受詞表「目標對象」。

I'm attracted by his math ability. ➡ by force ➡ 表「助力來源」。

不同的介系詞有不同的原型語意，我們必須先觀察情緒動詞側重的語意與哪個介系詞語意相符，才能決定該如何搭配。

單元6 介系詞的其他用法

➤ 介系詞搭配 BE 動詞

in	I'm in; she is out. ➡ in / out 是「在內/在外」，指「參不參加在內」
	She is into yoga. ➡ into 是「進入」，有「熱衷……」的意思
for	Are you for or against the plan? ➡ for 是「為了」，有「支持」的意思 ➡ against 是「牴觸」，有「反對」的意思
	He can't sleep for coughing. ➡ for 是「為了」，有「因為」的意思
on	The dinner is on me. ➡ on 是「在上」，有「在……身上」的意思
	He is on drugs. ➡ on 是「在上」，有「在使用……」的意思

➤ 介系詞後面不加名詞時，可以當作形容詞來使用：

off	She is off today. ➡ off 表示「脫離」工作
	The TV is off. ➡ off 表示「脫離」電源
	He is off on a trip. ➡ off 表示「脫離」此處
	We prefer to travel in the off season. ➡ off 表示「脫離」旺季

on	The radio is on. ➡ on 表示「在電源上」	
	She is on tomorrow. ➡ on 表示「在工作上」（上班）	
	What's on in Vieshow Cinemas now? ➡ on 表示「在螢幕上」（上演）	
	The demonstration is still on. ➡ on 表示「在平面上」 ➡ 在時間上出現	
up	Hey, what's up? ➡ up 表示「上來」 ➡ 出現發生 ➡ 最近有什麼新鮮事嗎？	
	Time is up. ➡ up 表示「上來」 ➡ 上到盡頭 ➡ 時間到了	

➤ 特殊語境下介系詞用法

Coming out	"Coming out" 或 "Coming out of the closet" 的意思是「同性戀公開出櫃」，這個用法源自英文俚語 "skeleton in the closet"（家中見不得人的醜事），因為同性戀者在傳統社會中較受歧視，故被比喻為櫥櫃裡的骷髏。「躲在衣櫥裡的人」意指隱藏有同性戀傾向的人，"coming out" 則代表「出櫃」。
Be into someone	正如同 "into something" 意指「進入其中」，也就是「熱衷於某事」，"Be into someone" 可以用來表達「對某人有興趣」或「喜歡某人」。舉例來說，有部電影叫做 "He's just not that into you"，中文就翻作「他其實沒那麼喜歡妳」。
Have a crush on someone	喜歡某人也可用「擠壓面」的意象："I have a crush on him / her." 這裡用 on 表示施力及接觸面的含意。

On and off	"On and off" 可以用來表示情侶「分分合合」、「藕斷絲連」的狀態 ➡ "My girlfriend and I have been on and off for a few years."
Down with something	"Be down with something" 可以用來表達「因為某個疾病病倒」，例如："He was down with the flu last week." 在不同語境下，"Down with something" 可以用來表示「打倒某件事物」，例如："Down with racism!"（打倒種族主義！）

 ## 4. 讀一段短文

Record-breaking Athlete

Michael Phelps made sports history by winning twenty-eight medals, 23 of them gold medals, at the 2008 Olympics in Beijing, China, at the 2012 Olympics in London, and at the 2016 Olympics in Rio de Janeiro. Born on June 30, 1985, Phelps was just 15 years old when he qualified for the Sydney Australia Olympics in 2000. Phelps shattered the 200 meter butterfly by swimming it in record time. He swam it in 1:54:58 seconds. He went on to break many more records at the 2004 Athens Olympics. In August 2008, he arrived at the Beijing Olympic games determined to break, former Olympic swimmer, Mark Spitz' 6-gold medal record. He qualified to compete in three team and five individual events. He swam 17 races in nine days and won gold medal in all eight events. On August 16, Phelps won his seventh gold medal of the Games in the men's 100-meter butterfly event, setting an Olympic record for the event. He did it in 50.58 seconds, edging out his nearest competitor by 1/100 of a second. When his team won the 4 X 100 meter medley relay, he stood on the podium overwhelmed with emotion as he received his eighth record-breaking medal.

In 2016, Phelps was chosen to be the flag bearer for the US Olympic team in Rio de Janeiro. He went on to win five more gold and one silver medal. On August 13, in the 4 × 100-meter medley relay, Phelps ended his career with another medal, his 23rd gold and his 28th medal overall. Incredibly, at age 31, Michael Phelps broke a 2,168-year-old ancient Olympic record, set by Leonidas of Rhodes, who had held the most Olympic individual titles of all time.

註解：1.「in + 一段時間」在……之內。2. "He went on to break...",「go on +
to V」繼續做下一件事。而「go on + V-ing」則是繼續之前做的事情。3. "...
Michael Phelps <u>broke</u> a ... Olympic record, <u>set</u> by Leonidas of Rhodes..." 整
句話的意思為，Michael Phelps 破了 Leoniidas of Rhodes 所創下的紀錄。
這句話主要動詞為 broke，Olympic record 後的 set 為過去分詞，意思為被
創下紀錄，by 則是接之前創紀錄的人。

5. 唱一首英文歌

In The Ghetto

(By Elvis Presley)

As the snow flies
On a cold and gray Chicago morning
A poor little baby child is born
In the ghetto
And his mama cries
Cause if there's one thing that she don't need
Its another hungry mouth to feed
In the ghetto

People, don't you understand
The child needs a helping hand
Or he will grow to be an angry young man some day
Take a look at you and me,
Are we too blind to see,
Do we simply turn our heads
And look the other way

Well the world turns
And a hungry little boy with a runny nose
Plays in the street as the cold wind blows
In the ghetto

And his hunger burns
So he starts to roam the streets at night
And he learns how to steal
And he learns how to fight
In the ghetto

Then one night in desperation
A young man breaks away
He buys a gun, steals a car,
Tries to run, but he don't get far
And his mama cries

As a crowd gathers round an angry young man
Face down on the street with a gun in his hand
In the ghetto

As her young man dies,
On a cold and gray Chicago morning,
Another little baby child is born
In the ghetto

https://www.youtube.com/watch?v=2Ox1Tore9nw (https://bit.ly/2PWgxZg)

 6. 看一部影片

A Lesson in Prepositions Brought To You By Sean Spicer's Bushes
https://www.youtube.com/watch?v=XfldlvS_mYg
(https://bit.ly/2zTnvTR)
"Preposition" (by The Bazillions)
https://www.youtube.com/watch?v=byszemY8Pl8
(https://bit.ly/2PWiFAe)

7. 做一點練習

Part 1：填空題

請依照文意，在下列空格中填入介系詞 in 或 on

1. All the students will work _____ a collaborative environment.

2. They need to concentrate _____ their studies.

3. They will be placed _____ a range of community settings.

4. The essay will be _____ a topic you have studied recently.

5. The researchers are reliant _____ external funding.

6. This course provides the opportunity to focus _____ your major area of interest.

7. You will study this _____ a social context.

8. The course is _____ the boundary of advanced engineering and science.

9. This degree appeals to students who are interested _____ working in the new fields and occupations created by digitization.

10. I don't know what we'll do at the weekend. It depends _____ the weather.

Part 2：克漏字（選項可重複）

(A) for	(B) to	(C) on	(D) in	(E) across
(F) by	(G) around	(H) inside	(I) within	(J) beyond
(K) beside	(L) with	(M) toward	(N) between	(O) from

    My neighbor said she wanted to ask me __1__ a small favor. Little did I know what was __2__ store __3__ me when I agreed to feed her cat. After my neighbor left __4__ her trip, I walked __5__ the street __6__ her house. Once I got __7__ the house, I was overwhelmed __8__ the stench of cat urine. I looked __9__ the house and couldn't believe what I saw. My eyes fell __10__ two salad dressing containers sitting __11__ a table __12__ the couch, which was completely covered __13__ dirty laundry, except for this one worn area by the table. The volume __14__ the TV was turned up all the way. In disbelief and despite my better judgment, I walked __15__ the restroom. __16__ the base of the tub I saw these red velvety mushrooms coming up __17__ the tub and tile floor. This filth was __18__ anything I'd ever seen __19__ my life.
    __20__ two minutes the cat was fed and I was out of there. Since she returned __21__ her trip, I have never been available to watch her cat again.

填空題答案：

1. in	2. on	3. in	4. on	5. on
6. on	7. in	8. on	9. in	10. on

克漏字答案：

1. A	2. D	3. A	4. C	5. E
6. B	7. H	8. F	9. G	10. C
11. C	12. K	13. L	14. C	15. M
16. G	17. N	18. J	19. D or C	20. I
21. O				

註解：1. "in store for sb" 即將發生在某人身上的事。2. "eyes fall on..." 注意到……。3. "in disbelief" 不相信。4. between A and B。5. "beyond anything I'd ever seen..." 超過了我此生看過的所有東西，就是程度誇張的意思。6. "within two minutes" 兩分鐘內。

Part 3：填空題

請依照文意，在下列空格中填入介系詞 until、since 或 for

1. Sue and Dave have been married _____ 1968.

2. I was tired this morning. I stayed in bed _____ 10 o'clock.

3. We waited for Sue _____ half an hour, but she didn't come.

4. "Have you just arrived?" "No, I've been here _____ half past seven."

5. Dan and I are good friends. We have known each other _____ ten years.

6. I am tired. I am going to lie down _____ a few minutes.

7. Don't open the door of the train _____ the train stops.

8. This is my house. I have lived here _____ I was seven years old.

9. Next week I am going to Paris _____ three days.

10. I usually finish work at 5:30, but sometimes I work _____ 6.

Part 4：克漏字（選項可重複）

(A) of	(B) to	(C) on	(D) in	(E) down
(F) at	(G) into	(H) inside	(I) from	

    Francis Macomber had, half an hour before, been carried __1__ his tent __2__ the edge __3__ the camp __4__ triumph __5__ the arms and shoulders __6__ the cook, the personal boys, the skinner and the porters. The gun-bearers had taken no part __7__ the demonstration. When the native boys put him __8__ __9__ the door __10__ his tent, he had shaken all their hands, received their congratulations, and then gone __11__ the tent and sat __12__ the bed until his wife came __13__. She did not speak __14__ him when she came __15__ and he left the tent __16__ once to wash his face and hands __17__ the portable wash basin outside and go over __18__ the dining tent to sit __19__ a comfortable canvas chair __20__ the breeze and the shade.

填空題答案：

1. since	2. until	3. for	4. since	5. for
6. for	7. until	8. since	9. for	10. until

克漏字答案：

1. B	2. I	3. A	4. D	5. C
6. A	7. D	8. E	9. F	10. A
11. G	12. C	13. D	14. B	15. D
16. F	17. D	18. B	19. D or C	20. D

Part 5：選擇題

1. She paid for lunch _____ advance, so we don't need to pay now.
   (A) on   (B) at   (C) in

2. I went to the wrong house _____ mistake.
   (A) on   (B) by   (C) with

3. Please make sure that you're _____ time for the class.

   (A) in   (B) on   (C) at

4. I was walking to the station and _____ chance I saw the glove that I'd lost on the ground.

   (A) by   (B) in   (C) on

5. I love eating out in London. _____ instance, one of my favorite restaurants has amazing Japanese food.

   (A) At   (B) For   (C) On

6. I think the cat is _____ danger on that high roof.

   (A) in   (B) on   (C) at

7. I picked up the laptop and _____ my surprise it fell apart in my hands.

   (A) to   (B) at   (C) in

8. I have a lot _____ common with my cousin. We both like many of the same things.

   (A) of   (B) with   (C) in

9. If the baby starts to cry, pick her up _____ once.

   (A) for   (B) at   (C) in

10. Did you forget your purse _____ purpose so you wouldn't have to pay?

   (A) on   (B) at   (C) in

填空題答案：

1. in	2. on	3. to	4. in	5. of
6. on	7. of	8. in	9. on	10. of
11. to	12. in	13. in	14. of	15. in
16. to	17. for	18. on	19. on	20. from
21. to	22. of	23. in		

選擇題答案：

1. C	2. B	3. B	4. A	5. B
6. A	7. A	8. C	9. B	10. A

註解：1. in advance 預先。2. by mistake 弄錯。3. on time 準時。4. by chance 碰巧。5. for instance 例如。6. in danger 有危險的。7. to one's surprise 讓某人驚訝。8. have...in common 有共同之處。9. at once 立刻。10. on purpose 故意。

10

規則之外

1. 你想說什麼？

為什麼語言法則會有例外的存在？

　　首先，我們必須重新探討語法規則的存在目的：語法是一套為了溝通而產生的「形意搭配」的法則，這套法則必定存在著一定的共通性，以便能夠讓說話者清楚了解彼此傳達的訊息。

　　因此，在多數情況下，我們會遵循常用的語法規則來溝通，好讓對方理解我們的訊息。但是有時我們會為了特殊的目的，表達特別的語意，這時就必須選擇不同於常規的特殊標記，這就是為什麼語法規則總有例外！

　　由此可見，語言中的規則或例外都是為了達成溝通目的而存在。

　　語法規則其實是「多數原則」，意即：大多數人，在大多數情況下，為著大多數的目的，所使用「溝通策略」通則。例外則是少數人，在少數情況下，為少數的目的，所使用的少數另類的「溝通策略」。

2. 英文怎麼說？

單元1 I'm loving it! 傳達什麼語意？

　　動詞的語意範圍分為兩大類：動態的「活動」（activity / action）或靜態的「狀態」（situation / state）。「活動」是變動的，會隨時間推移而有改變；「狀態」是相對穩定的屬性，較持久不變。

　　動態動詞又可分外在的體力活動（如：run）和內在的心力活動（如：think）；靜態動詞則表達感知（如："I know the answer."）或情緒狀態（如："I like her."）。

　　動態和靜態這兩類動詞最大的差別在於：動態動詞牽涉到力的運用變化，可隨時間不斷變動前進，所以可搭配表示 ongoing 的「進行式」，表示

持續存在。靜態動詞則表達持久不變的狀態，不涉及體力或心力的運作、不會隨時間改變，就不能用在進行式。

　　舉例而言，love 這個動詞屬於表達情感狀態的靜態動詞，所以在一般語法規則之下，love 通常不會和進行貌合用：

　　我們會說 "The fans love Jeremy Lin." ➡ 不會說：(×)The fans are loving Jeremy Lin.

　　這是一個通則，意即在大多數情況下大多數人為了大多數的目的所使用的原則。

　　但是麥當勞卻違反「狀態無進行」的通則，硬要說 "I'm loving it!" 這是為何？

　　麥當勞的廣告標語 "I'm loving it!" 看似文法錯誤，其實是為了表達特殊語意而刻意將 love 加上「-ing」，透過進行貌的動態語意把「心動」變成了「行動」。這個用法，並不是破壞規則，而是利用「形意搭配」的原則所做的特殊運用！

　　所有的狀態動詞加上「-ing」，就轉變為動態語意了：
　　I am having a cup of coffee.　　➡ drinking
　　I am seeing my advisor now.　　➡ meeting
　　He is being ridiculous.　　➡ acting

單元2 可數／不可數名詞的規則與例外

　　我們在第四章提到，可數／不可數名詞的區別在於可否「個體化」。rice和 sand 之所以為不可數名詞，是因為在大多數的情況下，大多數的人使用rice 這個詞的時候，不會把它「個體化」，不會再細分米粒，而是把一堆米當作一個整體來看，在認知和使用上，是「整體不可分」的概念。故rice 這個名詞在常態語法規則中屬於不可數名詞。

275

然而，判斷名詞可否「個體化」、屬於可數還是不可數名詞的決定仍取決於人的認知選擇。因此，可不可數的區別是以認知和使用的常態來區分，但有時為了表達特別的語意，就可能打破常規。

　　例如，在特別的米食大會上，有人想要強調多樣不同的米種，也可能刻意把 rice 加上「-s」："I bought a variety of "rices"." 這樣例外的用法，就是要表達例外的語意！

　　再舉一例：literature 一字在語法規則中為不可數名詞，指「文學」。
　　這是因為大多數人在大多數情況下使用 literature 這個詞是要為了表達「文類／學門」這種整體的概念，不會再做細分。
　　不過在少數情況下，literature 會作為可數名詞使用。外文系的名稱是 "Department of Foreign Languages and Literatures"。這是因為外文系為了表達少數特殊的語意，強調要教的是多種多樣的文學（如小說、散文、戲劇、英國文學、美國文學），而故意加上「-s」，藉由複數的標記表達多元化的文學研究，表示文學還可再細分為不同的文學類型。

　　所以，「規則」是溝通的常態，是大多數人在大多數的情境中，為了大多數的目的所使用的方式；「例外」就是少數人在少數特殊情境下，為了少數目的，所使用的特殊搭配方式！

單元3 現在分詞和動名詞如何區分？

　　第八章中提到現在分詞（present participle）的形式都是用來表達主動的關係，過去分詞（past participle）的形式則都是用來表達被動的關係：

現在分詞：Helping my mom, I volunteered to do the dishes.
過去分詞：Helped by my mom, I finished doing the dishes in 30 minutes.

　　分詞除了可出現在附屬子句，修飾主要主詞外，還可當形容詞，修飾相關的名詞：
現在分詞：a heart-breaking experience ➡ 令人傷心的經歷

過去分詞：a <u>heart-broken</u> man ➡ 被傷透心的男人

但由於「現在分詞」的形式和「動名詞」一致，都是 V-ing，這兩者有時不容易分清。以下兩例中，形式類似的 V-ing，因為執行不同的溝通功能，而有不同的身份。前者是形容詞性的現在分詞，後者為名詞性的修飾語：

現在分詞做形容詞 ➡ a sleeping baby ➡ 睡覺的嬰兒 ＝ a baby who is sleeping

動詞名物化 ➡ a flying machine ➡ 動名詞＋名詞組成的複合名詞（N＋N）

➡ 飛行器（專門術語）≠ a machine that is flying

這裡的 flying 在功能上是動名詞（動詞作名詞），因為 machine 不會飛，所以 "flying machine" 通常不是指「在飛的機器」（溝通意涵不合常理），而是指一個專門的術語「飛行器」；這是兩個名詞組成的複合名詞（N ＋ N compound）：

driving license 駕照 ≠ a license that is driving
swimming pool 游泳池 ≠ a pool that is swimming

如果 flying 和其他可能會飛的名詞合用，溝通意涵上較合理自然，就成為常見的現在分詞做形容詞，表示「正在飛」的東西：

a flying plane = a plane that is flying ➡ 在飛的飛機
a flying kite = a kite that is flying ➡ 在飛的風箏
a flying balloon = a balloon that is flying ➡ 在飛的氣球

單元4 介副詞為什麼要放在名詞前，代名詞後？

我們背過的規則是：介副詞要放在名詞前、代名詞後。例如：

I turned <u>on</u> **the radio**.
I turned **it** <u>on</u>.
I turned <u>in</u> **the homework**.
I turned **it** <u>in</u>.

如果我們從溝通的角度考量，這項規則其實有其道理。介副詞不同於一般的介系詞，多了副詞性的功能，因此可以移動，但是只能放在名詞前，不能放在名詞後。原因是名詞有無限延展的可能，如果名詞太長，介副詞放在名詞後面就會妨礙溝通，試讀下面這個句子：

I turned [the small radio that was on the round table near the large window in the beautiful living room in his new house] on.

若是長長一串名詞後才加上介副詞 on，可能早就忘了動詞是什麼了，容易造成理解上的困擾。另一方面，語意比重也是考量因素，名詞通常承載較新、較重要的訊息（new information），所以放在最後 "turn on the radio"。同理，on 放在代名詞後 "turn it on"，也可能有兩個原因：其一，與介系詞的用法有所區隔；其二，代名詞是已知訊息，語意上介副詞比代名詞的訊息更新更重要，因此傾向放在後面。

單元5 冠詞標記的例外

當一個名詞沒有單、複數及冠詞的標準標記時，這個名詞的溝通功能也從「標準、典型」語意轉變為其他較特殊的語意。

"go home" 和 "go to school" 中的名詞「home、school」 不再是指實體可數的建築物，而是指其「社會功能」：

She goes to school every day.

➡ 上學讀書受教育，而不是指去學校這個地點

She went to the school yesterday.

➡ 到學校這個地點做別的事

> **In summer 和 in the summer 有何不同？**

　　春夏秋冬這些季節名詞和專有名詞相仿，因為聽者只要聽到 summer 就知道講者指的「夏天」這個季節，既然「僅此一家，毫無疑義」，也就不需要額外用冠詞來標記。故在一般通則之下，季節名詞不需要以冠詞或定冠詞標記：

In summer, we like to go hiking.

　　不過如果想要強調的<u>不是</u>泛指夏天這個季節，而是某一年的「那個夏天」，就必須加上定冠詞："<u>the</u> summer of 2010"，定冠詞 the 用於標記「明確可認定」的那一個夏天：

The picture was taken in the summer of 2017.
The spring was foul this year—it was cold and wet for weeks.
It was a great summer that we all enjoyed.

　　總結而言，用於通稱時，季節名詞泛指四季節令 "It gets really cold in winter."，沒有特定的時間點，所以不需要以冠詞標記。不過在「特指」的情況下，要表達某一年的某一季節，則要用<u>時間詞</u>或<u>定冠詞</u>來標記「明確可認定」的那一個季節 "It got really cold last summer." 或 "It got really cold in the winter I went to Canada."。

➤ This 可以用來指涉還沒有出現過的事物嗎？

This / that / these / those 屬於指示代名詞（demonstrative pronoun）是用來代稱前文剛剛提過、或是在對話情境中出現的事物：

This ➡ 靠近說話者的 ➡ 說話者自己提過的論點

That ➡ 遠離說話者的 ➡ 對方提出的論點

空間物體：

This is really delicious; how do you make it?

What is that? I've never seen something like that!

話語論點：

Artificial Intelligence (AI) will surpass human capacity. This is the fear of humans.

"How shall we raise money?" "That is the question."

上述為指示代名詞的使用通則，不過有時也會有例外出現：

I have this friend, who is a novelist. ➡ 第一次提到的新訊息

在一般情況下，當闡述一件事的時候，剛開始聽者對傳達的內容還一無所知，必須先把指涉對象建立起來，所以第一次介紹的人物都用 a，之後才用 the 或是代名詞來指稱。

但是上述例句特別使用 this 來標記第一次出場的人物，這種例外用法是為了傳達特殊的溝通目的：提示聽者這個未知人物的獨特性和可辨識性，營造出一種「生動熟悉」的氛圍，彷彿這位特定朋友在對話的當下就站在講者和聽者旁邊。

由此可見，語法規則是多數人在多數情況下所使用的普遍「溝通策略」。例外則是少數人在少數情況下，為著特定的溝通目的，所使用的另類「溝通策略」！

單元6 動詞在非典型句式中的用法

有些動詞和特定句式結合後會產生新的延伸語意，例如：

He elbowed his way out.（他用手肘奮力推擠出人群。）➡ elbow 變成及物動詞，代表「用肘推，擠出」一條出路。

"I baked him a cake."（我烤了一個蛋糕給他）➡ bake 這個動詞後面接了兩個受詞，一個為間接受詞「him」，一個為直接受詞「a cake」。這樣的雙受詞句式（V-NP-NP）強調「我為送他而烤了蛋糕」的傳遞語意。

"She sneezed the napkin off the table."（她打噴嚏太大力，把餐巾紙吹到桌子下面了。）➡ sneeze 變成及物動詞，「打噴嚏」這個動作進入「使動結構」（caused motion construction），而得到特有的使動語意。

 ## 3. 還能怎麼說？

單元1 一對多的形意搭配

語法規則是為了方便溝通訊息而存在，但是規則有其侷限，標記形式和語意間並非總是「一對一」完美的配搭關係，有時會出現句子的表層形式相同（one form）但深層語意不同（different meanings）。我們可以在以下句子中看到這種語意上的歧義性：

I saw a man on a hill with a telescope.

關鍵在於介系詞片語 "on a hill" 和 "with a telescope" 是用來修飾 I 還是 "a man"？此句可以用下列三種方式來解讀：

> I saw a man on a hill with a telescope.
> 我在山上，用望遠鏡看到了一個男人（I was on a hill, and I saw a man using a telescope.）

> I saw a man on a hill with a telescope.
> 我用望遠鏡看到山上的男人（There's a man on a hill, and I was watching him with my telescope.）

> I saw a man on a hill with a telescope.

我看到山上拿著望遠鏡的男人（There was a man on a hill, who I saw, and he had a telescope.）

He fed her cat food.

關鍵在於動詞 feed 的受詞是 her 還是 her cat？此句可以用下列兩種方式來解讀：

> He fed her cat food.

他餵了她的貓（He fed a woman's cat some food.）

> He fed her cat food.

他餵她吃貓糧（He fed a woman some food that was intended for cats.）

One morning I shot an elephant in my pajamas.

關鍵在於介系詞片語 "in my pajamas" 是用來修飾 I 還是 "an elephant"？此句可以用下列兩種方式來解讀：

> One morning I shot an elephant in my pajamas.
> 有天早上，我穿著睡衣開槍打了一隻大象（I was in my pajamas while shooting the elephant.）。

> One morning I shot an elephant in my pajamas.
> 有天早上，我開槍打了一隻穿著我的睡衣的大象（I shot an elephant who was wearing my pajamas.）。

雖然形式和語意間不是完美的、一對一的搭配，但是語言仍舊可以達成流暢的溝通，這就是語法標記和使用情境間相互輔助、彼此關聯的結果。對話當下的情境、主題、人物、背景、時地、上下文等因素都有助雙方彼此理解，並減少誤解。

語言是活的，是變動的，因為使用語言的人是活的，是有創造力的。但

語言中的形意搭配原則是固定的，用 A 的形式就有 A 的語意，這是不變的！所以語言規則不是數學定理，而多數的使用原則；少數的例外則是為了另類語意而選擇的另類標記方式！

總結：
語言學習的重點是充分了解形式和意義的搭配原則，然後要表達什麼語意，就選擇什麼形式。這就是從理解到活用的不二法門！

 ## 4. 讀一段短文

> **Look Homeward, Angel.**
>
> He remembered yet the East India Tea House at the Fair, the sandalwood, the turbans, and the robes, the cool interior and the smell of India tea; and he had felt now the nostalgic thrill of dew-wet mornings in Spring, the cherry scent, the cool clarion earth, the wet loaminess of the garden, the pungent breakfast smells and the floating snow of blossoms. He knew the inchoate sharp excitement of hot dandelions in young earth; in July, of watermelons bedded in sweet hay, inside a farmer's covered wagon; of cantaloupe and crated peaches; and the scent of orange rind, bitter-sweet, before a fire of coals. He knew the good male smell of his father's sitting-room; of the smooth worn leather sofa, with the gaping horse-hair rent; of the blistered varnished wood upon the hearth; of the heated calf-skin bindings; of the flat moist plug of apple tobacco, stuck with a red flag; of wood-smoke and burnt leaves in October; of the brown tired autumn earth; of honey-suckle at night; of warm nasturtiums, of a clean ruddy farmer who comes weekly with printed butter, eggs, and milk; of fat limp underdone bacon and of coffee; of a bakery-oven in the wind; of large deep-hued string beans smoking-hot and seasoned well with salt and butter; of a room of old pine boards in which books and carpets have been stored, long closed; of Concord grapes in their long white baskets.

註解：1. covered wagon，有蓋起來的馬車。2. "smooth worn leather sofa" 磨的很平滑的沙發。3 gape（v.）為裂開、張開之意，變成現在分詞 gaping 開口大的，當形容詞用。4. deep-hued 是形容詞＋名詞變成的過去分詞，deep + hue+ed→ deep-hued 深色調的。5. 豆子燙到冒煙，被鹽巴、奶油調味。前面分詞為現在分詞，後面是被動地被調味，所以是過去分詞。

Don't Stop Believin'
(By Journey)

Just a small town girl

Livin' in a lonely world

She took the midnight train goin' anywhere

Just a city boy

Born and raised in south Detroit

He took the midnight train goin' anywhere

A singer in a smoky room

A smell of wine and cheap perfume

For a smile they can share the night

It goes on and on, and on, and on

Strangers waiting

Up and down the boulevard

Their shadows searching in the night

Streetlights, people

Living just to find emotion

Hiding somewhere in the night

Working hard to get my fill

Everybody wants a thrill

Payin' anything to roll the dice

Just one more time

Some will win, some will lose

Some were born to sing the blues

Oh, the movie never ends

It goes on and on, and on, and on

Strangers waiting

Up and down the boulevard

Their shadows searching in the night

Streetlights, people

Living just to find emotion

Hiding somewhere in the night

Don't stop believin'

Hold on to the feelin'

Streetlights, people

https://www.youtube.com/watch?v=1k8craCGpgs (https://bit.ly/2PODmxX)

註解：1. "Living in a lonely world, she took the midnight train going anywhere." 前後主詞一致，故可使用現在分詞。2. "Born and raised in south Detroit, he took the midnight train going anywhere" 前後主詞一致，男孩是在底特律出生被養大的，所以用過去分詞。

6. 看一部影片

Structural Ambiguity

7. 做一點練習

Part 1：填空題
請在下列空格中填入現在分詞或過去分詞

1. He saw his friend _____ (go) out with Sue.
2. The bus crashed into the blue car _____ (drive) down the hill.
3. Peter hurt his leg _____ (do) karate.
4. The umbrella _____ (find) at the bus stop belongs to John Smith.
5. The people _____ (dance) in the street are all very friendly.
6. I heard my mother _____ (talk) on the phone.
7. My uncle always has his car _____ (wash).
8. We stood _____ (wait) for the taxi.
9. _____ (look) down from the tower we saw many people walking in the streets.
10. The people drove off in a _____ (steal) car.

Part 2：選擇題
1. The people I work with are _____ with their jobs.
   a. satisfied
   b. satisfying

2. John was _____ by the the news report.

    a. disgusting

    b. disgusted

3. We thought that the instructions were _____ .

    a. confused

    b. confusing

4. It's an _____ little story. You should read it.

    a. amusing

    b. amused

5. Working late every day is _____ .

    a. tired

    b. tiring

6. I'm not really _____ in sport.

    a. interested

    b. interesting

7. Do you feel _____ about them?

    a. worried

    b. worrying

8. All this information is making me _____.

    a. confusing

    b. confused

9. I had a _____ weekend because of the rain.

    a. boring

    b. bored

10. Young children are often _____ of the dark.

    a. scaring

    b. scared

填空題答案：

| 1. going | 2. driving | 3. doing | 4. found | 5. dancing |
| 6. talking | 7. washed | 8. waiting | 9. Looking | 10. stolen |

選擇題答案：

| 1. a | 2. b | 3. b | 4. a | 5. b |
| 6. a | 7. a | 8. b | 9. a | 10. b |

▌ 註解：人的感受用-ed 過去分詞，形容事物則用 –ing 現在分詞。

Part 3：填空題
請在下列空格中填入現在分詞或過去分詞

1. A woman _____ (wear) a blue hat opened the door.
2. Champagne, _____ (produced) in France, is exported all over the world.
3. My sister works in a bakery _____ (make) cakes.
4. A million dollars worth of jewellery _____ (belong) to the President's wife has been stolen.
5. Pictures _____ (paint) by Picasso usually sell for millions of pounds.
6. A lorry _____ (carry) fruit crashed on the motorway.
7. This is a vegetarian restaurant. None of the dishes _____ (serve) here contains meat or fish.
8. The Harry Potter books, _____ (write) by JK Rowling, have all been made into films.

Part 4：多選題
請選出分詞子句主詞與主要子句主詞不符的選項

1.
(a) Stuck in the mud, Tim could see a man waving.
(b) Stuck in the mud, the man tried to free himself.
(c) Stuck in the mud, the man called for help.
(d) Stuck in the mud, the rescue services rushed to the man's assistance.

2.
(a) Breathing his last, the man passed away.
(b) Breathing his last, we saw the man pass away.
(c) Breathing his last, the old man shut his eyes.
(d) Breathing his last, the man's dog jumped up and gave a howl.

3.

(a) Soaring high above the fields, the eagle is a majestic bird.

(b) Soaring high above the fields, we could see the eagle clearly.

(c) Soaring high above the fields, the eagle can spot its prey easily.

(d) Soaring high above the fields, we watched the eagles for hours.

4.

(a) Rushing to catch the bus, the old man slipped and fell.

(b) Rushing to catch the bus, the old man's wallet fell out of his pocket.

(c) Rushing to catch the bus, the old man's face was covered in sweat.

(d) Rushing to catch the bus, the old man cursed his advancing years.

5.

(a) Having finished my homework, dad said I could go out.

(b) Having finished my homework, my sister wanted me to play football with her.

(c) Having finished my homework, I could relax and watch the television.

(d) Having finished my homework, mum was very pleased with me.

6.

(a) Giving an important speech, the chairman made a number of grammatical errors.

(b) Giving an important speech, we couldn't help laughing at the chairman's grammatical errors.

(c) Giving an important speech, the building was full of the chairman's supporters.

(d) Giving an important speech, the chairman began to shake uncontrollably.

7.

(a) Exploding in bright colors, the crowd loved the fireworks.

(b) Exploding in bright colors, the rockets looked beautiful.

(c) Exploding in bright colors, everyone cheered as the fireworks went off.

(d) Exploding in bright colors, the fireworks lit up the night.

8.

(a) Fumbling over his words, we laughed at Tim's mistakes.

(b) Fumbling over his words, Tim looked ridiculous.

(c) Fumbling over his words, Tim's supporters both looked shocked.

(d) Fumbling over his words, Tim's speech was a disaster.

9.

(a) With every limb aching, the runner crossed the line.

(b) With every limb aching, he finished the race just ahead of his rival.

(c) With every limb aching, the crowd roared him towards the finish line.

(d) With every limb aching, the spectators cheered as he crossed the line.

填空題答案：

| 1. wearing | 2. produced | 3. making | 4. belonging | 5. painted |
| 6. carrying | 7. served | 8. written | | |

選擇題答案：

| 1. a, d | 2. b, d | 3. b, d | 4. b, c | 5. a, b, d |
| 6. b, c | 7. a, c | 8. a, c, d | 9. c, d | |

註解：1. (a) 陷在泥土裡與 Tim 看到有人揮手，可知道陷在泥土的不是 Tim。
(d) "stuck in the mud" 陷在泥土裡，"the rescue services rushed to..." 救
援小隊趕去。前後語意不搭，故可知主詞不同。2. (b) 吸了最後一口
氣，我們看到男子去世了。呼吸最後一口氣的主詞是 the man，而此句
的主詞為 we。(d) 吸最後一口氣的並不是小狗，因為小狗還可以跳、可
以叫。5. (a) 做完功課，爸爸說我可以出去。做完功課的不是爸爸，所
以前後主詞不一。(b) 做完我的功課，我姐姐要我⋯⋯。除非是姊姊幫
我做功課，因此可知主詞前後不一。(d) 解題同上。這題因為發生在過
去，所以分詞構句用完成式表過去發生的事。

英文達人必讀系列

英文文法有道理！：入門版

2019年10月初版
2023年10月初版第二刷
有著作權・翻印必究
Printed in Taiwan.

定價：新臺幣380元

著　　者	劉美君
	呂佳玲
	徐志良
叢書主編	李　芃
執行編輯	蔡子潔
潤稿校對	劉彥珈
插　　畫	陳彥文
整體設計	菩薩蠻

出　版　者	聯經出版事業股份有限公司
地　　　址	新北市汐止區大同路一段369號1樓
叢書編輯電話	(02)86925588轉5305
台北聯經書房	台北市新生南路三段94號
電　　　話	(02)23620308
郵政劃撥帳戶	第0100559-3號
郵撥電話	(02)23620308
印　刷　者	文聯彩色製版印刷有限公司
總　經　銷	聯合發行股份有限公司
發　行　所	新北市新店區寶橋路235巷6弄6號2樓
電　　　話	(02)29178022

副總編輯	陳逸華
總　編　輯	涂豐恩
總　經　理	陳芝宇
社　　長	羅國俊
發　行　人	林載爵

行政院新聞局出版事業登記證局版臺業字第0130號

本書如有缺頁，破損，倒裝請寄回台北聯經書房更換。　ISBN　978-957-08-5380-3 (平裝)
電子信箱：linking@udngroup.com

國家圖書館出版品預行編目資料

英文文法有道理！ ：入門版/ 劉美君、呂佳玲、徐志良著 .
初版 . 新北市 . 聯經 . 2019年10月 . 292面 . 18×26公分
（英文達人必讀系列）
ISBN　978-957-08-5380-3（平裝）
［2023年10月初版第二刷］

1.英語　2.語法

805.16　　　　　　　　　　　　　　　　　　　108013395